Author Note

If you have been following the *A Season in Town* mini-series, you will have been wondering if Amelia and Gerard would ever get together. Here is their book, which I hope you will enjoy as much as I have enjoyed writing all three books for you. Amelia has helped other young women to find happiness. Can the Mistress of Hanover Square now find happiness for herself? Enjoy!

If you would like to contact me about any of my books please visit the website at www.lindasole.co.uk

Love to you all.

'You were prepared to marry me all those years ago. Dare I hope that you still find the idea agreeable?'

'Gerard…' Amelia gasped. 'Yes…'

She meant to say more, but he lowered his head to kiss her on the lips. Amelia responded with all the love that was in her, her arms going about his neck as her body melded with his. This was what she had longed for, dreamed of so many lonely nights! She had never expected to be so fortunate.

'My beautiful Amelia,' Gerard said. 'I am a fool! You are such a sensible woman. You understand everything. You would not do something stupid because of a foolish quarrel. I should have asked long ago. You are exactly the woman I need in my life. You will not expect more than I am able to give…'

Amelia withdrew a little. She waited for him to say the words she needed to hear, but he did not speak of love and she was conscious of her disappointment.

'I look forward to our wedding, Amelia. You will have the comfort and security of marriage and I shall have a beautiful, gracious wife…'

THE MISTRESS OF
HANOVER SQUARE

Anne Herries

™ MILLS & BOON®

First published in Great Britain 2009
Harlequin Mills & Boon Limited,
Eton House, 18-24 Paradise Road, Richmond, Surrey TW9 1SR

ISBN: 978 0 263 20988 4

MORAY COUNCIL LIBRARIES & INFO.SERVICES	
20 27 92 99	
Askews	
RF RF	

Printed and bound in Great Britain
by CPI Antony Rowe, Chippenham, Wiltshire

THE MISTRESS OF
HANOVER SQUARE

Anne Herries lives in Cambridgeshire, where she is fond of watching wildlife and spoils the birds and squirrels that are frequent visitors to her garden. Anne loves to write about the beauty of nature, and sometimes puts a little into her books—although they are mostly about love and romance. She writes for her own enjoyment, and to give pleasure to her readers. She is a winner of the Romantic Novelists' Association Romance Prize.

Recent novels by the same author:

MARRYING CAPTAIN JACK
THE UNKNOWN HEIR
THE HOMELESS HEIRESS
THE RAKE'S REBELLIOUS LADY
A COUNTRY MISS IN HANOVER SQUARE*
AN INNOCENT DEBUTANTE IN
   HANOVER SQUARE*

A Season in Town trilogy

And in the Regency series
***The Steepwood Scandal*:**

LORD RAVENSDEN'S MARRIAGE
COUNTERFEIT EARL

And in *The Hellfire Mysteries*:

AN IMPROPER COMPANION
A WEALTHY WIDOW
A WORTHY GENTLEMAN

Chapter One

Amelia stood for a moment on the steps of her house in Hanover Square, gazing across to the Earl of Ravenshead's London home, which was at the far side. She knew that he was not in residence and supposed that he was at his estate in the country. It was only because she had wanted to do some shopping for Christmas and deliver some gifts that she and her companion had themselves come to town for a few days. She had hoped that she might perhaps meet the earl, at the theatre or at some other affair, but it had not happened.

'Is something wrong?' Emily Barton asked.

Amelia looked at her in surprise and then realised that she had sighed. Her companion was a sensitive girl and always seemed to know when Amelia was out of sorts.

'No, I was merely wondering if I had forgotten anything. I should not wish to arrive at Pendleton and then remember something I had left behind.'

'I am sure you will not.' Emily smiled at her. 'I helped Martha pack your trunks and I am certain nothing was left out.'

'Thank you, my love. I know I can always rely on your good sense.'

'You are not upset by your brother's visit, I hope?'

For a moment Amelia's eyes clouded. Her brother, Sir Michael Royston, had paid her a brief but intensely unpleasant visit to complain. He always seemed to be in a temper these days and Amelia had come to dread his visits.

'No, dearest. As you know, my brother is…difficult. However, I am not upset.' She took Emily's arm. 'Come, we must not keep the horses standing. I want to make good time, for the sky has all the appearance of bad weather and I would like to get to Pendleton before it turns to snow.'

'I am looking forward to spending Christmas with our friends,' Emily said and smiled as she glanced across the carriage. They had been travelling for some time now and the streets of London had given way to pleasant countryside. 'Before I came to you, Amelia, Christmas was always a time of regret.'

'Was it, my love?' Amelia Royston looked at Emily in concern. She was aware of her companion's secret sorrow, but it was something Emily hardly ever spoke of. 'Are you happier now that you have been living with me for more than a year?'

'Oh yes, much. If only—' Emily broke off and shook her head. 'No, we shall not think of things that make us sad. Do you think that the Earl of Ravenshead will be at Pendleton this year?'

'Susannah said nothing of it when she wrote to invite us,' Amelia said, and a faint colour stained her cheeks. It almost seemed that Emily was reading her thoughts. 'Why do you ask, Emily?'

'Forgive me, perhaps I ought not to have spoken, but I thought…in the Season and at Helene's wedding earlier this year…I did think that perhaps there might be something—' Emily broke off and shook her head. 'It was not my place to ask…'

'Have I not told you that you may say anything to me, Emily? We are friends and have no secrets from each other. Since you ask, I shall tell you that I did think Gerard might speak some eighteen months ago, but he was called to France on family business. When we met him in London this year he paid me some attention, but…' Amelia sighed. 'I think now it was merely friendship he had in mind for us. There was a time when we might have married, but my brother sent him away. He married another woman some months later, which must mean that he did not suffer from our parting as I did.'

'You cannot be sure of that, Amelia. The earl may have married for various reasons. Perhaps it was on the rebound?' Emily frowned. 'I think you told me his wife has since died?'

'Gerard told me she was ill after the birth of their daughter and never recovered. I think that perhaps he is still grieving for her.'

'He will surely wish to marry again, if only for the sake of his daughter.'

'Yes, perhaps—though I am not sure I should wish to be married for such a reason.'

'I did not mean…please do not think I meant that he would marry you for the sake of his child,' Emily apologised and looked upset. 'I believe he likes you very well, Amelia.'

'Yes, I believe we are good friends,' Amelia agreed.

She leaned her head back against the squabs, closing her eyes. It would be very foolish of her to give way to emotion. She had cried too many tears when Gerard went away the first time. He had vowed that he loved her with all his heart, asked her to be his wife and then simply disappeared. When she was told he had joined the army, she had suffered a broken heart. She had not understood then that her brother had forced him to walk away from her—and threatened him and used violence. His desertion had left her feeling abandoned and distraught. When she first saw him again in company some four years later, she had been overwhelmed, and it had taken all her self-control not to show her feelings.

Gerard had been polite and friendly, but then, when someone had attempted to abduct Amelia when she was staying at Pendleton the summer before last, Gerard had been so concerned for her. She had believed then that he still cared, had begun to hope that he might speak, but he had been called away to France.

They had met again this summer. Gerard had been as generous, polite and kind as ever, but still he had not spoken of marriage. Of course there was no reason why he should. Too much time had passed, more than five years. If he had ever felt anything for her it had gone, or at least faded to a gentle affection. It was foolish of her to hope that he might feel more than mere friendship.

She opened her eyes and saw that Emily was looking upset.

'You have not distressed me, dearest.' Amelia smiled at her. 'We are almost there. I am so looking forward to seeing Susannah and Harry again.'

'I should never wish to distress you, Amelia. You have done so much for me, taking me in when many would have turned me from their door, because of my shame…'

'Do not look like that, Emily. You have more than repaid me for any kindness I have shown you. As for your shame—I will not have you speak of yourself in such a way. Come, smile and look forward to spending Christmas at Pendleton.'

* * *

'Amelia dearest,' Susannah exclaimed and kissed her on both cheeks. 'You look wonderful. That colour green always becomes you so well—and Emily, how pretty you look!'

'Oh, no…' Emily shook her head and blushed. 'It is this bonnet. I admired it in a milliner's window and Amelia bought it for me without my knowing. She said it was the very thing to brighten my winter wardrobe and of course she was right. She has such excellent taste.'

'Yes, she does.' Susannah looked fondly at Amelia. 'I may be biased, but I think Amelia is everything that is perfect and good.'

'Between the two of you, you will turn my head. I shall become impossible and start expecting to be treated like a duchess.'

Susannah trilled with laughter. 'You deserve to be a duchess,' she said. 'You must both come up to the nursery and see my little Harry. He is such a darling. His father thinks he is the most wonderful child ever born. I cannot begin to tell you all the plans he is making for when he can walk and go to school.'

'I always knew Harry Pendleton would be a doting father,' Amelia said, much amused.

'He spoils me dreadfully,' Susanna confessed as she led her friends up to their chambers. 'I've given you the apartments we had when I first stayed here, Amelia. I was so terrified of Harry's relatives and this vast house. I could not imagine how I should cope with it, but everything runs like clockwork. I hardly have to do a thing—just as Harry's mama told me it would be. And we always have guests so it is never too big or lonely, because people love to stay here. We shall have some twenty or thirty invited guests this Christmas, but it is quite possible that as many more will simply arrive on our doorstep. I tell Harry it is because he is such a generous host, but he thinks it is because they are all in love with me.'

'I dare say it is a mixture of both,' Amelia told her and smiled. She was delighted that her friend had not changed one bit since she became Lady Pendleton. She might not be quite as impulsive as when she had first visited town as Amelia's guest, but if anything her confidence had grown.

Susannah took them to the nursery, where the young heir was being prepared for bed by his nurse. After some twenty minutes or so admiring the admittedly beautiful child, Amelia and Emily were taken to the apartment they were to share during the Christmas period. It had three bedrooms and a sitting room, which was pleasant if one wished to escape from the rest of the company at times, and was quite a privilege.

Amelia allowed Emily to choose the bedchamber she liked best, and was pleased when her friend chose the one Susannah had used during that first visit. It meant she could take the room she preferred, and felt perfectly at home in.

After Susannah left them to settle in, Amelia walked to the window and looked out. Her view was of the lake and park, and, as she watched for a moment, she saw three horsemen canter to a halt and dismount. They had obviously been out riding together for pleasure and were in high good humour. Her breath caught in her throat as she heard laughter and caught sight of one familiar face. So Gerard *was* to be one of the guests this Christmas!

Amelia realised that she had been hoping for it, her heart beginning to thump with excitement. Oh, how foolish she was! Just because Gerard was here did not mean that he would speak of marriage. Why should he indeed? Had he wished to, he had had ample opportunity to do so before this.

She turned away to glance in the mirror. She was still attractive, but she was no longer a young girl. It was quite ridiculous to fancy herself in love; the time for such things had passed her by. The most she could hope for now would be a marriage of convenience, as Emily had suggested on the way to Pendleton. If perhaps Gerard were looking for a mother for his daughter, he might consider Amelia a suitable choice.

Amelia shook her head, dismissing her thoughts as a flight of fancy. There were a dozen young and beautiful girls Gerard might think of taking as his wife. Why should he look at a woman of her age? She had just turned eight and twenty. Besides, he was probably still grieving for the wife he had lost. Why had he married only a few months after their parting? Her brother Michael had behaved disgracefully to Gerard, of course, but why had he not told Amelia at the time the real reason behind his sudden departure? She would have run away with him had he asked her then.

No, if he had ever loved her, his love had faded and died.

She must not spend her time dreaming of something that would never happen!

Her thoughts turned to her companion. She knew that this time of year was often sad for Emily, because of her secret sorrow. None of their friends knew of Emily's secret, but she had told Amelia the truth when they first met. In doing so she had risked losing the chance of a good position, for many would have turned her away. Amelia had admired her honesty. She had done everything she could to make Emily forget the past, but nothing could take away the ache Emily carried inside.

Amelia was thoughtful as she prepared to go downstairs. She was almost sure that Mr Toby Sinclair would be a guest at

Pendleton that Christmas. He had paid Emily some attention earlier in the year, but nothing had come of it. If he were to offer for her…but nothing was certain. Amelia would not put the idea into her companion's mind, but if it happened she would be delighted.

If it did not, perhaps there was something she might be able to do to help the girl she had come to love almost as a sister.

Amelia was glad that she had seen Gerard from her window; the knowledge that he was here at Pendleton made it possible for her to meet him without that element of surprise she might otherwise have felt. She was able to greet him in the drawing room later that evening with perfect serenity.

'How nice to see you here, sir,' she said, offering her hand and giving no sign that her heart was beating rather too fast. 'People are arriving all the time. I think Susannah will have a great many guests this Christmas.'

'Yes, I imagine she will,' Gerard agreed. He held her hand briefly. 'How are you, Miss Royston? I trust you have had no further trouble since I last saw you?'

'None at all, sir—except for a raid by some foxes on our hen houses. But I know you did not mean that.' Amelia laughed softly. 'You are referring to the abduction attempt made the summer before last when we were all here together, I imagine?'

'Yes, I was. I am glad nothing more has happened to disturb your peace.' He looked at her thoughtfully. 'I am glad that you are here this Christmas. I was hoping that I might have a private conversation with you concerning my daughter? I would rather like your advice.'

'I should be delighted to help you if I am able.' As he smiled,

Amelia's heart stopped for one moment, and then raced on madly. 'Of course, my experience with children is limited to my orphans and the children of friends—but I am fond of them.'

'It is your feeling as a woman of compassion that I need,' Gerard assured her. One of the other guests was headed towards them; from her manner and gestures she was clearly intent on speaking with Amelia. 'This is not the time, however—perhaps tomorrow we might take a walk in the gardens?'

'Yes, certainly,' Amelia agreed. Her smile and quiet manner continued undisturbed. Gerard had asked for help with his daughter and she was quite willing to give it if she could, even if she could not help wishing that his request to walk with her had stemmed from a very different desire. Seeing him, being close to him, had aroused feelings that were not appropriate for a woman who was unlikely to marry. She closed her mind to the tantalising visions of herself in his arms…his bed. That way lay disaster and heartbreak! She must remember her dignity at all times. As a young woman she had not hesitated to confess her love, but things were different now. 'I am available to you at any time, my lord.'

'Do you not think we could be Gerard and Amelia?' he asked. 'We are friends of some long standing, I think?'

'Yes, indeed we are,' Amelia agreed. For a moment the look in his eyes was so intense that she could not breathe. He should not look at her so if he wanted nothing more than friendship.

Their conversation was ended as they were drawn into the company. Susannah's guests were of all ages and included some young people, who had been allowed to come down to dinner because it was nearly Christmas. The eclectic mix of young and old, Harry's relatives and friends of the couple, made for a lively evening. The younger members were sent to bed after their meal, but the older guests continued in their merry way until long past midnight.

It was not until the moment that she had decided to retire that Gerard approached Amelia once more.

'Shall we say ten o'clock for our walk?' he asked. 'If that is not too early for you?'

'I am always an early riser.'

'You must wrap up well, for I think it may be a cold morning.'

'I enjoy walking in any kind of weather, except a downpour,' Amelia assured him.

Their arrangements made, Amelia went upstairs to the apartment she shared with Emily. She saw that Emily was looking thoughtful and asked her if she had enjoyed the evening.

'You did not find the young company too much, dearest?'

'It was a delightful evening,' Emily assured her. 'Mr Sinclair and I joined in a guessing game with some of the young people at the dinner table. I do not know when I have had such fun.' A wistful expression came to her eyes. 'I was an only child and I doubt I shall have…' She blinked hard, as if to stop herself crying. 'I am certain Mr Sinclair means to make me an offer, Amelia. What shall I do?'

'I believe you should tell him the truth. He will keep your confidence—Toby Sinclair is a true gentleman. If he still wishes for the marriage, he will make it clear to you.'

'And if he does not?' Emily lifted her head as if to seek guidance and then nodded as she answered her own question. 'I must bear it. You are quite right, Amelia. I cannot be less than truthful, though it may make things awkward for the rest of our stay here.'

'Perhaps if you could prevent him speaking for a few days, and then tell him just before we leave. If he needs time to consider his feelings, he would have his chance before following us to Coleridge.'

'You are so wise and sensible,' Emily said and looked relieved. 'I shall do my best to avoid being alone with him until the day before we leave.'

'Try not to brood on the outcome.' Amelia kissed her cheek. 'I believe it may all turn out better than you imagine, dearest.'

Having done her best to reassure her friend, Amelia went to her own room. She dismissed her maid as soon as the girl had undone the little hooks at the back of her gown, preferring to be alone with her thoughts. It was easier to settle Emily's doubts than her own, for she had no doubt that Toby Sinclair was deeply in love. It was more difficult to understand Gerard Ravenshead's feelings.

Sometimes his look seemed to indicate that he felt a strong emotion for her, but at others his expression was brooding and remote. They were friends, but *was* that all? These days it seemed that Gerard thought of her as a mature lady in whom he might confide his worries concerning his daughter. He could have no idea of the passionate and improper thoughts his nearness aroused in her. She must be careful to conceal her feelings, otherwise there might be some embarrassment.

'No! No, Lisette...I beg you...do not do it...forgive me...' Gerard Ravenshead's arm twitched, his head moving from side to side as he sat in the deep wing chair in the library at Pendleton. He was dreaming...a dream he had had too many times before. *'No, I say! Stop...the blood...the blood...'* He screamed out and

woke to find himself in a room where the fire had gone cold and the candles burned out.

Unable to sleep, he had dressed and come down to read for a while and fallen into a fitful sleep. He hoped that his nightmare had woken no one. Having gone for some months without one, he had thought they were finished, but something had brought it all back to him.

Gerard rose from the chair and walked over to the window, gazing out as the light strengthened. It was dawn and another night had gone.

The library was an impressive, long room with glass-fronted bookcases on three walls, a magnificent desk, occasional tables and comfortable chairs, and three sets of French windows to let in maximum light. Gerard was an avid reader and, when at home in his house in Hanover Square, often sat late into the night reading rather than retiring to his bedchamber, where he found it impossible to sleep. Indeed, he could hardly remember a night when he had slept through until morning.

Gerard was a handsome man, tall, broad in the shoulder with strong legs that looked particularly well in the riding breeches he most often wore. His coats had never needed excessive padding at the shoulder. His hair was very dark but not black, his eyes grey and sometimes flinty. His expression was often brooding, stern, perhaps because his thoughts caused him regret. At this moment he wore a pair of buff-coloured breeches and topboots and his fine linen shirt was opened to the waist. A glass of wine was to hand, but he had scarcely touched it. Gerard had long ago discovered that there was no forgetfulness in a wine bottle.

Before falling into a restless sleep, he had spent the night wrestling with his problem. His daughter was in need of feminine company, and not just that of nursemaids or a governess. He too was in need of a female companion: a woman with whom he could share his hopes and dreams, a woman he could admire and respect. In short, he needed a wife. Having made one mistake with the young French girl he had married out of pity, he did not wish to make another. Easy enough to find a mistress or even a young woman willing to become Countess Ravenshead, but there was only one woman Gerard wanted as his wife—the woman he had been denied when he was a young man and head over heels in love.

He touched the scar at his right temple, the only blemish on a strong and handsome face, his eyes darkening at the memory it aroused. Amelia's brother had instructed his servants to beat him when he dared to ask for her hand as a young man; he had not been wealthy enough to please the proud Sir Michael Royston! However, it was not fear of Sir Michael's displeasure that made Gerard hesitate to ask Amelia Royston if she would be his wife now. Guilt weighed heavily on his conscience, because he had not told anyone the whole truth concerning his wife's death. It was the reason for his nightmares.

'Damn you, Lisette. Let me be...' His eyes were dark with memories as he relived the dream. *'So much blood...so much blood...'*

She *had* been ill for a long time after the birth of her child, but it was not that illness that had caused her death. Lisette had died by her own hand.

He found her with her wrists cut in a bath of warm water. She was still alive when he dragged her from the bath, but barely breathing. He had tried frantically to save her, sending his servant for the doctor, but his efforts were in vain and she was dead when the doctor arrived. Lisette had been buried and Gerard mourned the loss of a young life.

He had not loved her, but she haunted his dreams because he blamed himself for her death. He had married her out of pity, because she was young, alone and with child, abandoned by her lover in a country that was not her own. He knew that the father of her child was an English officer, but Lisette had never named him. His own dreams turned to dust, Gerard had done what he believed was the right thing—a good thing—but he had been unable to love her; when Lisette finally understood that, she had taken her own life.

'I am so sorry...so very sorry...'

Gerard had never been able to confess the truth to another living soul. He carried it inside, where it continued to fester. If he allowed his guilt to haunt him, it would ruin his life. Gerard had no idea whether or not Amelia would marry him if he asked her. What would she think if she knew the truth concerning his wife's death?

He had been on the point of asking her to be his wife once, but an urgent message had sent him hurrying to his daughter's side in France. Little Lisa was a demanding child and she did not like her papa to leave her for long periods. Realising she needed more than her nurses, Gerard had brought her to England and placed her in the charge of an English nanny, but neither Lisa nor her papa was truly content.

Gerard had reached the conclusion that he would never know true happiness unless he asked Amelia Royston to be his wife. He could not marry her without confessing his secret, which was one of the reasons why he had hesitated so long, for he feared that she would turn from him in disgust. He had wanted to die on the battlefield the first time he lost Amelia; to let himself hope and then lose her a second time would destroy him.

This was ridiculous! He was a man of six and thirty and should be able to face up to the truth without fear of rejection. It might be better if he forgot about marriage altogether. He had broken Lisette's heart, causing her to commit suicide. Perhaps he would do better to remain unwed.

Amelia saw Gerard waiting for her the next morning as she went down to the hall. He was wearing a long coat with several capes, a warm muffler bound about his throat and a fur hat in the Russian style. He smiled his approval as he saw that she too was wearing a thick cloak and muffler, her gloved hands tucked inside a fur muff that hung suspended from a chain about her neck.

'I see you are prepared for the weather, Amelia. There is a fine frost this morning.'

'As there should be for Christmas Eve,' she replied. 'I think it will be just right for a brisk walk about the gardens, sir.'

'My daughter would not agree with you.' Gerard looked rueful. 'I believe I was wrong to leave her so long in France. She finds our English weather cold and damp and asks constantly when do we return to Paris.'

'Do you think of leaving England permanently?' Amelia asked, doing her best to conceal her feeling of acute disappointment.

'I considered it for a while,' Gerard confessed. 'However, I have decided that I should prefer to live in England where I have friends rather than mere acquaintances. Lisa must come to terms with the situation. I believe she will be happier once the summer comes.'

'I think you may have been in the habit of giving her her own way?' Amelia tipped her head to one side, her eyebrows slightly raised.

'Yes, I have spoiled her,' Gerard admitted and laughed. 'She is a little charmer and I fear that I may have given in too often to her whims—which may be why she is giving poor Nanny such a difficult time. I hear complaints that she is sometimes sulky and unresponsive, though with me she is very different.'

Amelia was thoughtful. 'Is the nanny well recommended?'

'Her references were good. She came from a family with whom she had served for more than six years. However, I have wondered if she is a little too strict with the child. I may have been too lenient, but I would not have Lisa's life made a misery. It is not easy for a man alone…' Gerard glanced at Amelia, a rueful look in his eyes. 'I feel in need of a lady's advice. Some ladies take little interest in their children. They feel their duty is done once the heir is produced, but you make it your business to care for unfortunate children. You might be able to tell me what to do for the best as far as my daughter is concerned.'

Amelia kept her smile in place despite her disappointment. It was as she had feared—he wanted only to discuss his daughter. 'I would need to see Lisa and her nanny together. It would be best if it happened casually. If Nanny knows she is being observed, I should learn nothing.'

'You understand at once, as I knew you would,' Gerard said, looking pleased. 'I brought Lisa to Pendleton with me, though I did not allow her to come down to dinner last evening for she is not ready yet. However, she will be present at the children's party this afternoon. Susannah has lots of small presents and prizes for the young ones. I shall be there. Perhaps…if it is not too much trouble?' He arched his brows at her.

'I had intended to be there anyway. I enjoy these things and Susannah will need a little help to organise the games and present giving. It will be no trouble to observe your daughter and her nanny.'

'How generous you are…' He paused as Amelia gave an impatient shake of her head. 'It will be good to have a lady's opinion in this matter. I have no female relations that I may call upon.'

'Does your late wife not have a family?'

'I have no idea. I met Lisette after a bloody battle between the French and the Spanish troops. She had been ill used and I took pity on her. I married her to protect her and to give her unborn child my name. She never spoke of her family. I imagine they were killed during the conflict…' Gerard was looking straight ahead, a nerve flicking at his temple. 'I knew nothing about her, except that she was French and clearly of gentle birth.'

'You love the child very much, do you not?'

'I fell in love with her when she was born. I was present and helped bring her into the world for there were few doctors available to us—and so she became mine.' Gerard glanced towards her. 'After I left England, I was a disappointed man, Amelia. At one time I had nothing to live for. Indeed, I might have welcomed death on the battlefield. I married Lisette because it seemed the best way to protect her and I had abandoned all hope of happiness…but when her child was born I loved the child from the first moment of seeing her.'

'Yes, you mentioned something of this once before.' Amelia looked thoughtful. 'You said that your wife was ill for a long time after the child's birth?'

'She took no interest in the babe at all. I was able to secure the services of a wet-nurse. Often I cared for the child myself, changing her and feeding her as she began to take solid foods. Lisette had no interest in anything for a long time. When she recovered a little…' He shook his head, as she would have questioned him. 'After she died, I engaged the services of a nurse, and when the war was over I made the decision to keep Lisa in France with me. At that time I was not sure what to do for the best.'

'You thought you might live there because your child's mother was French?'

'I must confess that for a while I considered leaving the child in France with a nurse,' he admitted. 'I was a soldier, a single man—and my estate was in some trouble. I have rectified that now, though I am not as rich as Pendleton or Coleridge.' He gave Amelia a rueful look. 'When we first met I had hardly any fortune at all. I dare say that was the reason Sir Michael did not consider me a worthy husband for his sister.'

'He had no right to send you away.' Amelia hesitated, then lifted her gaze to meet his because she needed to ask. 'Why did you not send me word of what happened? Surely you knew that I would have gone with you had you asked? I would not have allowed Michael to prevent our marriage if I had known. I suspected that he had had a hand in it, but when you told me what he did to you—' She broke off and sighed. 'It was a wicked thing that Michael did to you—to us…'

'I ought to have known you would elope with me, despite what your brother said when he had me beaten,' Gerard admitted. 'I suppose I was humiliated and angry—even bitter. I was not certain that you loved me enough to defy him. At that time I did not expect to be my uncle's heir. He had a son who should have inherited. Had my cousin not died of a putrid chill, I must have made my living as a soldier. Perhaps your brother had some right on his side, Amelia.'

'No, he did not,' she contradicted at once. 'Your lack of fortune meant nothing to me, Gerard.'

'I am no longer a pauper. I have worked hard and my business ventures prosper. However, your own fortune surpasses mine these days. I well remember that you had nothing when I asked you to be my wife.'

'I did not expect that to change. It was a surprise when my great-aunt asked me to live with her—and when she left everything to me. She had told me that I would have something when she died, but I had no idea that she was so wealthy.'

'It was a stroke of luck for you, I suppose.'

'Yes…though it has its drawbacks. My brother and sister-in-law are resentful of the fact that I inherited a fortune they believe should have gone to them. Michael has been unpleasant to me on more than one occasion since my aunt died.'

'They had no right to expect it. Lady Agatha might have left her money anywhere.'

'Indeed, she might,' Amelia said. 'I believe her deceased husband also had relatives who might have hoped for something—but they at least have not approached me on the matter.'

'And your brother has?' His brows arched, eyes narrowed and intent.

'Several times,' Amelia said. 'It has been the subject of endless arguments between us. Michael thinks I should make most of the money over to him. I have no intention of doing what he demands, but it has made for bad blood between us.' She hesitated, then, 'I have not spoken of this to anyone but Emily—but his last visit was almost threatening. I was a little disturbed by it, I admit.'

'Sir Michael is of a violent temperament…'

Amelia was silent for a moment, then, 'You are thinking it might have been he who tried to have me abducted at Pendleton the summer before last? I believe you thought it then?'

'It is possible, but I may have been mistaken. My own encounter with him may have coloured my thinking. If it was him, why has he not carried the threat further? Why stop at one attempt?'

'I do not know. For a long time I thought that there might be another attempt, but nothing happened.'

'It is puzzling. The likely explanation seems that it was actually Susannah who was the intended victim and you were mistaken for her. As you know, there was some awkwardness between the Marquis of Northaven and Harry Pendleton at that time.'

'That is one possibility, and yet I cannot think that we are alike. Emily is convinced that my brother means me harm. She overheard something he said to me some months ago and she suggested that he would benefit if I died.'

'Would he?'

'At the moment he is the largest, though not the only, beneficiary.'

Gerard nodded. 'It might be wise to change that and let it be known that you have done so, Amelia.'

Amelia's expression was thoughtful. 'I cannot think that Michael would wish to see me dead—even for a fortune. My brother is bad tempered and arrogant, but I would not have thought him a murderer.'

'It would not hurt to take some precautions. I could arrange for you to be watched over—as I did once before. And changes to your will might help if you would consider making them.'

'Yes, I may do so after the New Year. We are to attend Helene and Max's ball at Coleridge. Shall you be there?'

'Yes, I believe so,' Gerard said. 'As you know, both Harry and Max are particular friends of mine.'

'And their wives are good friends of mine,' Amelia said. 'I should be grateful if you could arrange some kind of protection, for Emily as well as me. I have no idea how it may be done and it may not truly be necessary. I shall, of course, pay the men myself.'

'As you wish,' Gerard said. 'The breeze is very cold. I think we may have some snow. Should we return to the house before we freeze to death?'

'Yes, perhaps we should,' Amelia replied.

She had the oddest feeling that he had been on the verge of saying something very different, but at the last he had changed his mind. Nothing more of note was said between them, and they parted after returning to the house. She pondered on what might have been in Gerard's mind as she went in search of her hostess.

It was good of him to say that he would find suitable men to protect her if he thought her in danger from her brother's spite. If, of course, it was her brother she needed protecting from…but who else could it be?

'What made you think I would be interested in such an outrageous proposition?' The Marquis of Northaven looked at the person sitting opposite him in the private parlour of the posting inn to which he had been summoned that evening. He had considered ignoring the note sent to his lodgings in town, but curiosity and a certain intuition had brought him here. However, to the best of his knowledge he had never met the gentleman before. 'Kidnapping is a hanging offence…'

'I had heard that you have a score to settle with a certain gentleman.'

'Where did you hear that?' Northaven was alert, suspicious. The other man's features were barely visible in the shadows, his face half-covered by the muffler he wore to keep out the cold.

'One hears these things…of course there would be money once the ransom was paid.'

'Money…' Northaven's mouth curved in a sneer, a flash of hauteur in his manner. 'I have not yet run through the inheritance my uncle left me.'

'Then forget I asked you. I had thought you might care to see Ravenshead brought down, but if you do not have the stomach for it there are others willing, nay, eager to do my bidding.'

'How would this bring Ravenshead down?' Northaven asked, eyes narrowed, menacing.

'He imagines he will marry Amelia Royston. I do not wish to see that happen. Once I have finished with her, she will marry no one!'

The Marquis of Northaven shivered, feeling icy cold. He had done much in his life that he was not proud of, but something in the tone of the person who was asking him to arrange Amelia Royston's downfall was disturbing. Northaven had seduced more than one young woman, but contrary to what was said and thought of him, he had taken none against their will. Indeed, they usually threw themselves into his arms—and why should he say no? Handsome beyond what many thought decent, he had an air of unavailability that made him irresistible to many ladies. He was by no means a white knight, but neither was he the traitor some thought him. He might cheat at cards when desperate; he might lie if it suited him and would not deny that he had sailed close to the edge a few times, but a cold-blooded murderer he was not.

Northaven had been angry with the men who had once been his friends. He had hated the holy trilogy, as he was wont to call Harry Pendleton, Max Coleridge and Gerard Ravenshead. He hated them because they despised him, believed him worse than he truly was, but with the turn in his fortunes of late much of his resentment had cooled. He would have dismissed the proposition being made to him out of hand, but he was curious to hear more.

'Supposing I were interested in bringing down Ravenshead,' he said. 'What would you be willing to pay—and what do you plan for Miss Royston?'

'I was thinking of ten thousand guineas. Her fate is not your affair. All you need to do is to deliver her to me.'

The words were delivered with such malice that Northaven's stomach turned. He imagined that Miss Royston's fate might be worse than death and it sickened him. He was well aware that Amelia Royston had once thought him guilty of the callous seduction and desertion of her friend; he had allowed her to believe it, but it was not true. A few months previously he might have left her to her fate. He had then been a bitter, angry man, but something had happened to him the day he watched a young girl marry the man she loved—the man she had risked everything to save when she thought he was about to die.

No woman had ever loved Northaven enough to take a ball in the shoulder for him. Susannah Hampton had been reckless and could easily have died had his aim been slightly to the left. The moment his ball had struck her shoulder, Northaven had felt remorse. He had been relieved when Susannah made a full recovery. Something drove him to mingle with the crowd on her wedding day. When her eyes met his as she left the church on her husband's arm, they had seemed to ask a question. He had answered it with a nod of his head and he believed she understood. His feud with her husband was over.

He had not fallen in love with her. Yet she had touched him in a way he had never expected. He had suddenly realised where he was headed if he continued on his reckless path: he would end a lonely, bitter man. For a while the resentment against his one-time friends had continued to burn inside him, but of late he had felt more at peace with himself.

Perhaps at last he had found the way to redeem himself.

'Let me think about it,' he said. 'Ten thousand guineas is a fair sum—and I have no love for Ravenshead. Give me a few days and I shall decide.'

'Meet me here again in two days and I will tell you more. We can do nothing over Christmas. Miss Royston goes to Coleridge in the New Year—and that will be our chance…'

Chapter Two

Gerard cursed himself for a fool as he parted from Amelia. He had let yet another chance slip, but after discussing his daughter and her brother the time had not seemed right. If he had asked Amelia to marry him in the same breath as telling her that she ought to think of changing her will, she might have thought he was asking her for reasons of convenience to himself. He had made his circumstances clear so that when he did speak there would be no misunderstanding. He was not in need of a rich wife, though Amelia was extremely wealthy. Her fortune was yet another reason why he hesitated—but the burning problem besetting him was whether her opinion of him would suffer when he told her the truth of Lisette's death.

To conceal the details from her would not be honest. If they were to come out at some time in the future, she might feel that he had deceived her and there would be a loss of trust. All in all, Gerard considered that he had done what he could to prepare the ground for a future proposal. He felt they were good friends, but he could not be sure that anything of their former love was left on Amelia's part, though every time he saw her he was more con-

vinced that she was the only woman for him. She was beautiful, charming and the scent of her always seemed to linger,
making him aware of a deep hunger within. He wanted her more
than he had ever wanted anything in his life. Without her…

'My lord…' The footman's voice broke through Gerard's
reverie. He turned as the man approached him. 'This was delivered for you early this morning, sir.'

'For me?' Gerard stared at the parcel wrapped in strong brown
paper and tied with string. 'Was there a card? Do you know who
delivered it?'

'It was a gentleman's man, sir. I do not know his name, but
he said his gentleman had bid him deliver this to you here.'

'I see…thank you.' Gerard frowned as he took the parcel.
He had left gifts at the homes of some friends in London;
however, he had told no one but Toby Sinclair that he was
coming here for Christmas. The gift might have come from one
of the other guests, but it was more normal to exchange them
after dinner on Christmas Eve. He shook the parcel gently and
discovered that it rattled. Intrigued, he took it into a small
parlour to the right of the hall and untied the strings, folding
back the paper.

There was no card, but inside the paper was a wooden box.
He lifted the lid and stared at the contents. At first he thought
that the doll must be a present for Lisa. However, the head was
lying at an odd angle, and, as he lifted it out, he saw that the porcelain head had been wrenched from the stuffed body. It was
broken across the face and the body had been slit down the
middle with a knife or something similar.

Gerard felt cold all over. There was something disturbing
about the wanton destruction to what had been a pretty fashion

doll, the kind that was often used to show off the wares of expensive couturiers rather than a child's toy.

It could hardly have been broken accidentally. No, this had been done deliberately. He could not imagine who had sent such a thing to him or why. However, he felt that the broken doll was a symbol of something—a threat. The implication was sinister for it must be a warning, though he could not think what he was being warned about or why it had been sent to him at such a time.

Gerard realised that he must have an enemy. His first thought was that he had only one enemy of any note that he knew of and that was the Marquis of Northaven. Northaven had been bitter because Gerard, along with Harry and Max, had ostracised him after that débâcle in Spain, blaming him for the fact that the French troop had been expecting an attack. Northaven had engineered a duel with Harry, which had almost ended in tragedy, but since then none of them had heard much from him. It was as if he had dropped out of sight.

Somehow, it seemed unlikely that the doll had come from Northaven. The man had always denied betraying his friends to the Spanish; he had been prepared to fight any of them in a duel to clear his name—but this doll was something very different. It was meant to disturb, to sow confusion and anxiety—though its message was obscure. Was the sender threatening his daughter?

Gerard felt sick inside as he pictured his daughter being mutilated as the doll had been. Surely the sender could not be threatening Lisa? She was an innocent child who had harmed no one. Besides, what had he done that would cause anyone to hate him to this extent?

'Gerard…' Harry entered the room behind him. 'I thought I saw you come in here.'

'Yes. I wanted to open this…' Gerard held the box out to him. 'One of your footmen gave it to me a moment ago. Apparently, it was delivered earlier this morning.'

Harry looked at the doll, his eyes narrowing as he saw what had been done to it. 'Good grief! What on earth is that about?'

'I have no idea. I wish I did.'

'A threat, do you think?' Harry's mouth was a grim white line. 'To your daughter—or a warning?'

'Perhaps both…'

'There was no message?'

'None that I could find.'

Harry picked up the box and looked inside. Then he saw a small card lying in the discarded paper and string and held it out to Gerard.

'If you value her, stay away from her. This is your one and only warning and sent in good faith. Ignore it and the one you love may end like this.' Gerard frowned as he read the words aloud. 'What can that mean—how can I stay away from my own daughter?'

'Are you sure the doll is meant to represent your daughter?' Harry asked. 'Only a few of us even know she exists, Gerard. Perhaps the person who sent this does not know you have a child.'

Gerard stared at him and then nodded. 'You are right. Only a handful of my friends know about Lisa. So if the doll isn't her…' His gaze narrowed. 'You don't think—Amelia…?'

'It makes more sense,' Harry said. 'Whoever sent this used a fashion doll, not a child's toy. Amelia is an extremely elegant woman and it is more likely that the doll represents her. We suspect an attempt to kidnap her was made that summer at Pendleton. Max had an idea that the reason no further attempts were made to kidnap her was because you were no longer around.'

'Yes, he mentioned something of the kind some months ago, but I did not think it possible. Good grief!' Gerard was horrified. 'You think they tried to abduct Amelia because they thought I might be about to ask her to marry me—and then I returned to France. Nothing happened while I was away, but now I am back…'

'And you receive this warning.' Harry looked concerned. 'If that is the case, Amelia could be in grave danger.'

Gerard frowned. 'She told me this morning that Miss Barton had asked her if her brother would benefit from her death. Apparently, he has been demanding that she hand over most of the fortune her great-aunt left her.'

'Is Royston such a brute?' Harry pondered the question. 'I do not know him well, but I would not have thought it. He might bully her into giving him money, but murder?'

'Northaven?'

'I am not sure that the murder of a woman is his style. He would be more likely to force a duel on you if he wished to pursue a quarrel.'

'My thoughts entirely. It must be Royston—I can think of no one else who would be affected if she were to marry me.'

'You cannot think of anyone who has cause to hate you?'

'None that I know of,' Gerard replied, but looked thoughtful. 'Everyone makes enemies, but I cannot think of anyone who would wish to harm me or mine. Royston does not like me. He had me beaten when I asked for Amelia's hand as a young man—but surely he has not harboured a grudge all this time? Besides, why harm his sister? If his quarrel is with me, why not have me shot? There are assassins enough to put a ball between my shoulders on a dark street.'

'Royston had you beaten when you asked for Amelia?'

Harry's brows shot up as Gerard nodded. 'The scar at your temple! I knew something had happened but you never spoke of it… You have never sought retribution?'

'How could I? Whatever happened, Royston is Amelia's brother. I love her, Harry. I would do nothing to harm her. He has no reason to hate me that I know of—I swear it.'

'Then this threat must have been made in order to gain control of her fortune,' Harry said grimly. 'If you marry her, he loses all chance of inheriting if she dies.'

'Good grief! If I ask her to marry me, I could be signing her death warrant.'

'And if you do not, she remains vulnerable,' Harry pointed out. 'You cannot allow this threat to alter your plans.'

'I am damned whichever way I go!' Gerard cursed. 'I must arrange protection for her. She must be watched around the clock.'

'And for yourself,' Harry warned. 'Do not shake your head, Gerard. You need someone to watch your back, my friend. I am not certain that we have reached the heart of this business. You need to investigate this affair immediately. I shall question my servants. Perhaps one of them may know something of the man who delivered that thing.'

Gerard had replaced the broken doll and closed the box. 'The footman knew nothing, but someone else may have seen the messenger who delivered this thing. Any clue would be welcome, for at the moment I have little to go on.'

'You know you may call on me for assistance?'

'Yes, of course. Please say nothing of this to your wife or Amelia for the moment. I do not wish to throw a cloud over the celebrations this Christmas. Besides, I believe Amelia must be safe enough here for we are aware of the danger…' He frowned.

'Does it not strike you as odd that I was warned? If the rogue wants Amelia dead—why warn me of the possibility?'

'Perhaps he simply wants to prevent you speaking to her?'

'Perhaps…' Gerard looked thoughtful. 'Or someone else sent it to alert me to danger. Something puzzles me, Harry. I think there is more to this than we yet know, but I confess I have no idea what it may be.'

Amelia was thoughtful as she went upstairs to change. Speaking to Gerard confidentially had made her think about her situation. It was hard to think that her brother could mean her harm, but she could not deny that he had several times spoken to her in a manner that might be thought threatening.

Perhaps it would be sensible to take some precautions, though she would hate to think her life might be in danger. Of course, if she were married, her brother would have no hope of her fortune—which might be why he had several times made it plain that he would never agree to her marrying Gerard. She was her own mistress, of course. Michael must know that he could not stop her marrying whomsoever she wished.

Amelia looked out of her bedchamber and watched her companion walking towards the house. Emily Barton's head was down and her manner one of thoughtfulness. She was quite alone.

Emily had a gentle beauty with her dark honey-blonde hair and blue eyes that were startling in a pale face. However, because of her modest manner and way of dressing, she was often thought unremarkable until she smiled, when she could look stunning. Amelia frowned, because of late Emily had seemed quieter than usual. She was clearly brooding.

Amelia suspected she knew what was troubling her. Emily

had been scrupulous in confessing her shame when she applied for the position as Amelia's companion.

'I must tell you that I have a secret, Miss Royston.' Emily had looked at her steadily. 'Only my parents and a few servants knew, for my father did his best to hide my shame.'

'Your shame—are you telling me that you have borne a child out of wedlock?' Amelia had sensed it instinctively.

'I…was forced,' Emily told her, cheeks pale, eyes dark with remembered horror. 'He was not my lover—but he held me down as he raped me, and, later, I knew that I would bear his child.'

'My dear,' Amelia cried. 'It is shocking that men can be so vile. Please tell me what happened then.'

'My father never believed that it was not my fault, but I swear to you that I am innocent of duplicity in this.' Emily's eyes brimmed with tears, though she did not weep. 'If this makes me unacceptable as your companion…'

'No, do not think it.' Amelia smiled at her. 'What you have told me makes me more determined to give you a home. You will live with me, meet my friends and learn to be happy again, my dear.'

'You are so very kind…'

'I know what it is to have a broken heart, Emily.' She shook her head as the young woman raised her brows. 'Put your shame behind you, my dear. I absolve you of blame.'

If only Emily had been able to put her shame and unhappiness behind her! Amelia knew that she still had days when she was deeply unhappy.

She must do something to help her companion. For some time now Amelia had been considering the idea of trying to find Emily's child. The babe had been taken from her at birth and she did not even know where her daughter was. If she could be told that the little girl was well and healthy, living happily with her foster parents, perhaps this deep ache inside her might ease.

Amelia had hesitated because she did not wish to cause her companion more pain, but to see Emily unhappy even when she was in company was hard to bear.

Instead of brooding on her own problems, she would think about Emily. Surely there must be a way of finding the child?

Having changed into a fresh gown, Amelia prepared to go down and join Emily. She would say nothing to her for the moment, but after Christmas she would see what could be done.

Alone in his bedchamber, Gerard paced the floor. It seemed he was caught between a rock and a hard place—if he spoke to Amelia and she accepted his offer of marriage, it might place her in danger. Yet if her brother did plan her death in order to inherit her fortune, she needed protection. If she married, she would no longer be at the mercy of her grasping relatives.

He was aware of a burning need to protect her. Amelia was his, the love of his life. He could not give her up because of an obscure threat. He would make every effort to keep her safe. It would probably be best to let her know he believed she might be in some danger, but he was sure that she was safe enough for the moment. Harry would alert his servants to be on the lookout for strangers, and by the time she was ready to leave Pendleton he would have measures in place for her protection. He would summon the men he had used once before.

He could at least do this for the woman he loved, though he was still undecided whether to speak to her of marriage. Did he have the right? Amelia was still beautiful, a woman of fortune and charm and she must be much sought after. He had heard whispers, her name linked with various gentlemen, but nothing seemed to come of the rumours. Gerard had no idea whether she had received offers. If she had, she had turned them down—why? Was she suspicious of the motives behind every proposal that came her way? Did she imagine that no one could love her for herself? Surely not! And yet if her brother had been browbeating her because of her fortune, it would not be surprising if she thought others interested only in her wealth.

Gerard decided that he would tell no one else of his suspicions until Christmas was over, because he wanted it to be a happy time for Amelia and his daughter. He certainly did not wish to cast a shadow over the festivities for Susannah and her guests.

'Susannah asked me to help with the younger children,' Emily said to Amelia as they went downstairs together that afternoon. 'She thinks that they will need help to unwrap their presents and Nanny has been given time off.'

Amelia saw the happy smile on her face. Emily loved children and the knowledge that her own daughter was living with another family must be torture for her. She wondered if Emily had ever tried to discover the whereabouts of her child, but supposed it was unlikely. She had devoted her life to her ailing mother until that lady died and had then been forced to look for work. Perhaps Amelia might mention the possibility to Emily another day, but now was not the time.

'I think Susannah is very brave to have the children's party without her nanny, for I am certain that some of the ladies have no idea of looking after their own children.'

'I think it will be great fun. I always wished that I had brothers and sisters, and envied those who did.' The wistful expression had come back to Emily's face.

Amelia saw it and made up her mind that she would ask someone to make enquiries concerning the lost child for her. However, it would be better to say nothing to Emily for the moment in case the child could not be found.

'I am certain that we shall enjoy ourselves this afternoon,' Amelia said. 'I am eager to meet Gerard's daughter. She has been brought up in France until the past few months, and I dare say she may not understand English as well as she needs to if she is to communicate with the other children. I know that Gerard's nanny will be present, so we shall have help.'

The two ladies smiled at each other as they approached the large salon where the celebrations for the younger guests were taking place. Entering, they saw that the room had been decorated with silver and gold stars; there was also a crib with wooden animals and a doll representing the Baby Jesus and two of the servants were dressed as Joseph and Mary. Some of the other servants were dressed as the three kings, and they had big sacks of gifts. These would be distributed to the children at the end of the entertainment.

All kinds of delicious foods that might appeal to children had been set out on a table: sweet jellies, bottled fruits, cakes and tiny biscuits, also fingers of bread and butter with the crusts cut off and spread with honey.

'Amelia…Miss Barton.' Gerard approached them with a smile. 'May I have the pleasure of introducing my daughter, Lisa, to you? Lisa—this is Miss Amelia Royston—and Miss Emily Barton. Greet them nicely, my love.'

'*Bonjour*, Mademoiselle Royston, *bonjour*, Mademoiselle

Barton,' Lisa said and dipped a curtsy. 'I am pleased to meet you.' She tipped her head and looked at Gerard. 'Was that correct, Papa?'

Her manner was that of a little coquette. She was pretty, an enchanting little doll dressed in satin and frills, her dark eyes bright and mischievous; ringlets the colour of hazelnuts covered her head and were tied with a pink ribbon. Amelia adored her at once, completely understanding why Gerard had fallen in love with his daughter. For although Lisa did not carry his blood, she was undoubtedly his in every other way and the affection between them was a joy to see.

'It was charming, Mademoiselle Ravenshead.' Amelia smiled at her and held out her hand. 'Your English is very good. I see that you have been attending your lessons. Shall we go and see what Lady Pendleton has given us for tea?'

'Papa always speaks to me in English.' Lisa hesitated, then placed her tiny hand in Amelia's. She looked at her in a confiding manner. 'I am hungry, but Nanny said that I was not to eat anything. She says that the food is not suitable for me.'

'Oh, I think it would be a shame if you were not to have any of it,' Amelia replied. 'Perhaps not too much chocolate cake, but I think a small piece and some bread and honey could not hurt anyone.'

'We always had honey for tea in France,' Lisa told her with a happy smile. 'Nanny says a boiled egg is better, but I like honey for tea.'

'Well, do you know, so do I. Shall we have some?'

'Yes, please. Can I have a piece of cake? Nanny doesn't allow me cake.' Lisa looked sorrowful and then a smile peeped out. 'I have cake sometimes with Papa.'

'I think Christmas is an exception, don't you? Besides, Lady Pendleton would be very upset if all this lovely food went to waste—do you not think so?'

'Yes, I should think so,' Lisa said, giving her a naughty look. 'Could I have some of that red jelly, please?'

'I think perhaps that would be acceptable,' Amelia said. 'We shall have bread and honey and a jelly each—and then a piece of cake. How does that sound?'

'I beg your pardon, Miss Royston, but I do not allow my charge to eat such rich food as a rule.'

Amelia turned her head to look at the woman who had spoken. The child's nanny was a severe-looking woman with iron-grey hair and a thin mouth. She was perhaps fifty years of age and had doubtless ruled more than one nursery with a rod of iron. Amelia took an instant dislike to her, but hid it behind a polite smile.

'I believe we should relax the rules a little, Nanny,' she said pleasantly. 'This is Christmas, after all, and the earl asked me especially to make sure that his daughter enjoys herself. Lisa will not eat too much.'

'It is just that I do not wish her to be sick all night, ma'am.'

'I do not think it likely,' Amelia said. 'Please do what you can to help with the other children, Nanny. Lisa will be quite safe with me.'

The woman nodded and moved away. From the set of her shoulders, Amelia guessed that she was angry. She hoped that her refusal to accept Nanny's authority would not lead to some form of punishment for Lisa later.

'Do you like to play games?' she asked Lisa, making up her mind that she would speak to Gerard on the subject of his daughter's nanny later.

'I do not know, mademoiselle. I have never played any—except that Papa takes me up on his horse with him sometime. We run and chase each other in the garden when Nanny cannot see us. Is that a game?'

'Yes, one kind of a game but there are many others. Do you not have puzzles or a hoop to play with?'

'Papa gave me things when we came to England, but Nanny says I should study my books. She says playing with toys is a waste of time.'

'Does she indeed?' Amelia kept her voice light and without criticism. 'Lady Pendleton has several games for us to play today—musical chairs and pass the parcel, and I have seen some spilikins. I think that you and I might play these games together. It is Christmas, after all—and there are prizes to be won.'

Amelia smiled as she saw the little girl's face light up. Gerard was right to be concerned about his daughter's nanny. Lisa was clearly a high-spirited child and needed discipline, but not to the extent that she was forbidden time to play or the food that she enjoyed.

Two hours later, Amelia had fallen totally in love with her new friend. Lisa had blossomed, becoming a natural, happy little girl, as they joined in noisy games of pass the parcel and musical chairs. Susannah had been in charge of the music and saw to it that every child managed to win a small gift, which was most often sweetmeats or a trinket of some kind. Lisa won a little silver cross on a pink ribbon, and as a gift she was given a doll with a porcelain head and a stuffed body. It was wearing a pink satin dress that matched hers and, when the party ended, she ran to show it to her father.

'Beautiful,' he said and kissed her, gazing at Amelia over the child's head. 'Has this scamp of mine been good, Amelia?'

'Oh, I think so,' Amelia said. 'We have enjoyed ourselves, have we not, Lisa?'

'Oui, merci, mademoiselle,' Lisa said and curtsied to her. 'Will you come and see me again, please? I would like you to be my friend.' There was something a little desperate in the child's look as she saw her nurse coming to claim her. 'Please…'

'Yes, certainly. I shall come in the morning,' Amelia said. 'I have a gift for you, Lisa—and I think we could go for a walk together in the park or even a ride in the carriage since it is cold. You, your papa and me—how would that be?'

'I should like it above all things, *mademoiselle*.' Lisa threw herself at Amelia and hugged her.

'Come along, Miss Ravenshead,' Nanny said. 'You are over-excited. You will never sleep and I shall be up all night with you.' The woman shot a look of dislike at Amelia.

Mindful that it would take time to replace her, Amelia made no reply. However, she turned urgently to Gerard as Nanny led the child away.

'I must speak to you privately. I have made certain observations and I think you should consider replacing that woman.'

'You do not like her either?' Gerard looked relieved. 'I am so glad that I asked you to take note, Amelia. She was recommended to me, but I have thought her too sour. I was not sure if I was being unfair—and I know that children need discipline…'

'Not to the extent that all the joy of life is squeezed out of them,' Amelia said as they walked from the room into a smaller parlour where they were alone. 'Lisa is high-spirited, but she is a delightful child and has good manners. I think Nanny is too strict with her. She is not allowed to play or to have honey for tea—and that I must tell you is a terrible deprivation.'

'And entirely unnecessary,' Gerard said and laughed. 'I knew I might rely on you, my very dear Amelia. I was afraid that my partiality for Lisa made me too lenient. I have a nursemaid. I shall put her in charge and dismiss Nanny. Oh, I will give her a year's wages and a reference, but she shall not have charge of my daughter again.'

'Oh dear, the poor woman. I feel terrible now for she has lost her employment, and at Christmas—but I confess that I did not like her. I once employed a woman of that sort at the orphanage and had to dismiss her soon after, because she ill treated her charges. I do not understand why some people feel it is necessary to treat children as if they were criminals.'

'Some can be little monsters. I remember that I used to put frogs in the bed of my nanny.'

'Did you? I did that once and she went to my father. He sent me to bed and I was given nothing but bread and water for two days—and I had to apologise.'

'My father thrashed me. It did me the world of good, for as he said—think what a shock it was for the poor frog.'

'The frog…' Amelia went into a peal of delighted laughter. 'Oh, no! That is a great deal too bad of you, sir. You have a wicked sense of humour.'

'Yes, I have at times,' Gerard admitted. 'Though I have not laughed so very much of late. Amelia…may I tell you something?'

'Yes, of course.'

He led her towards a little sofa. 'Please sit down. This is not easy for me. I have wished to tell you something that almost no one else knows, but I fear it may give you a bad opinion of me.'

'Have you done something wicked?' she asked with a smile.

'I have not told you the whole truth about something.'

Amelia's smile faded. This was clearly serious. 'Please explain. I do not understand.'

'I told you that my wife died after a long illness?' Amelia nodded. 'It was not quite the truth. She had been ill, but she had recovered in her physical health at least, though I know now that she must still have been suffering in her mind.'

'Gerard! Please explain. I do not understand.'

'Lisette seemed happy enough while she was carrying the child, but afterwards...she complained that I did not love her—that I thought more of the child...'

'Surely any father would love their child? Perhaps she was pulled down by the birth? I have heard that some women are deeply affected by childbirth.'

'Yes, it may have been that...' Gerard hesitated. Now was his chance to tell her the whole truth, but he was reluctant. 'I may have neglected her. I tried to be good to her, to give her my protection and all that she needed, but perhaps it was not enough for her. I am not the man I was when we first met, Amelia. I have become harder, I think, less caring of others.'

'Oh, Gerard! I cannot think that you deliberately mistreated your wife?'

He stroked the little scar at his temple. 'No, not deliberately, but I may have been careless perhaps. Lisette was vulnerable, easily hurt. I should have been kinder.' He paused, then, 'It may not be possible for me to love anyone completely. Something died in me the night your brother had me thrashed. At first I believed that you knew—that you felt insulted by my love. I suppose that I became afraid to show love, and Lisette suffered because of my lack.'

Gerard hesitated. He wanted to tell her that Lisette's death was his fault, to tell her of the night when Lisette had crept into his bed and offered herself to him—of the way he had turned from his wife, because she was not the woman he had loved so deeply. It would be right and fair to make Amelia aware of what he had done, but he could not bear to see her turn from him in disgust. He knew that Lisette had been terribly hurt—that it had driven her to a desperate act.

'What happened—how did she die?'

'One day when I was out she ordered a bath and then…' He paused, almost choking on the words. 'When I returned I found her. She had slashed her wrists and bled to death. I pulled her from the water and did what I could for her. She died in my arms…' His face twisted with pain. 'I did not mean to hurt her. She must have been desperately unhappy and I was not there for her. Something in me must be lacking. How could I not know that my own wife was so desperate that she would take her own life? I have blamed myself for her death ever since.'

He had told her the truth, leaving out only a few details that he felt unable to communicate.

'Gerard…' Amelia was on her feet. She held out her hands to him, her expression understanding and sympathetic. 'My dear—how terrible for you! It was a tragedy for a life was lost—but it was not your fault. Lisette could not have recovered completely from the birth. How could you have known she was unhappy if she did not tell you?'

'She may have been unwell, but I was not aware of it. I should have known.'

'You rescued her when she was alone. You married her, were

kind to her so she turned to you, gave you her heart. If she felt unsure of your love, it may have made her desperately unhappy, but the blame is not all yours.'

'You see things so clearly…' Gerard moved closer, his eyes searching her face. 'So you do not hate me? You will not turn away in disgust? You understand that I am not as I once was?'

'I could never hate you. Surely you know…'

'I know that you are a wonderful, wise and lovely woman,' Gerard said passionately. 'I would be honoured if you would become my wife, Amelia. You were prepared to marry me all those years ago. Dare I hope that you still find the idea agreeable?'

'Gerard…' Amelia gasped. 'Yes…'

She meant to say more, but he lowered his head to kiss her on the lips. Amelia responded with all the love that was in her, her arms going about his neck as her body melded with his. This was what she had longed for, dreamed of so many lonely nights! She had never expected to be so fortunate.

'My beautiful Amelia,' Gerard said. 'I am a fool! You are such a sensible woman. You understand everything. You would not do something stupid because of a foolish quarrel. I should have asked long ago. You are exactly the woman I need in my life. You will not expect more than I am able to give.'

Amelia withdrew a little. She waited for him to say the words she needed to hear, but he did not speak of love and she was conscious of a slight disappointment.

She looked at him uncertainly. 'I had thought you meant to ask me before, but then you seemed to withdraw and I was not sure you cared for me.'

'I have always admired and cared for you,' Gerard replied. 'We should have married years ago had your brother not had me beaten for having the temerity to approach you.' He paused, then, 'I fear Sir Michael will not take the news kindly, Amelia.'

'Michael may be pleased for me or stay away from my home. I am not obliged to him and he may not deny me this time. However, *you* should take care, for I know he can be a spiteful man, Gerard.'

'I shall take care for myself and for you. I do not forget that someone made an attempt to abduct you, Amelia. It will be my first duty to protect you, my dearest.'

'Thank you. I feel it unlikely that Michael would do more than vent his displeasure on me verbally—but it is always best to be careful.' She looked at him, her doubt writ plain on her face. 'Do you wish to announce our engagement at once?'

'That is entirely up to you, Amelia. If you wish for more time to consider…'

'No, I think not,' Amelia told him. 'I have given you my answer and I shall not change my mind.'

'Then you have made me the happiest man alive,' Gerard said. 'I have a Christmas gift for you, Amelia—but it is not a ring. I was afraid to tempt fate. However, I did commission a ring. I shall send to my jeweller and have it delivered at Coleridge.'

'Perhaps we should announce our engagement at the ball there,' Amelia suggested. 'We shall consider ourselves pledged, Gerard—but tell only our best friends until the ball.'

'As usual you have solved the thing,' he said and leaned forwards to kiss her softly on the lips. 'I look forward to our wedding, Amelia. You are a good friend and you will be a wonderful wife. Lisa already adores you and this is the best thing I can do for her. You will have the comfort and security of marriage and I shall have a beautiful gracious wife…we shall all get on famously.'

Amelia allowed him to kiss her, but she did not cling to him as she had the first time. At the back of her mind a tiny doubt had formed. She did not want to think it, but she was afraid that Gerard had proposed to her because he needed a suitable wife and a mother for his delightful daughter! Much as she knew she would love Lisa, she could not help thinking that if things had been different she might have been the child's mother. She would be a good mother to Lisa, but her heart ached when she thought of what might have been.

Did Gerard imagine that she had remained single because she had not received another offer? Amelia frowned as she went up to change for the evening. She might have been married soon after Gerard disappeared, but she had refused every man her brother brought for her to meet. Michael had tried to push her into marrying a marquis, but she had not allowed him to bully her.

Since she came into her fortune, she had received six offers of marriage. Not one of the gentlemen had made her feel that she wished to be married, even though she believed that at least one had been in love with her. Despite the hurt Gerard's apparent desertion had inflicted, she had never ceased to love him. No other man could ever replace him in her heart.

Amelia's feelings now were mixed. Gerard had proposed and she had accepted, but the doubts had begun to creep in. Was he truly in love with her—or did he simply wish for a convenient arrangement? He needed a mother for Lisa, and he wanted a wife who would not make too many demands.

She tried to remember his exact words, but had only a vague

memory for his proposal had swept all else from her mind. She thought he had told her that he cared for his wife, but he could never love with all his heart, because something had died in him the night Michael sent him away. Lisette had wanted more and because of that she had become desperately unhappy. Amelia imagined that she had still been low after the birth of her child, for more than one young one woman had been known to suffer a deep melancholy after giving birth.

Amelia frowned. Gerard's words as he proposed seemed to indicate that he was looking for a comfortable marriage that would not make too many demands on his emotions. Was he saying that *she* must not expect too much—that he simply needed a complaisant woman to care for his child and his home?

Did he care for her at all?

What nonsense was this? She was such a fool! Amelia's thoughts were confused as she changed for dinner that evening. For years she had regretted the love she had lost. She had felt the years slipping away, her youth lost. There were times when she believed she would die an old maid, unfulfilled and unloved.

Recently, after meeting Gerard again, she had begun to long for him to speak. Now he had proposed and she had accepted, and yet she was beset by doubts. A tiny voice in her head was telling her she should not hope for a love match. Gerard was older and he had undoubtedly changed from the young man who had declared his love so passionately. He had spoken of caring for Amelia and of looking forward to her becoming his wife— not the words of a man desperately in love. Not the passionate declaration she had hoped to hear!

Gerard *had* asked her to marry him because it was a conve-nient arrangement. He wanted a wife—a mother for his beautiful daughter. Had he not asked her to give him her opinion of Lisa's nanny? She had done so and her thoughts coincided with his, which had made him feel she would make an ideal wife and mother. In her first rush of delight that he had spoken, Amelia had imagined that he was proposing because he loved her as she loved him. However, she was certain that he respected and liked her—and was that not a perfectly sound basis for marriage?

She took a turn about the room, her thoughts tumbling in confusion as she came to terms with her situation. Was a marriage of convenience acceptable? Could she be happy as Gerard's wife, knowing that he cared for her but was not in love with her?

Of course she could! Amelia scolded herself for the feeling of disappointment she had been experiencing since leaving Gerard. She was no longer a green girl. She ought not to expect romance at her age. Her heart told her that Gerard was the only man she would ever love. If she behaved foolishly and changed her mind, because his proposal was not the declaration of love she desired, she would be cutting off her nose to spite her face— and that would be ridiculous.

Amelia was faced with the choice of remaining unwed for the rest of her life or marrying the man she loved, understanding that he did not feel romantic love for her. Had she been that young girl of so many years ago, she would have demanded an equal partnership where both partners loved, but the years had taught her some hard lessons and she was a woman of sense. The prospect of remaining single all her life was one she had faced, because there seemed no alternative. However, she now had a chance of some happiness. She would have a husband who cared for her in his own way and she would have a family; she was still young enough to give Gerard an heir. In her mind she saw pictures of their sons growing through childhood to manhood, hearing their laughter as an echo in her head and seeing their smiling faces. If she did not marry, she would never have a child of her own to love. She might not have the passionate love she had longed for, but she would have a family, children and companionship.

It was enough, she decided. She would make it enough, and perhaps Gerard would recapture some of the feeling he'd once had for her. His kiss had told her that he was not indifferent in a physical sense. He found her desirable. Perhaps in time true love would blossom once more.

A marriage where the feeling was stronger on one side than the other was not unusual. People married for many reasons, quite often for money or position. She acquitted Gerard of wanting her fortune—he had made it plain to her at an earlier time that he had enough for his needs. He wanted a companion, a sensible woman who would love his daughter and not make too many demands. Could she be that woman? Amelia decided that she could. She had had years of learning to hide her emotions; it should not be too difficult to give Gerard the kind of wife he desired. It would be a convenient arrangement for them both.

Amelia picked up her long evening gloves and pulled them on, smoothing the fingers in place. She glanced in the mirror and smiled at the picture she presented. She looked serene, untroubled. No one would ever guess at the ache in her heart.

She was about to open her door when someone knocked and Emily walked in. It was obvious that she was distressed and Amelia forgot her own problems instantly.

'Something is wrong! I can see it in your face, Emily.'

'Mr Sinclair…I could not prevent him from speaking,' Emily said, her voice catching. 'I told him that I must have time to consider…and I think he was angry with me for his face went white. He inclined his head and walked away from me without another word. I should have called him back, but I could not speak.'

'Oh, my poor Emily,' Amelia said. 'Could you not find the words to tell him the truth?'

'I was afraid of what I might see in his eyes,' Emily confessed. 'We must somehow manage to speak to each other while we are both guests here…' She gave a little sob. 'I am in such distress for I would not hurt him for the world and I am sure he was hurt by my hesitation. Yet how could I tell him the truth?'

'Do not distress yourself, my love,' Amelia said. 'You have done nothing wrong. Many other ladies ask for time when first asked that question. When next it happens, you will be ready to make your confession.'

'Yes, I shall. I intend to seek Mr Sinclair out tomorrow evening after the celebrations. One of us may leave the following day—I could go home if he did not wish to leave.'

'Do not be so pessimistic, Emily.' Amelia was encouraging. 'I still believe that Mr Sinclair will be more understanding than you imagine—and now, my love, you must wish me happy. The Earl of Ravenshead has asked me to be his wife and I have accepted him. We shall not announce our engagement until the ball at Coleridge, but I wanted you to know.'

'Amelia!' Emily's face reflected surprise and then pleasure. 'I am so very happy for you, dearest. I have thought that perhaps you liked him and he liked you, but I was not sure what your intentions were regarding marriage.'

'It will be…a convenient arrangement for us both, for my brother will have to accept that he is no longer my heir. Especially if I should have a child, which I hope will be the case.'

'A convenient arrangement?' Emily looked puzzled. 'It is not my business to pry, but are you sure that is all it is? I am sure the earl has a deep regard for you, Amelia.'

'Ah, yes, we are comfortable together—good friends,' Amelia said, avoiding Emily's probing gaze. She was doing her best to appear dispassionate, but Emily knew her too well. 'Shall we go down, my love? We do not wish to keep Susannah and her guests waiting.' She saw a doubtful look in her companion's eyes. 'You must not think that I would wish to dispense with your company, Emily. While I should be happy to see you marry a gentleman of your choice, I should be sad to lose you. Be assured that your home is with me until you decide to leave.'

'You are always so generous,' Emily replied. 'Thank you for making that plain to me. Like you, I have met only one man I would care to marry, but you know my thoughts and I shall say no more, for this is Christmas Eve.'

Amelia noticed how thoughtful her companion was as they went downstairs and joined the other guests. She smiled and nodded to the company, but was quiet and merely nodded her head when Toby offered her his arm to take her into dinner. Obviously, he had controlled his hurt feelings and was deter-mined to remain Emily's friend. Amelia had always thought him a likeable young man and now found she approved of his manners—he was everything he ought to be as a gentleman.

Gerard took Amelia in to dinner. He told her in a whisper that he had confided their secret to Harry and Susannah, also to Toby Sinclair.

'For the moment I have asked that they keep the news to themselves,' he said. 'We shall make our announcement at Coleridge, as we planned.'

'I have told Emily, for it would have seemed secretive and unkind had I excluded her. She would have been worried that her position might not be secure had she heard something from another person.'

'I doubt that Miss Barton will need to work as a companion for long,' Gerard said. 'You must have observed that a certain gentleman has a distinct partiality for her company?'

'Yes, I know that Mr Sinclair has made Emily an offer, but she is a little nervous of her situation in life and asked for more time.'

Gerard raised his brows. 'She feels that she may not suit the ambitions of his family, because she is employed as a companion?'

'I believe she does feel something of the kind, but I hope the matter will be resolved satisfactorily.'

'Toby will inherit a decent estate when his father dies, but I am certain he will make his own fortune. Although he is close to his family, I do not think he would allow them to dictate to him in such a matter—and I see no reason why Emily should not be acceptable to them. Toby is of good family, but he is not the heir to an illustrious title, merely his father's baronetcy. I see no cause for anyone to object to his choice.'

Amelia nodded. She had wondered if she might ask for Gerard for help in trying to find Emily's child, but she had hoped to find a way of concealing the mother's identity. Even if that was impracticable, now was not the time or place to reveal it.

'Well, we must hope for a happy outcome,' she said. 'I was wondering when you thought would be a suitable moment for us to marry? Do you wish for some time to make your arrangements or would you prefer the wedding to be held quite soon?'

'Personally, I believe the sooner we marry the better for all concerned,' Gerard said. 'I know that my daughter would be happy to have a new mama—and I am certainly looking forward to our wedding. Do you wish for a longer engagement or shall we settle it for a month after the ball?'

'I think a month after the ball should be adequate time,' Amelia replied. 'It will give me a chance to make necessary changes. Will you wish to live at Ravenshead on a permanent basis?'

'Are you thinking that you would like to spend a part of the year at your estate, Amelia?'

'I like to spend some part of the summer in Bath and I must visit London several times a year to oversee my children's home, but I dare say I shall like Ravenshead very well.'

'There will be time enough to decide once you have visited,' Gerard told her. 'We must have the lawyers draw up the settlements, Amelia. I should not wish to control your fortune, though I will help you to manage it if you so wish. It might be a sensible idea to put a part at least in trust for your children.'

'That is an excellent notion,' Amelia agreed, a faint blush in her cheeks. 'I have a great deal of property—mostly houses. Great-Aunt Agatha acquired a considerable portfolio during her lifetime. I have wondered whether it might be better to sell most of them and re-invest the money. I should greatly appreciate your opinion, Gerard. I have my man of business, naturally, and my lawyers—but there has been no one I could turn to with my problems. No one I could truly trust. I have good friends, of course, but one does not like to ask advice in these matters.'

'I am sure Harry would have been happy to help you, Amelia. He has an excellent head for business. However, you have me now, my dearest. Any concern—the slightest worry—you may address to me, and I will do my best to take it from you.'

'Thank you, Gerard. You are most kind…' Amelia spoke carefully. He seemed so considerate, but was it merely the kindness he would offer to any friend?

Gerard looked at her oddly. She thought he was about to speak once more, but they had reached the dining room and Amelia found that she was sitting between Gerard on her left side and an elderly gentleman she knew slightly on the other. The time for confidences had passed, and though she made polite conversation with both gentlemen throughout dinner there was no chance of talking privately to Gerard.

Amelia glanced round the dinner table. Everyone was smiling and looking pleased. Susannah was a generous hostess and her cooks had excelled themselves. Course after course of delicious food was served to the guests and it was late before Susannah rose to take the ladies through to the drawing room. The gentlemen remained to drink port and smoke their cigars, while the ladies took tea in the drawing room.

It was nearly eleven o'clock when the gentlemen joined them at last, and then the present-giving ceremony took place. Susannah and Harry had bought gifts for all their guests. The footmen took these round on silver trays and there was a great deal of exclaiming and cries of pleasure as the small gifts were unwrapped to reveal things like Bristol-blue scent bottles for the ladies and enamelled snuffboxes for the gentlemen.

Amelia had already exchanged personal gifts with Susannah and Harry and would open those she had received in privacy. She had purchased a silver-gilt card case for Gerard, which she planned to give him the next morning after breakfast.

Chapter Three

It was five and twenty minutes to twelve when the guests separated. The older members of the family said goodnight and went up to their rooms, whilst the younger guests donned cloaks and greatcoats and went out to the waiting carriages. They were driven to Pendleton church, where they joined villagers for the midnight mass. This was a special part of Christmas as far as Amelia was concerned. She felt that this year it was even more so, because she was sharing it with her fiancé. Now that she had made up her mind, the thought warmed her and she felt a little thrill of happiness. How much better life would be in the future, even if her husband were not desperately in love with her.

Amelia left the church on Gerard's arm, feeling happy. The bells had begun to ring and it was almost a forerunner of their wedding day. As they paused for a moment for the carriages to come forwards to pick them up, their breath made patterns on the frosty air.

'Gerard…' Amelia began, but was shocked when he suddenly

pushed her to one side so that she stumbled and fell against a prickly holly bush. 'What...?' Before she could finish her sentence, a shot rang out, passing so close to her that she felt a puff of air. She was struggling to recover her balance, as Gerard took out a pistol and fired at something in the shadows.

Almost at once, Amelia found that Harry and Susannah were at her side, assisting her. Everything else was confusion as people shouted and rushed about, some of the men setting off in pursuit of the would-be assassin.

'Amelia dearest,' Susannah cried, looking at her anxiously. 'Are you hurt? I do not know what happened...'

'The earl saw him just in time,' Emily said, for she too had rushed to Amelia's side. 'I noticed someone lurking over there in those trees. However, I did not realise what he meant to do until I saw him lift his arm.'

'Did you see his face, Miss Barton?' Harry asked. 'I'm dashed if I noticed anything until I heard the shot.'

'He was wearing a dark hat and a muffler,' Emily told him. 'I am sorry. I know that is of little use to you, but it was all I saw.'

Harry nodded and looked grim. 'Forgive us, Amelia. We expected something might happen, but not like this...on such a night. What kind of a man would attempt murder on Christmas Eve?'

'What do you mean?' Amelia stared at him. Her wrist stung where a thorn had penetrated her glove and she was feeling a little sick inside. 'Why did you expect something to happen?'

'Come, get inside the carriage, ladies,' Harry said. 'We must take you home. Gerard will explain later. He is coming now...' He glanced at the earl, who had gone after the assassin. 'Any luck?' Gerard shook his head and Harry swore.

'Amelia, forgive me for pushing you into the holly,' Gerard apologised. 'I knew I must act quickly—but have you been hurt?'

'A mere scratch,' Amelia told him. 'Had that ball found its mark, I might be dead.'

'I think it was meant more as a warning to me,' Gerard said. He climbed into the carriage with her and Emily. Susannah had gone with some of the other ladies and Harry. 'I received a threat this morning, when I returned from our walk, Amelia. It was somewhat obscure and I was not truly certain of its meaning, though I had an idea that I was being warned to stay away from you.'

'To stay away from me?' Amelia stared at him in dismay. 'What can you mean?'

'I think someone had guessed that I meant to ask you to marry me—and whoever that person is he has decided that he does not wish for the marriage to go ahead.'

'He would rather see me dead than as your wife?' Amelia's hand shook and she felt cold all over. 'Who could be so evil? I do not understand who would do such a thing.'

'Your brother threatened you,' Emily reminded her. 'He warned you against renewing your acquaintance with the earl.'

'Is this true?'

Amelia met Gerard's concerned look. 'Yes. Michael has warned me that you are interested only in my fortune many times. I told him that I did not believe you to be so mercenary—and he did tell me that I would be sorry if—' She broke off and shook her head. 'I cannot believe that my brother would try to shoot me like that.'

'He knows that if you marry me he would no longer have a chance of claiming your fortune for himself. I am sorry to say that there are some men who would stop at nothing where a large amount of money is concerned.'

'Michael is a bully—but I am not certain he would murder for gain.'

'At the moment he is our most likely suspect.' Gerard reached for her hand and held it. 'Do not fear, Amelia. You will be protected. I have already set measures in hand to have you watched all the time. I had not thought it necessary while we stayed at Pendleton. I imagined that you might be at risk once we announce our engagement, but my men will be in place by then.' His expression was grave. 'Unless you wish to withdraw in the circumstances?'

'I refuse to let anyone dictate to me!' Amelia lifted her head proudly. 'Whoever this person is, the threat would not go away if we postponed the announcement of our engagement, Gerard.'

'You are as brave as I imagined.' Gerard squeezed her hand comfortingly. 'I had planned to tell you all this after Christmas. I did not want to spoil the celebrations for Susannah and her guests—but I am afraid that this unpleasant incident will cast a shadow over things.'

'Can you not let people think it was merely a poacher or some such thing?'

'At half an hour past midnight?' Gerard smiled. 'I could try, Amelia, but I doubt I should be believed. We might tell everyone that it was an attempted robbery.'

'That would be much better—and it may even be the truth,' Amelia said. 'You say that you were warned, Gerard—how exactly were you warned?'

'I was sent a doll that had been mutilated. A note in the wrappings said that if I cared for her I must stay away from her.'

'Could that not have meant Lisa?'

'Very few people even knew that I had a daughter until today,' Gerard said. 'Besides, why should I stay away from my own daughter—who could that benefit? She does not have a fortune…'

'No one could benefit from her death. It would in any case seem that I am the target after what happened this evening.' Amelia looked at him steadily. 'It is most unpleasant, Gerard… that someone should wish to kill me for money.'

'It is wicked!' Emily burst out, obviously upset. 'I think he should be ashamed of himself! Oh, do not look at me so, Amelia. It must be Sir Michael behind this monstrous plot. Who else could it be?'

'I do not know—yet I am loathe to think my brother would stoop so low.'

'You think well of most people,' Gerard said as the carriage began to slow down. 'Forgive me for allowing that evil man to get near enough to take a shot at you this night, Amelia. I promise it will not happen again.'

He jumped out as soon as the carriage drew to a halt, helped Amelia down and sheltered her with his body as he hurried her into the house. Once inside, he saw how pale she looked and took her into his arms for a moment, holding her close. Amelia wanted to cling to him and weep, but controlled her feelings. Gerard would not care for a clinging wife. She stood unmoving within his arms and he let her go as they heard the other guests, who had attended mass with them, arriving.

'Perhaps you would prefer to go straight up?'

'Yes, I should. I do not wish to discuss the matter further at the moment. Excuse me, I shall see you in the morning.'

Amelia went quickly up the stairs, followed immediately by

Emily. She was conscious of an irritation of the nerves. When Emily tried to follow her into her bedroom, she turned to her with a hasty dismissal.

'Please excuse me, Emily. I would prefer to be alone.'

'Yes, of course.'

Emily looked a little hurt at her tone, but Amelia was in too much distress to notice. It was bad enough that someone should try to shoot her, but to know that they all thought it was her brother who was behind the plot to murder her was lowering. Amelia had suffered much at the hands of her brother and sister-in-law—but murder was too terrible to comprehend.

She took off her bonnet and shawl, feeling glad that she had put on a gown that fastened at the front and told her maid not to wait up for her. At the moment her mind was in such turmoil that she could not speak to anyone.

Amelia slept fitfully and was awake long before the maids brought breakfast to her room. However, she had recovered from her irritation of the nerves and asked that the breakfast be laid in the sitting room. Wearing a pretty new lace peignoir, she went through to the little parlour and found that Emily was already there.

'Good morning, my love. May I wish you a Happy Christmas?'

'Thank you—Happy Christmas to you, Amelia. I hope you will like my gift. It is not much, but was chosen with care.'

'I am sure I shall.' Amelia presented her with an exquisitely wrapped parcel and smiled as Emily gave a cry of pleasure on opening it. Inside was an evening purse made of delicate links of gold, which fastened with a crossover clasp set with diamonds. It was a very expensive gift and reflected Amelia's true regard for her companion.

'This is so beautiful…you are always so generous to me…' Emily's lashes were wet with tears. 'To think that anyone could wish—' She broke off and wiped her hand across her cheek. 'I know you will not wish me to mention it, but I have not slept for thinking of what happened. Had the earl not been so alert you might not be here this morning…'

'You must not let a silly incident upset you. It will not happen again,' Amelia said and opened her parcel. Discovering a scarf she had admired some weeks before Christmas, she went to embrace her friend. 'This is exactly what I wished for, Emily. How sweet of you to remember it.'

'I bought it the day after we saw it,' Emily said and helped herself to some toast and honey. 'Lady Pendleton gave me a lovely scent flask with silver ends last evening, but this purse…it is the most beautiful thing I have ever owned.'

'I am glad you are pleased with it, my love. Has Mr Sinclair given you a gift?'

'No—but I think he has one for me. I believe he intended it to be a ring…' She fiddled with her toast. 'I bought a horn-and-ivory card case inlaid with gold for him, but I am undecided as to whether I should give it to him or not.'

'I am certain that you should exchange gifts with Mr Sinclair, Emily. He is a close friend and I also have a gift for him. You may deliver mine at the same time if it makes you feel better, my love.'

'Yes, I think it would. I should not feel so particular. May I ask what you have bought for Mr Sinclair?'

'I purchased a rather fine diamond stickpin. It has the shape of four hands linking and I thought it might appeal to him.'

'It will be the very thing for him,' Emily said and laughed delightedly. 'He was so very desperate to become a member of the Four-in-Hand Club and he delights in wearing the special waistcoat.'

'I am very fond of that gentleman,' Amelia said with a smile. 'He played his part in the fortunes of both of my protégées. Susannah and Helene have both been lucky. I should be happy to see you settled as well, Emily my love.'

A delicate blush appeared in her companion's cheeks. 'I think I may say without fear of boasting that Mr Sinclair does care for me—but whether he could accept my shame…'

'Emily, that is enough! The shame belongs to the man who forced you, my love. I will not have you hang your head. I was thinking that I would ask you to be my bridesmaid—and, of course, Susannah and Helene will be matrons of honour if they can spare the time from their busy lives—and Lisa must be a bridesmaid also, of course.'

'I should be honoured,' Emily told her and finished eating her toast. 'Mr Sinclair asked me if I would be paying my usual morning visit to the nursery and I said yes. I have a gift for Susannah's son—and also a little ring that I had as a girl, which I mean to give to Lisa.'

'How thoughtful of you, my love,' Amelia approved. 'I bought a doll for Lisa…just in case she was staying here with her father this Christmas. I think I shall come with you this morning—if you would not mind waiting until I dress?'

'I should be delighted. I usually go for a walk after I visit the children, but it snowed early this morning. Not enough to make walking impossible, but I felt…' She floundered to a halt.

'Yes, I understand.' Amelia nodded. 'I too shall be very careful when and where I walk until Gerard has his men in place. It may be as well to remain indoors for the moment—and we may blame the weather for it is inclement.'

'You wish to keep last night's incident as private as possible? I doubt that it will be possible, Amelia. Not everyone will keep it to himself or herself. I dare say the incident will be whispered of, if not openly admitted.'

'Yes, I fear that it may.' Amelia sighed. 'We, however, shall make light of it—there was a rogue near the church who sought to rob us. It is a weak excuse but it will suffice. Excuse me while I dress.'

'There is no hurry. I have something to do first—besides, you have not yet opened all your letters.'

'I have rather a lot of them, but I shall open one or two before I dress.' She looked with pleasure at the pile of letters waiting for her.

One of Amelia's chief pleasures in life was in writing to her friends. It was a good way of keeping in touch with many acquaintances she hardly ever saw. Amongst the cards and greetings she had received that Christmas morning was one from a lady for whom she had profound sympathy. The lady was very much in the position Amelia had been for years, at the mercy of her family. Except that Marguerite had no chance of marriage at all and Amelia might have married if she had wished.

Something must be done for her friend, Amelia thought. A Season in town would not solve Marguerite's problem, but perhaps she could think of some way of getting her away from her family for a while. She wrote a long and cheerful letter and sealed it. It had occurred to her that she would need someone she trusted to help her care for Lisa. Marguerite adored children and she might enjoy helping with Lisa's education.

Glancing at the clock, Amelia realised that it was time she paid her visit to the nursery. Lisa would have had her breakfast and she would be waiting for the gift Amelia had promised her. She hoped the child would be pleased with the doll she had chosen.

Amelia spent a pleasant half an hour in the nursery, playing with Lisa, who had been given several presents, including a pretty doll from her father. Lisa was delighted to have two dolls, especially as Amelia's had curly hair.

'She is like me,' she said and put the doll up against her face. 'Thank you, Mademoiselle Royston.'

'You may call me Amelia. We are going to be friends, Lisa.'

'Papa says you are to be my mama.' Lisa's eyes were large and apprehensive. 'Will you live with us, Melia?'

'Yes, I shall live with you and your papa,' Amelia replied. 'That is why I want us to be friends, dearest. As you grow up, it will be I who buys your dresses and teaches you to be a young lady. You will have a governess, but she will be kind and I shall make certain that your studies include games as well as the dull things.'

Lisa's face lit up, then a shy expression came into her eyes. 'Will you love me, *mademoiselle*?'

'I already love you,' Amelia said and took her into her arms, hugging and kissing her. 'You are a delight to me, Lisa—and perhaps one day you may have brothers or sisters to play with you.'

'I should like that but…Papa will not send me away when you are married?'

'No, of course not. Why should you think that?'

'Nanny told me it would happen if I did not do everything she told me.'

'That lady has been dismissed. I shall choose another nurse to help look after you, and I assure you that she will be kind.'

'I love you,' Lisa said as she climbed on Amelia's knee and put her arms about her neck. 'Nanny hasn't left yet, Melia. I saw her in the garden as I looked from my window. She was talking to someone—a man. I have seen her talk to him before, but she said that if I told Papa she would whip me.'

'She was very wicked to threaten you like that.' Amelia controlled her anger. 'Your papa has dismissed her. If she has not already left this house, she will do so within a few hours. I dare say your papa thought it would be unfair to make her leave at Christmastide. However, she will not be allowed near you again.' Amelia touched her hair. 'You must always tell Papa or me these things, Lisa, if someone hurts or frightens you—or if you see someone who makes you feel uncomfortable.'

'I will tell you. Papa might think I was telling tales—and gentlemen do not approve of such things.'

'There are times when telling a grown-up the truth is important. If someone frightens you, Lisa—or threatens you—you must tell us. Please promise me you will?'

'I promise.' Lisa slid from her lap as some of the other children came running into the nursery schoolroom. They were all clutching new toys of some kind. 'I must not keep you, *mademoiselle*. Nanny said that mothers only spend a few minutes with children; they are too busy to waste their time with us.'

Amelia smothered a sigh. Gerard had not dismissed that woman a moment too soon!

'When we are all living together, you will spend a part of your day with your papa and me when he has the time. It is true that gentlemen have their business to keep them busy, but I assure you that I shall take you for walks and I think your papa might teach you to ride a pony.'

'Ride a pony?' Lisa's face lit up. 'Truly? Would Papa truly teach me to ride himself?'

'I am sure that he will, as soon as he considers you are ready.' Amelia kissed her cheek. 'I must go now, my love, but I shall ask your papa if he will take us both for a little carriage ride after dinner.'

Amelia received an enthusiastic hug. She was smiling as she went downstairs. As she turned towards the large drawing room where she knew many of the other guests had gathered, she was unaware that she was being watched from the gallery above.

Turning away to return to the room she would have to leave in the morning, Lisa's former nanny, Alice Horton, gave a spiteful smile. The Royston woman was riding for a fall. She had not hesitated to use her position and influence to have Alice dismissed from her position, but she would not see herself installed as the Earl of Ravenshead's wife. There were plans afoot that would prevent their marriage. When *he* had first approached her, Alice had been reluctant to give him any information about her employer or his daughter. However, she had no such scruples now.

He had paid her well for the news that Lisa was to have a new mama very soon. Alice had enough money to see her through the next few months without having to apply for a new position—and if she did what *he* asked, she might never have to work again…

Amelia saw Gerard standing near the window in the large salon. He had been in conversation with Harry, but as soon as he noticed her, he said something to his friend and came to greet her.

'Have you been to see Lisa? Toby told me that he saw you with Miss Barton on your way there.'

'I took her my gift. I had bought her a doll. She received several dolls, but mine had curly hair like hers and that pleased her.' Amelia lifted her hand to her own neat, dark locks. She had allowed her maid to dress it in a softer style and believed it suited her. 'I have made Lisa a promise on your behalf, Gerard. She seemed to think that she must not expect us to visit her for more than half an hour in the mornings. I told her that when we were married I should take her for walks—and that you would teach her to ride a pony. I hope I have not spoken out of turn?'

'Of course you have not,' Gerard assured her instantly. 'I had intended to buy the child a pony quite soon—and I shall certainly teach her to ride it myself. Since we shall be spending much of our lives in the country there will be plenty of time for such pleasures. You must feel free to do as you think best, Amelia. I am confident that your sure judgement will bring many benefits to both Lisa's life and my own.'

'I shall do my best to be the mother she lacks.'

'You will be the best mother she could have—the only one she has known.'

'I am glad you feel as I do,' Amelia said. 'I know that in many families the children are confined to the nursery until they are old enough to come out—but I do not approve of such rigid rules. Naturally, they must study and there are times when they might be a nuisance to guests, but when it is just the family I hope we shall often be together.'

He gave her a look of warm approval. 'You are a constant delight to me. I knew you would be generous towards my daughter—but this is more than I could have expected.'

'I love her. She is a delightful child, Gerard.'

A tiny pinprick of hurt entered her heart, because it was so obvious that he wanted and needed a mother for Lisa. Would any woman have done—or did he feel something stronger toward her?

'Yes, she is.' He smiled and took a small box from inside his coat. 'This is my gift to you for today, Amelia. I shall be sending for the family jewels and you may make your choice of them— though I warn you that they will need to be refurbished for they are heavy and old-fashioned. This is something I thought might please you.'

Amelia unwrapped the box and took out the beautiful diamond brooch inside. It was shaped like a delicate bouquet of flowers and the heads trembled as she took it from its box.

'This is beautiful,' she said and pinned it to her gown. She reached into the pocket of her gown. 'I have a small gift for you, Gerard—it is a mere trinket…' In value, it was a similar gift to the one she had given Toby Sinclair, something she might have given to any member of her close friends and family. Not what she might have chosen had she known they would be engaged by Christmas Day.

He took the box and dispensed with the wrappings, revealing the silver-gilt card case. 'More than a trinket, Amelia. Thank you.'

Amelia shook her head, changing the subject. 'Emily was saying that she would not walk alone, because of what happened last night. I too think it would be best to take care for the moment. I wondered if we might take Lisa for a little ride in your carriage after dinner?'

'I see no reason why we should not go for a drive,' Gerard said. 'As for what happened last night, the matter is in hand. Any strangers seen on the estate will be stopped and questioned.'

Amelia recalled what Lisa had told her about the nanny speaking to a man in the gardens—a man the woman had spoken to before. However, she had no reason to suppose that the man could have anything to do with the incident outside the church. As unlikely as it seemed, Nanny probably had a follower.

Dismissing the nanny from her mind, she smiled as Susannah came up to them. She was wearing the pearl-and-diamond pendant that Amelia had given her as a Christmas gift and the next few minutes were taken up with her delight and her gratitude. By the time Amelia and Gerard spoke again, the nanny had been forgotten.

It was a pleasant morning. Amelia exchanged gifts with several friends, enjoying some music before nuncheon. After they had eaten, Gerard sent for his carriage. Lisa's nurse brought her downstairs. She was wearing a pretty pink coat and hat and had a fur muff that her papa had given her. She was excited to be going for a drive, chattering about the many gifts that she had received that morning.

'I had four dolls altogether, Papa—was I not fortunate?' she said as they went out to the carriage. 'One was broken.'

Gerard's attention was caught. 'A broken doll—who gave you that, my love?'

'I do not know, Papa. I asked Nurse Mary. She said there was no card.'

'I shall have a look at the doll later,' Gerard said. 'It was a shame the doll was broken.' His eyes met Amelia's over Lisa's head.

'I did not mind,' Lisa said. 'I had so many pretty things. I did not expect so many presents. Nanny said it was obscene for one small child to have so many expensive clothes as I have. What does obscene mean, Papa?'

'I think it means that I spoil you,' Gerard said, but his mouth had pulled into a grim line.

Amelia touched his hand. He glanced at her but his expression remained grim.

'I have been spoiled too,' Amelia said and smiled at the child as she touched the brooch she was wearing. She had fastened it to the scarf Emily had given her, and she was wearing a new black velvet cloak she had purchased in London; it had a fur lining and was very warm. 'I was given this lovely scarf and this brooch—do you see how it trembles as I move?'

'Did Papa give it to you?' Amelia nodded. 'It is very beautiful—but you are *très ravissante*, Melia. Papa will be lucky when you marry him.'

'We shall all be lucky to have each other,' Amelia said. 'Look, Lisa—can you see the deer over there? I think they have come closer to the house than usual. I know that Susannah has food put out for them when the weather is inclement.'

'They are lovely…' Lisa said, pressing her face to the carriage window. 'Papa, do we have deer at Ravenshead?'

'I believe not,' he said. 'We might have some brought into the park if you would like that, Lisa.' His face had relaxed. He smiled as he met Amelia's eyes. She nodded slightly, understanding his feelings. The broken doll was worrying, but might simply be a coincidence.

'Oh, yes, please. I should love that, Papa—and could I please have a puppy…?'

'Is there anything else, miss?' he asked, brows rising indulgently.

'Oh, no, Papa,' Lisa said and put her hand into Amelia's. 'But Melia did say I should tell you anything I wanted.'

'Did she, indeed?' Gerard laughed. 'I can see that I am to be petticoat-led now that I have two beautiful ladies in my life.'

Amelia was pleased that he had managed to put his worries to one side, and yet she sensed a shadow hanging over them.

She glanced out of the carriage window. A light dusting of snow clung to the trees and shrubs, but it was beginning to melt. A pale sun had brightened the day. Shadows might gather in the distance, but for today Amelia would try to forget them and think only of pleasant things.

Lisa was singing a little French song when Amelia took her up to the nursery and handed her back to Mary. The little girl turned to her, hugging her as she took her leave.

'Thank you for my lovely afternoon, Melia.'

'You are very welcome, Lisa. It was a pleasure for me.'

Amelia smiled and left the child with her nurse. The future was looking so much brighter. Children were a blessing and already the ache she had carried deep inside her was easing. She was a mother to Gerard's daughter and in time they would have others of their own.

She hastened to the apartments she shared with Emily, because the hour was late and she would have to hurry if she were to change and be ready in time for dinner. As she entered the little parlour, the sound of sobbing met her. The sight of Emily weeping desperately brought her to a halt.

She went to her at once. 'Emily, dearest—what is wrong?'

'Oh…Amelia…' Emily lifted her head to look at her. 'Forgive me. I did not mean you to see me like this…' She wiped her hand across her face. 'I should have gone to my bedchamber.'

'Do not be foolish. You should not hide your tears from me, Emily. Can you not tell me what is wrong?'

'I spoke to Mr Sinclair when we exchanged gifts,' Emily said, her body shaken by a deep, hurtful sob. 'He gave me a beautiful sapphire-and-diamond ring and I…told him that I could not marry him. He asked me why and I told him that I had given birth to a child…' She bent her head, the tears falling once more.

'Emily, my love.' Amelia knelt down beside her and took her hand. 'Did you explain that you were forced?' Emily shook her head and Amelia gave her fingers a gentle squeeze 'You should have made that plain. He did not understand the circumstances.'

'He did not give me a chance,' Emily said. She took a kerchief from her sleeve and wiped her face. 'He looked so stunned, Amelia. It was as if I had thrown a jug of cold water over him. He drew back, shaking his head and looked…as if he could not bear the sight of me. I think he must hate me now.'

'Emily! I am certain it was merely shock. He did not understand the circumstances. Mr Sinclair is a gentleman. I do not believe he would have done that to you deliberately.'

'I begged him not to look at me that way. I pleaded for a chance to explain, but he said that he must have time—and then he walked away and left me. It is over. He has a disgust of me now.'

'He was shocked, that is all. I am sure that when he has recovered from his…' Amelia paused, searching for the right word.

'Disappointment?' Emily lifted her head. 'I saw it in his eyes, Amelia. He was stunned, disappointed, even revolted—I think he could not bear the idea that I had been with another man.'

'It must have been upsetting for him, but he may have thought you had a love child, Emily. You must try to understand that he had put you on a pedestal. He may have misunderstood you. He may think that you took a lover. You must tell him the truth.'

'I could not! I do not think I could bear to face him again.'

'Emily dearest,' Amelia said, 'I understand that it would be too difficult for you to tell him everything—but I could speak to him. I could explain how badly your family treated you. I am hopeful that once he has had time to think about things he will still wish to marry you.'

'No! Please do not,' Emily begged, a sob in her voice. 'I cannot bear to speak of it.' She jumped to her feet and ran into her own bedroom, shutting the door and locking it behind her. Amelia knocked at the door.

'Emily. Please listen to me. You must not let this destroy you. If Mr Sinclair truly loves you it will all come right. Do not throw away your chance of happiness too soon.'

'Please do not ask me to see him. I shall not come down this evening.'

'Emily…'

Amelia sighed as she heard a renewal of wild sobbing from her companion. In the hall downstairs the longcase clock was chiming the hour. She realised with a start that she would be late for dinner. She must hurry and change her clothes. Emily would come to her senses when she had cried herself to sleep. In the morning they would talk about things calmly—and she would have a few words with Mr Sinclair. If he had behaved as badly as Emily claimed, he was not the gentleman she had thought him!

Amelia apologised to the company when she joined them in the drawing room. She spoke to Susannah, telling her that Emily had a headache and would not be joining them that evening.

'I am so sorry.' Susannah was concerned. 'I hope it is nothing serious. Should we send for the doctor?'

'No, I am sure that will not be necessary,' Amelia told her. 'I am sorry if Emily's absence has unbalanced your dining table.'

'As it happens she is not the only guest missing,' Susannah replied. 'Toby Sinclair received a message from home and left us two hours ago. His parents had not joined us for Christmas because Mr Sinclair was feeling a little unwell. He had insisted that his son join his friends, but perhaps he has taken a turn for the worse. Toby seemed in a strange mood. He was abrupt—distant—and that is not like him...not like him at all. Harry thinks that his brother-in-law must be quite ill to send for his son.'

'I am sorry to hear it. Illness in the family is distressing, especially at this time of the year.'

'Had it been at any other time Harry would have gone to his sister immediately, but we cannot desert our guests. Lady Elizabeth is staying with her daughter this Christmas, so Harry's sister will not be completely alone should anything happen.'

'We must hope that it is not serious.' Amelia was thoughtful as she joined the guests moving into the long dining room. If Toby Sinclair had received bad news, it was understandable that he had left—but he ought to have left a note for Emily.

Gerard came to offer her his arm. 'You look serious, Amelia. Is something wrong?'

'Emily has a headache. I am sure she will be better in the morning.'

'I am sorry she is unwell. I understand that Toby has taken himself off in a hurry—there wouldn't be a connection?'

'Perhaps—but I cannot tell you, for it is not my secret.'

'Then you must keep it.' He paused, then, 'I have spoken to

Lisa's nurse and looked at the doll. It is not the same as the one I had sent to me. I believe it may just be a coincidence—I must hope so, otherwise it would be serious. If I believed the child was threatened, I should take her back to France.'

'I think we must talk about this matter. I know your opinion—but I am not sure.' Amelia shook her head as his brows lifted. 'We shall not discuss this tonight. The morning will be soon enough, but I must tell you that I believe your theory about my brother may be wrong.'

'Yes, you may be correct. We shall talk tomorrow, Amelia. We must make arrangements for the future and discuss this other business.'

'Yes, the morning will be time enough. We shall enjoy this evening, for Susannah has gone to so much trouble for us all.'

Chapter Four

Throughout dinner Gerard was very aware of the woman sitting beside him. She was lovely, but more than that she had an air of serenity, a presence that was lacking in so many other ladies. He was not certain why she had accepted his proposal of marriage. Was it only that she wished to be married and felt comfortable in his presence? They were good friends and shared an interest in many things. Marriage to Amelia would, he had no doubt, be pleasant and comfortable whatever the case, but he was not looking for someone to place his slippers by the fire and arrange for his favourite meals to be served. He wanted so much more! He wanted a woman who would welcome him to her bed with open arms.

The scent of her perfume was intoxicating. She seemed to smell of flowers and yet there was a subtle fragrance that was all her own. The sight of her, the way she turned her head, the way she moved, her voice…her smile…all these things set him on fire with longing. He wanted to take her in his arms and make love to her that very night, but was not sure that she would welcome a show of passion.

Amelia's manner gave little away. Her first reaction to his

proposal had seemed positive, but since then she had become more reserved. He was not sure why. The incident at the church had been upsetting, of course—but he did not think Amelia would allow that to upset her. She had insisted that she wished to go on with the engagement.

Was it something in Gerard himself that had caused her to withdraw? He knew that his rejection of Lisette the night she had crept into his bed had been the reason for her desperate unhappiness. He had not been able to tell Amelia that he had rejected Lisette's attempt to ask for his love. After her death he had regretted his curt manner that night. He had married her on a whim, indulging his sense of honour and pity—and he had still been angry with Amelia and her brother. Later, when he began to realise that there was only one woman he wanted despite what had happened, he had regretted the impulse that had urged him to wed a woman he did not know or love. However, he had meant to honour his promise, but, in rejecting Lisette when she tried to give herself to him, he had hurt her. He believed it was his rejection that had driven her to take her own life. Perhaps there was more, perhaps he was incapable of making a woman happy…

'Susannah is a wonderful hostess, is she not?' Amelia remarked, breaking into his thoughts. 'When I recall how anxious she was the first time she stayed here, I cannot believe how much she has matured.'

'Harry seems very content with his family,' Gerard replied. He smiled inwardly, wondering if Amelia guessed how aroused he was when she turned to him and made some intimate remark. It was fortunate that the table hid the evidence of his intense need at that moment. He must think of other things!

Several times since the incident outside the church he had

wondered if he had placed Amelia's life in danger by propos-ing. Harry was aware of his anxious thoughts and had been forthright in his opinion.

'I have no idea who this enemy of yours is, Gerard—but to give in to him would be more dangerous, believe me. If it is Royston, Amelia would be at his mercy, and if it is not…' He shook his head and frowned. 'She would never truly be safe— and nor, my friend, would you.'

'Then we are working in the dark. I have searched my memory for someone I have offended, but I can think of no one—at least, no one who would think it worthwhile to kill Amelia simply to spite me. I am still of the opinion that the plotter is Royston.'

'You may well be right, but Susannah is very close to Amelia. She thinks that Amelia is doubtful about her brother being the culprit.'

'It would be hard for any woman to accept such an idea,' Gerard said. 'I have not tried to impress my feelings on her, but for the moment I can see no other reason for the attempt on her life.'

Gerard felt Amelia's loss keenly when the ladies retired to the drawing room to take tea. He wished that he could follow at once, but custom dictated that he remain with the gentlemen to drink port and discuss politics and sport. When the gentlemen at last made their move towards the drawing room, Harry invited him to play a game of billiards. Not wanting to offend his friend, he agreed.

They had been playing for half an hour or so when he caught the smell of the perfume he always associated with Amelia and turned to see her watching them. The wistful expression he surprised in her eyes set him wondering. Was she wishing that they might be alone? Did she burn to be in his arms? He realised that despite their long friendship he hardly knew her. Gerard well remembered the passionate girl who would have given herself to him one never-forgotten night—but who was she now? Beautiful, serene, sophisticated, she was surrounded by friends, loved by those who knew her best, envied by many—but who was the woman behind the mask? How did she really feel about their marriage? He wished he knew.

'I came to say goodnight,' she said. 'I must see if Emily is feeling better. I shall speak to you in the morning, Gerard—shall, we say at nine?'

'If that is not too early for you.' He inclined his head, then went to her, taking her hand and turning it to drop a kiss into the palm. 'Sleep well, my dearest. I hope you find Miss Barton much recovered.'

'Thank you.' Amelia smiled as she bid both men goodnight and then walked from the room.

'You know that I shall be happy to stand up with you at your wedding,' Harry said and lined up a coloured ball, striking it with the white so that it rolled into the pocket. 'Have you agreed the day yet?'

'We are thinking of a month after the ball at Coleridge,' Gerard said. 'I hope that I am doing the right thing…if I thought I was putting Amelia's life in danger by marrying her…'

'If you have an enemy, we shall find him out,' Harry said and potted another ball. 'I have told my men to be on the lookout for strangers, but I doubt that whoever it was the other night will try anything more just yet. I have been wondering if that shot was just another warning.'

'We cannot even be certain that the target is Amelia...' Gerard frowned, missing his ball. His heart was not in the game. All he could think about was Amelia. He wanted her so badly. He would be a fool to let whoever was threatening her have his way.

Amelia sighed as she went into the private sitting room she shared with Emily. She wished that she might have had more time alone with Gerard that evening, but it was not possible. There were so many guests staying and she was acquainted with all of them; mere politeness decreed that she must spend a little time with as many as she could.

She saw that her blue cloak with the fur lining was lying on one of the chairs. She had told Emily that she might wear it that morning, because the weather had turned so cold and she had her new black one, which was even more sumptuously lined. Emily must have left it lying there. That was unusual, for she was by habit a tidy girl. Amelia's maid knew that she had loaned the cloak to her companion and had left it where it was instead of putting it away as she normally would.

Amelia went to her companion's door and knocked softly. 'Are you awake, dearest? Is your headache still bad? Would you like to talk to me about anything?'

There was no reply. Amelia did not persist; she did not wish to wake Emily if she was sleeping. She knew that it was Emily's heart that ached rather than her head, and she felt annoyed with Toby Sinclair. Really, she had thought better of him! Surely he could have accepted that Emily had had a child? It was shocking, but not the crime some thought it, in Amelia's opinion, especially since Emily had been forced. Toby might at least have asked her about the circumstances. Obviously, he had wanted to get home quickly after the news that his father's health had taken a turn for the worse, but he could have left a note for Emily. To leave her without a word—to run away like a disappointed schoolboy—was not what Amelia would have expected from him.

If he really could not face the fact that Emily had given birth to a child, even though she was forced and not willing, he could have found a way of telling her. To simply abandon her like this was so hurtful. It was no wonder that Emily had taken to her bed this evening. She was suffering from a broken heart.

Amelia went to her own bedchamber. She allowed her maid to undo the hooks at the back of her gown and then dismissed her. She sat down at her dressing table, picked up her brush, but then just stared at her mirror.

She was anxious about Emily. The girl was assured of a position with her for as long as she needed it, but there was very little she could do to help with the pain of a disappointment in love. Amelia had once suffered much as her companion was suffering now. She had not even known why Gerard had gone away without speaking to her or telling her he was leaving. For years she had alternated between distress and disappointment at his desertion, but then she had finally understood that her brother was to blame. Michael had acted in a high-handed, ruthless manner, not caring who he hurt!

He had not been a good brother to her. Indeed, there were times when she had come close to hating him. His last letter had been a hateful tirade about her selfishness towards her family that had left her in tears—but would he truly wish her dead so that he could get his hands on her fortune?

Amelia shuddered at the thought. They had quarrelled so

many times, but although she had sensed violence in him he had never actually harmed her—except by sending Gerard away.

Her thoughts turned to the man she had never ceased to love. She had thought there was something of the man she had known when she was young in him that evening…a simmering passion that had made her catch her breath.

She longed for him to want her, to love her—need her, as she loved and desired him. Was she a fool to believe that their marriage could work? If all he truly wanted was a complaisant wife who would care for his child, he might feel cheated when he realised that she was in love with him.

It must not matter! She knew that a marriage that was not equal in love might lead to hurt in the years to come, but perhaps if she were careful to hide her feelings he need never know. He wanted a companion rather than a wife so that was what she would be. Besides, it would break her to leave him now. If she waited, gave him time to know her, he might begin to feel the passion he had once had for her.

Smiling a trifle ruefully, Amelia went to bed. She might be foolish, but she thought that she had seen passion in Gerard's eyes that evening…

Amelia slept a little later than usual. She was woken by her maid pulling back the curtains and yawned, sitting up and blinking at the bright light.

Glancing at the clock, she saw that it was half past eight. 'Has it been snowing again, Martha?'

'Yes, Miss Royston. It has stopped now, but I believe there was a heavy fall last night.'

'What have you brought me this morning?'

'I thought you might like a light repast in bed instead of going down to the breakfast room. Since you slept in, Miss Royston—'

'How thoughtful you are,' Amelia said. 'I shall need some warm water at once for I have an appointment at nine this morning.'

'I should have woken you sooner, miss—but you were so peaceful.'

'I have half an hour; it is plenty of time if I hurry.'

'I will fetch the water now, miss.'

'Oh…' Amelia said as the girl turned away. 'Have you seen Miss Barton this morning?'

'No, miss. I went into her room to ask if she wished for breakfast in bed, but she was not there. Her bed had been made, but Miss Barton often makes her bed.'

'Yes, she does, because she is a thoughtful girl,' Amelia said. She broke a piece of the soft roll, buttered it and ate a piece as she poured a cup of the dark, slightly bitter chocolate she liked to drink when she indulged in breakfast in bed. It was not often she did so and wished she might linger longer this morning, but she did not want to be late for her meeting with Gerard.

By the time Martha returned with her hot water, Amelia had finished her roll and her cup of chocolate. She washed hastily and dressed in a simple morning gown that she could fasten herself. For once she left her hair hanging loose on her shoulders, merely brushing it back from her face and securing it with a comb at either side. Since she scarcely glanced at herself, she had no idea that she looked much younger and more like the girl she had been when she first met Gerard.

The beautiful mahogany longcase clock in the hall had just finished striking when Amelia went downstairs. She found that

Gerard was waiting for her. He looked handsome, elegant in his coat with three layers of capes across the shoulders, his topboots so glossy that you might see your reflection in them. He was frowning, but as she called to him he turned and smiled. Amelia's heart did a somersault, leaving her breathless for one moment. She truly thought that he had the most compelling eyes of any gentleman of her acquaintance and they seemed very intent as he looked at her.

'Forgive me if I have kept you. I slept later than usual and did not think to ask my maid to wake me. I am normally up much earlier.'

'We have all been keeping late hours at Pendleton. I should have suggested ten rather than nine, but I thought we should be sure of being alone. I have the carriage waiting…'

'We have not been much alone,' Amelia said as they went outside together. 'I have been thinking about what happened the other night outside the church, Gerard.'

'I have thought of it constantly.' His eyes dwelled on her face for some moments. 'We shall talk in the carriage. I would not care to be overheard.'

'Surely here there is no one that would wish us harm?'

'Our friends would not,' Gerard agreed, taking her arm and leading her out to the carriage. He helped her inside and she found that a warm brick had been brought so that she might place her feet on it, and a thick rug provided for her knees. 'I hope you will be comfortable, Amelia. It is a bitterly cold day.'

'I dare say your coachman will feel it, but we shall not be out long.'

'Coachman has his comforts, a warm coat and a blanket, I am sure,' Gerard told her. 'You say that we are safe here with friends and to a certain degree I concur, but servants talk—and sometimes they pass on information for money without realising what harm they may do.'

'Yes, I am sure that is so,' Amelia said. 'I believe someone may have mentioned the fact that we had been talking together—for no one but our close friends know that we are engaged.' She frowned. 'Of course, Lisa knows. When did you tell her you were thinking of marrying me—before or after you dismissed Nanny?'

'I believe it was before…' He stared at her. 'You think Nanny may have heard something and passed on the information?'

'Lisa told me yesterday that Nanny did not leave Pendleton immediately. She saw her talking to a man in the gardens—a man that she had seen Nanny speak to before.'

'Why did you not tell me that yesterday?'

'I did not think it important at first. I imagined Miss Horton might have a follower, but when you said just now that servants talk, I realised that she could have been selling information—perhaps because she had been dismissed.'

'Yes, you are right. I should have forced her to leave the house instantly.'

'It would not have changed anything. If she already had the information…'

Gerard swore angrily and then apologised. 'Forgive me. I should not use such language in your presence, Amelia. I have been careless. I did not imagine that my servants would gossip to strangers.'

'It makes little difference. Our enemy would have heard as soon as our engagement was announced.'

Gerard looked concerned. 'I have wondered if I was wrong to ask you. If I have put your life at risk…'

'If my marriage to you renders me liable to be murdered, then it is best that I am aware of it. This threat will not go away if we deny it, Gerard. We must discover who wishes me ill. There is some mystery here and it needs to be solved.'

'You do not accept that it is your brother?'

'I am loathe to do so. I know that Michael resents the fact that Great-Aunt Agatha did not leave him anything. He has tried to bully me into giving him at least half of my fortune. We have quarrelled because I refuse to do as he wishes. Had my aunt wished him to share in her fortune, she would have left him money. I might have done something for him before this had he behaved in a civilised manner. Perhaps—if you believe it is Michael…' She shook her head. 'No! I shall not be blackmailed into giving him my aunt's money. She would not have wished me to do so.'

'I do not think he would be content with a part of it. If he is willing to murder you, then he wants it all.'

'Well, he shall not have it.' Amelia lifted her head proudly. 'I have my own plans for part of the money—though some must be put in trust for our children.'

'You are thinking of your charity?'

'That and other things. I have helped two young ladies find happiness. I know of at least two more deserving cases…' She halted as Gerard raised his brows. 'You do not approve?'

'I am happy with whatever you choose to do, Amelia. I told you that I did not wish to control your fortune and I meant it.'

'It will be *our* money. I should not dream of giving large sums away without first consulting you.'

'I am not your brother, Amelia. Your fortune is not my first concern.'

'Have I made you angry, Gerard? I beg your pardon. I did not mean to.' She looked at him uncertainly.

'I am not angry, but I would not have you think I asked you to marry me for your fortune.'

'I did not.' She hesitated, then, wishing to change the subject, 'Shall we travel to Coleridge together?'

'Yes, certainly.' He was silent for a moment. 'I have made arrangements for you to be protected—Lisa too. If you feel that my theory is wrong I must think carefully. Sir Michael seemed the most obvious since he would inherit.'

'Have you considered that this person may have something other than money on his mind—or her mind? I suppose it could be a woman…'

'A scorned mistress?' Gerard looked amused. 'I have none to my credit, Amelia. When I first returned from the wars there was a lady in France, but we parted as friends when I returned to England the first time. There has been no one since.'

'Oh…' Amelia digested his statement in silence. Most gentlemen had mistresses before they married. She found no cause for distress in an old affair. 'Then we are at least certain it is a man. My sister-in-law has no love for me, but she would think murder most vulgar.'

'Vulgar?' Laughter gleamed in his eyes.

'You do not know Louisa. She is very strict—rude when she chooses, but *never* vulgar.'

Gerard laughed. 'She sounds formidable?'

'She would consider murder beneath her—and she would not approve of her husband being involved with anything of the kind. Indeed, if she suspected something untoward she would have a deal to say on the subject.'

'Then perhaps I should look elsewhere for a motive.'

'I cannot think of anyone I have offended other than my brother.' Amelia sighed and looked distressed. 'Perhaps you are right—there is no other explanation.'

'Unless I have an enemy…'

'Gerard?' Amelia's eyes widened. 'Have you thought of someone?'

'Unfortunately, no. I dare say I have enemies, though none I would have thought…there is Northaven, of course. He may hate me enough to threaten, but to kill you…' He shook his head. 'I cannot think it, Amelia. He might wound me in a duel if he could or knock me down, but truth to tell I do not see him as a murderer.'

'I do not see my brother in that light. A bully—yes.'

'It is difficult. All we can do is wait until *he* shows himself—whoever he is. I have agents who may discover something, but…it might be best to delay the announcement of our engagement.'

'You would give in to him? Surely that way he wins? And if my fortune is his object…' Amelia waved her hand in distress. 'As you say, it is difficult. If you wish to withdraw—'

'Damn it, no! You cannot think it, Amelia?'

'No…forgive me. I hardly know what I am thinking.'

'All I want is to make you happy.'

'Then we shall not allow this person to dictate to us. I dare say there is some risk if we go ahead and announce the engagement but there is risk in any case. At the moment our enemy is merely a shadow. Perhaps when he sees he cannot bully us he will step out into the light.'

'You are both wise and brave,' Gerard murmured, taking her gloved hand to kiss it. 'Now we shall talk of happier things? How many guests shall we invite to our wedding—and do you think we should hold an engagement ball?'

'Oh, I think we shall give a ball on the eve of the wedding. I believe that will be sufficient. Shall we all go down to Ravenshead after the Coleridge ball? I think I should like to see your home, Gerard—and we must discuss what I ought to do with Aunt Agatha's estate. I told you that I thought we should sell some of the property, but she loved that house and I am very fond of the garden…'

Amelia was feeling more settled in her mind when they returned to the house an hour or so after they left it. They had discussed most aspects of the wedding and settled that they would keep Amelia's home and also the house in Bath and Gerard's London house, which was larger than her own. Most of the other property would be sold or let to tenants, and the money invested in some form of trust for their children. However, the identity of the person who was trying to prevent their marriage remained a mystery. She knew that Gerard still felt her brother the most likely culprit, though he intended to set his agents the task of discovering if either of them was being watched. There was nothing more they could do for the moment except be vigilant.

Amelia parted from Gerard and went upstairs to her own apartments to change into a more suitable gown. She noticed that the blue velvet cloak she had loaned Emily was not lying on a chair in the sitting room. She could not recall if it had been there when she left earlier that morning, because she had been in too much hurry. Either Emily had taken it and gone out or she had tidied it away. Perhaps she was in her room now.

Amelia knocked at the door. Receiving no answer, she opened it and went in. As the maid had said earlier, the bed had been made and the room was tidy, as always. The gold purse Amelia had given Emily for Christmas was lying on the dressing table, as were one or two other gifts. It was a little odd that Emily should leave them lying there; she would normally have put them in her dressing case for safety. Amelia had an odd sensation, a feeling that Emily might have done something foolish. Surely she had not run away? Or something more desperate! Chills ran down Amelia's spine as she recalled her childhood friend Lucinda's terrible fate. A few years ago, Lucinda had taken her own life in her desperation—but Emily would surely not be so foolish.

Going to the armoire, she looked inside, feeling relieved as she saw the leather dressing case and Emily's clothes. At least she had not run away. Amelia was certain that her companion would not have left without at least taking some of her clothes and the dressing case. Besides, the girl was too conscientious to go off without at least leaving a letter—and, she believed, too sensible to take her own life.

A little reassured, Amelia went to change her clothes. Shortly after, she paid a visit to the nursery, where she talked to Lisa and some of the other children. She was asked to read a story from a book that one of the children had received as a Christmas gift. She read aloud, taking Lisa and one of the others on to her lap. The others crowded about her, clutching at her clothes and staring up into her face adoringly as she acted out the story for them.

She was unaware that Gerard came to the door and watched for a few minutes before leaving.

* * *

It was almost nuncheon before Amelia was able to break away from her audience and go downstairs to join the others.

She was at the buffet table, helping herself to cold chicken, a dish of potatoes and turnips and some green vegetables when Gerard came up to her.

'I saw you just now,' he said. 'It is good of you to give so much of your time to the children, Amelia.'

'I enjoy it. Lisa asked if I would read to her and the others wanted to listen. I believe they enjoyed themselves—and, after all, Christmas is for the little ones, do you not think so? Our Lord was born at this time and it is for his sake that we hold these celebrations.'

'You deserve a large family of your own, Amelia.'

'I hope to have several children—if God wills it.'

She looked up into his face and her heart began to race wildly. The way he was looking at her set her on fire and she wished that they were somewhere else—anywhere that they might be alone. She wanted so desperately to be in his arms, to feel his mouth on hers—but most of all she wanted his love. She felt what was becoming a familiar ache about her heart. Gerard had loved her once, but he had told her that something had died inside him when her brother sent him away and he believed that she had merely been toying with his heart. Would he ever be able to love her as she loved him?

'Gerard—' she began and broke off as a footman came up to them, offering a silver salver to him.

'This was delivered for you a few moments ago, sir.'

'For me?' Gerard frowned and opened the sealed note. He swore softly and then looked at Amelia in some bewilderment.

'I do not understand—this note implies that you are a prisoner. I am to pay the sum of forty thousand pounds or you will die…but you are here…'

'Yes…' Amelia shivered as a trickle of ice slithered down her spine. 'But Emily is not…' She glanced round the room, which was filling up with guests. 'I believe she went out early this morning and, as far as I know, she has not returned.'

'Would she stay out so long in this weather?'

'I cannot think it. She was feeling unhappy. I wondered if she had run away, but her things were all in her room.'

'Who would snatch Miss Barton and demand such a huge ransom?'

'Someone who did not know me well,' Amelia said. 'On Christmas Eve I was wearing a dark blue cloak with fur lining. I had bought myself a new black one for Christmas, and because the weather was so very cold I loaned the blue one to Emily. If she was wearing it when she went out, she could have been mistaken for me.'

'Good grief!' Gerard was astounded. 'We must send at once and make certain she is not in her room.'

'I shall go up myself,' Amelia said. 'She was not in her room when we returned from our drive. I thought she wished to be alone and did not search for her. I should have alerted you before this, but I did not imagine that she was in danger. Excuse me…'

Amelia left her food untouched as she went immediately in search of her companion. She ran up the stairs. The sitting room was empty and so was Emily's room. Nothing had been moved since Amelia's last visit.

Her maid came from the other bedchamber, carrying an evening dress. Amelia asked her if she had seen Emily.

'No, Miss Royston. I came up to fetch this dress. I was going to iron it for you for this evening. Is something wrong?'

'Emily appears to be missing,' Amelia said. 'Please continue with your work, Martha—but make inquiries as you go. I am worried about Miss Barton.'

'Yes, miss. Of course. I'll ask if anyone has seen her this morning.'

Amelia went back down the stairs. Gerard and Harry were talking together in the hall. They turned to look at her. Amelia shook her head.

'Martha hasn't seen her. Her room is just as it was when I was last there.'

'I have alerted my butler,' Harry told her. 'He will make sure that all the servants are asked for their last sighting of her. If we know what time she left, we may discover how long she has been missing.'

'What can we do?' Amelia asked. 'How long have we been given to find the ransom, Gerard? I do not have that kind of money available, but I will sell some investments—anything I can to recover my poor Emily.'

'We will all contribute,' Harry assured her. 'However, it may be possible to recover her without giving this rogue a penny.'

'I cannot risk Emily's life. She was taken because they thought she was me…' Amelia could not prevent a sob of despair. 'If only we knew who had taken her. I shall never forgive myself if anything happens to her.'

'You cannot blame yourself,' Gerard said and frowned. 'I must confess that I should have been devastated had they managed to get their hands on you, Amelia.'

Amelia's eyes flashed with anger. 'Are you saying that Emily's life is less important than mine? That is unfair, Gerard. She is a lovely person and I am very fond of her.'

'I did not mean to imply that she was less worth saving.' Gerard ran fingers through his hair. 'Of course we shall do what we can, but once they know they have the wrong person…'

'Are you saying that they will kill her?' Amelia was rapidly becoming distraught. 'No! How do we let them know that I will pay?' She looked at him wildly. 'This is all my fault. If I had given my brother what he wanted… Oh, no! It is too much.'

At that moment there was a disturbance at the door and then two people entered, their clothes sprinkled with a dusting of snow.

Amelia looked towards the door and saw her companion. She gave a scream and ran to her. 'Emily, my love! I have been out of my mind with worry! Where have you been?'

'I went for a walk…' Emily sobbed and threw herself into Amelia's arms. 'I was snatched from behind and thrust into a carriage. I had a blanket over my head and I did not know what was happening. After some time, perhaps half an hour or so, the carriage stopped and I was carried into a house. I was left alone in a bedroom. It was a very cold house. I screamed and tried to get out but both the window and door were locked. As they carried me in, I heard one of them say that if the money did not come through I was to be killed…'

'Emily…' Amelia drew back in shock to look at her face. 'How terrifying for you, my love. What happened? How did you escape?'

Behind her, at that moment, she heard what seemed to be a quarrel break out. Turning her head, she saw that the man who had entered the house with Emily was the Marquis of

Northaven. From the look of it, both Harry and Gerard were threatening him.

'Please, you must not be angry with the marquis,' Emily cried. 'It was he who saved me and brought me back. Had he not come, I should still have been in that room.'

'Is this true?' Gerard demanded. 'Explain yourself if you please, sir.'

'I think we should speak privately,' Northaven said. He took a few steps towards Emily. 'I am sorry that you were subjected to such an ordeal, Miss Barton. I tried to warn the earl that he must be careful, but I did not expect that they would take you. I understood Miss Ravenshead was their quarry.'

'You tried to warn me…' Gerard frowned as something clicked into place. 'Was it you that sent the doll?'

'Yes. A clumsy trick, I think, but I was not sure how else to do it. I wanted to alert you to the fact that Miss Royston might be in danger.'

'Why did you not say so plainly?' Gerard glared at him.

'Would you have believed me if I had signed my name? Would you have received me had I tried to warn you in person?' Northaven lifted his head proudly. 'I do not pretend to be without vice. I have done many things that I might wish undone—but I am not a murderer, though you persist in thinking me one. If I caused the death of comrades by loose talk, I regret it—but it *was* careless talk, no more.'

'I think you need to do more explaining,' Gerard said. 'Amelia, please take Miss Barton upstairs and see that she is cared for. You might wish to send for the doctor?'

Emily shook her head in alarm. 'I am not harmed. I was frightened, but I am well enough now.'

'I shall take you upstairs, my love.' Amelia put a protective arm about her. 'You are cold and trembling. You shall go to bed with a warming pan and a tisane. I shall sit with you and you may tell me all about it.'

Amelia drew her companion from the room. She would have liked to listen to all the marquis had to say, but she knew that Gerard did not wish either her or Emily to hear all the details lest it frighten them more. They had both had a terrible shock and it was only thanks to the Marquis of Northaven that things were not much worse. Amelia could hardly bear to think of what might have happened.

'Were you far from the house when they took you?' she asked Emily as they walked upstairs together.

'Only in the knot gardens,' Emily told her. 'It must have been within sight of the house, but of course it was very early. I dare say even the servants had not risen.' She gave a little sob. 'I lay awake all night. I was tossing and turning and thought that a walk might clear my head. I had forgot what we said—besides, I did not imagine anyone would try to snatch me. It was you I believed in danger.'

'My poor Emily.' Amelia squeezed her hand. 'You were taken because they thought you were me. A huge ransom was demanded, but I should have paid it, my love. We were trying to think how it could be done when you came in. I could not have borne it had anything happened to you.'

'Amelia! I am so glad you did not have to pay—and I am sorry if you were worried. I did not dream that anyone would try to kidnap me.'

'I dare say they would not had you not been wearing my blue

cloak,' Amelia said. 'You must not wear it to walk in again until this rogue has been caught and dealt with, Emily.'

'Have you any idea of who it could be?'

'No, not truly. I suppose you heard nothing?'

'They spoke of someone of whom they were afraid,' Emily told her. 'However, they did not name him.'

'I know everyone thinks it must be my brother and I fear it may be so, though I do not wish to believe it.'

'It is so wicked. I do not know who could do such things.' Emily shivered. 'I was to have been strangled had the money not been forthcoming—but that was after I told them who I was. I believe they realised their mistake too late. They spoke of a ransom note and said that if the money was not paid they would amuse themselves before disposing of me.'

'My love! How awful for you. I am so sorry that you were exposed to such wickedness.'

'It was fortunate for me that the marquis came to get me.'

'How did he know that you had been taken—and where to find you?'

'I have no idea. I did not think to ask. I was simply grateful that he got me out of that house before...' A fit of shuddering overtook Emily. 'I have never been as frightened in my life.'

'I am certain that Gerard and Harry will wish to know where the marquis got his information,' Amelia said. 'Come, dearest, let me help you undress. Martha will bring you a pan filled with hot coals and a tisane. Tomorrow I shall take you home.'

'No, please do not. I want to go to the ball as we planned,' Emily said. 'I shall not let this frighten me—nor shall I dwell on what happened with Mr Sinclair. At one time last night I considered taking my own life, but what happened made me see that I want to live. It will be hard to meet Mr Sinclair again, but I shall bear it.'

'My poor love.' Amelia kissed her brow. 'You are a very brave girl. You must forget Mr Sinclair; if he could not behave in a proper manner, he is not worth breaking your heart over.'

Chapter Five

'Well, I am waiting,' Gerard said. 'I am grateful to have Miss Barton back, but this begs an explanation. How did you know that there was a plot to kidnap Miss Royston and how did you know where to find Miss Barton?'

The marquis made a wry face. 'I thought they had Miss Royston until I got there and realised that they had snatched the wrong lady. I persuaded them to drink some rum to keep out the cold and laced it with laudanum. As soon as they became groggy I snatched Miss Barton and brought her here. *He* will know that I tricked them and I dare say my life may be at risk, but I do not value it so highly that I shall lose sleep over it.'

'You have still not told us how you knew what was going on,' Harry objected. 'And who is behind this business?'

'Don't look at me like that, Pendleton,' the marquis said. 'If you must know, I was offered money to help capture Miss Royston. However, I believe he sensed that I was not going to do his bidding and so he moved ahead of time. I was told the abduction was planned for when she journeyed to Coleridge.'

'You were offered money—how much?'

'Ten thousand pounds.' Northaven laughed ruefully. 'A pittance, I dare say, when you consider her fortune. A few months ago I might have taken his money. I was in debt and the bitterness inside me was much stronger than it is now. You may thank a lady for that—and, no, I shall not name her.'

'Why did you not come to us—tell us who we have to deal with?' Gerard demanded.

'If I knew his name, I would have told you. He keeps to the shadows and hides his face—though I have seen it since our first meeting. I let him believe that I would help him, learning what I could of his intentions. I have tried to follow him, and I think he spotted me, which may be why he did not trust me in the end. However, I knew where they meant to hold Miss Royston for the first few hours—and I was on my way here early this morning. I had decided that I could not handle this alone and meant to ask you to listen to my story. As I walked towards the house, I saw what I thought was Miss Royston being snatched. There was no time to warn you so I followed them. They had not changed the rendezvous—and, thankfully, his rogues still trusted me.'

'You have no idea of his identity?'

'I know that he calls himself Lieutenant Gordon, but I doubt it is his name—though I believe him to have been an officer, for he has the manner of a military man. However, I do not recall that he ever served with us.'

'It was not Sir Michael Royston?'

'Miss Royston's brother? Good lord, no! I would have known his voice. I played cards with him quite recently.'

'Could he not be in league with this rogue?'

'He could, but not to my knowledge.'

'Why were you approached?'

'He believed that I might want to bring you down, Gerard. He must have heard of our quarrel, which is known well enough in certain circles. His plans for Miss Royston were not simply to ransom her, believe me. Had you paid what he asked, he would have taken the money—and then I believe he meant to despoil her and kill you.'

'My God!' Gerard turned pale. 'He must hate me.' He took a turn about the room, then returned to where Harry and the marquis stood. 'What have I done to him that he should hate me so?'

'Only you can answer that,' Northaven said. 'Have you ruined a man at the tables or taken his woman?'

'No…unless…Lisette—' Gerard broke off and smote his forehead with the palm of his hand, a look of disbelief in his eyes. 'I do not know. My wife…was carrying the child of her lover when I married her. She was honest with me. Lisette told me that he had died and that she was alone in the world. I married her to protect her, but if her lover were severely wounded and then recovered…to discover that she had married me…he may blame me for her death.'

'That may be your answer,' Northaven said, eyes narrowed in thought. 'If Gordon believes that you took her from him, he may wish to take what you love in revenge. Since Miss Royston is wealthy and you have your own fortune, he thinks that he may also have some financial gain from it.'

'But I did not take her from him…' Gerard shook his head. 'When I found her she was close to death. She was lying at the side of the road, bruised and beaten. She told me that some French soldiers had raped her—more than one, I believe. I nursed her back to life and then I married her to keep her safe. She was very ill after the birth, but then she recovered…' He paused, a nerve flicking in his cheek. 'Lisette took her own life. I believe because she wanted more from me than I could give her.'

'Good grief!' Harry cried, shocked. 'I had no idea… My dear fellow. I am so sorry.'

Gerard shrugged off his sympathy. 'I told no one until recently. Miss Royston knows some of it, but not all—and I ask you both to keep my secret. I believe Lisette took her own life because I did not love her.'

'*He* blames you for her death,' Northaven said grimly. 'It is as plain as the nose on your face! This Lieutenant Gordon—whoever he is—*he* blames you for the death of the woman he loves.'

'In a way I am guilty, though I never meant to hurt her. I thought Lisette understood that I had married her simply to offer my protection, but she wanted me to love her. I failed her…and her death has haunted me ever since.'

'I believe you have established a motive, Ravenshead—now you need to know who he really is. She did not give you the name of her lover?'

'No. I never asked; I believed him dead and it did not matter.'

'Does he know the child is his?' Harry asked. 'If so, he may feel that you have stolen her as well.'

'I doubt he knows it,' Gerard said. 'She had not seen him since he rode away to battle some weeks earlier—one of his friends told her he had been killed. She was trying to discover more when she was set upon by those rogues who raped her and left her for dead.'

'Then it is best that Gordon never knows the truth,' Harry said. 'Until you can discover the identity of your enemy, Gerard, you must be very careful.'

'Yes, you are right,' Gerard agreed. He looked at Northaven. 'Are you willing to help us?'

'Of course. You had only to *ask*.' Northaven's eyes gleamed. 'Tell me what I may do for you and I shall do my best to oblige.'

Amelia sat with Emily until she drifted off into sleep. After some tears and a fit of the shudders, she had finally settled. Leaving her to rest, Amelia decided to change for the evening. She was thoughtful as she sat for her maid to dress her hair into the new softer style, caught up in an intricate swirl at the nape of her neck. During one of her crying bouts, Emily's deep sadness at the loss of her child had come tumbling out.

Amelia had comforted her as best she could. She had made up her mind that she would definitely speak to someone soon about employing an agent to make inquiries. It might not be possible to trace the child, and even if Emily's child could be found they might not be able to recover her. She would have a family, perhaps a mother and father who loved her—but perhaps it would be enough for Emily to have news of her daughter.

Amelia would do what she could to find the child, but she would say nothing until she knew whether or not it was possible. Having settled that much in her mind, she went down to the parlour where guests had begun to gather for drinks before dinner. She saw Susannah and several of the other guests but there was no sign of Gerard or Harry.

'They went out earlier and have not yet come in,' Susannah said when Amelia asked. 'Harry told me what Northaven had done. I could hardly believe that he had acted so heroically. He was not always courteous to me in the past—and yet I am not sure that he is black as he is often painted.'

'I owe the marquis a debt of deep gratitude,' Amelia said. 'I do not forget that he once fought a duel with Harry and that you were wounded, my love. However, I do not believe he meant to injure you—and perhaps he has gone some way to redeeming himself by bringing Emily back to us.'

'Oh, I forgave him for that long ago.' Susannah smiled. 'He watched us when we walked from church after our wedding, you know. There was something in his eyes…I think he meant me to know that Harry was safe from him, as he has been.' Susannah looked thoughtful. 'He is undoubtedly a rake and has almost certainly done things that would shock us if we knew the whole—but everyone is entitled to a second chance.'

'Yes, I am sure you are right.' Amelia frowned. 'I wanted to speak to Harry, but it will keep.'

'Is there something I can help you with, Amelia?'

'No, Susannah. I need a man's advice about something, my dear. I had thought to ask Harry, for I believe that Gerard has enough on his mind at the moment—but another day will do.'

'Well, I dare say they will not be long, though Harry told me not to hold dinner.'

'I expect they have some business.'

'I dare say they do. It seems very odd that the Marquis of Northaven is involved; Harry was much against him at one time.'

'Gentlemen are contrary creatures,' Amelia teased. 'They can be at odds one minute and the best of friends another.'

'Do you think we can trust him?' Harry asked as they entered the house, shaking a light dusting of snow from their coats. 'I must admit I should not have given him a chance to speak had he not brought Miss Barton back to us. I should probably have told the footmen to throw him out.'

He went over to the magnificent mahogany sideboard in his

library and poured brandy for them both, giving one to Gerard and holding the other to warm it in his hands before sipping.

'At the moment I do not have much choice,' Gerard confessed. 'His tale of a Lieutenant Gordon might be a falsehood, but I am inclined to believe him. Lisette had a lover. She believed he had been killed, but it is possible that he still lives. Men fall in battle and are reported dead and then turn up somewhere…' He sighed with frustration. 'If he went looking for her and heard tales of her death, it would explain why he hates me. He probably thinks I am a monster and that I treated her ill. I gave her everything I could, but she needed so much more.'

'If you could speak to him, tell him what happened…'

Gerard shook his head, dismissing the idea. 'I doubt he would listen. In his place I would want revenge.' He groaned his frustration. 'What am I to do, Harry? How can I marry Amelia, knowing that by doing so I am endangering her life? When I thought she was in danger from her brother it was one thing, but now…'

'You cannot be sure of anything. This tale of Northaven's may be a ruse. He could still be in league with the rogues. Besides, you cannot wish to withdraw? You do not wish to jilt Amelia Royston? Think how it would look? Susannah would never speak to you again.'

'Of course I do not wish to jilt her! Good God! It is the last thing I want—but if the marriage is rendering her the target of a madman…'

'I can only advise you to wait. We shall see that she is protected, of course. Northaven says that he will try to discover the true identity of this man…get as close to him as he can and then bring you news of his whereabouts. We must hope that he will keep his word.'

'Yes, though, if he drugged the rogues who snatched Miss Barton, Northaven's life could be at risk. Lieutenant Gordon will have him shot on sight.'

'He knew that was possible when he agreed. This may be his way of atoning, Gerard. Even if he did not betray us that time in Spain, it was his loose talk while drunk that led to the deaths of several men. The French knew we were coming. Our mission was secret. Only the four of us knew, for we did not tell the troopers where we were going. They followed us blindly to their deaths—and Northaven did not turn up that morning. He says that he woke too late after a night of heavy drinking and gambling, but I am still not certain I believe him.'

'We sent him to Coventry and branded him a coward and a traitor,' Gerard observed grimly. 'He always swore that he was innocent, but in his heart he knew that his loose tongue was to blame. He provoked you into a duel and would have killed any of us in anger—but I believe he has changed, though I have no idea why.'

'He said it was a woman.'

'If rumour does not lie, he has ruined more than one in his time. *She* must be remarkable if she has reformed him. I am not certain that his story is the true one, but I have no other clues. So far this Lieutenant Gordon has managed to cover his tracks. I have set my agents to looking for him, and I am having Northaven watched too. I do not trust him entirely even yet.'

'Then you must carry on as if nothing has happened. If you change your plans, Gordon will become suspicious. There is no guarantee that he will leave Miss Royston in peace, even if you give her up. If I were in your shoes, I would double the number of men watching over her and Miss Barton and go ahead with your plans.'

'I must make Amelia aware of the danger—but I think you are right. We did not tell many people, but these things get out. To draw back now would look as if we had quarrelled. I shall just have to be vigilant.'

'It is all you can do for the moment. I shall come to Coleridge a few days after you, Gerard. In the meantime I will send some of my grooms with you. I know you have your own men, but they will do better in the shadows. My grooms will be armed and ride with you.'

'Thank you, but I hardly like to involve you in this business, Harry. You have a wife and child to think of and this may be a nasty affair before it is ended.'

'We swore to help each other that day in Spain,' Harry reminded him grimly. 'We survived that day because the three of us defended each other's backs. You were there for me when I needed you—I shall not desert you in your time of need.'

'You believe that all this may be because of Lisette's lover? Someone she knew before you married her?' Amelia stared at Gerard in the moonlight. He had come to her as she was about to go up to bed, requesting that she stroll with him in the gallery. The candles had burned low in their sockets, but the moonlight filtered through the long windows, giving them light enough to see each other's faces. Had it not been for the subject under discussion, it might have been romantic. She did not think that he had mentioned that Lisette had had a lover before this, though perhaps she had not perfectly heard him. 'Gerard—how can that be? I am at a loss to understand. Why should this man blame you for what happened?'

'I do not know. Northaven said that Gordon hates me and I

can only think he must be bitter because Lisette died. I told you that she took her own life some months after the birth of her child. If he went looking for her in the Spanish village where we lived and was told that she slashed her wrists, he would be horrified, angry. In his shoes I might want revenge.'

'Why did she marry you if she had a lover?'

'She believed he was dead. She was alone and in desperate need.'

'Lisette died four years ago, Gerard. Why has this man never tried to kill you in all those years? Why now?'

'I have no idea. I cannot even be sure that Northaven is telling me the truth. He could have planned the whole thing to gain some advantage for himself.'

'Surely he would not?' Amelia looked thoughtful. 'There must be some other reason that has kept this man from moving against you, Gerard. Something must have changed. Perhaps he did not know how Lisette died and then discovered it.'

'I wish I knew…' Gerard hesitated. 'You know in what danger you stand. Would you prefer it if I went away? I should still try to discover my enemy, but you would be safer. And in time I could return. It would be merely a postponement.'

'You know my answer. I refuse to hide in the shadows. Besides, he would not be fooled. If this man knows so much about us, he would soon learn the truth. If we let him part us, it would be for ever. Do you want that?'

'No! Damn it, no.'

'Then we have no alternative but to go ahead with our plans.'

'It is odd that he knows where we are. I told only a few people I was coming here this Christmas.'

'Most of my acquaintances knew I would be here,' Amelia

said. 'However, I told no one that I expected to see you for I did not know if I should.'

'It is a mystery,' Gerard said. 'I may have been followed, of course. I feel like a blind man stumbling about in the dark. As Harry says, we cannot be certain even now for it is all merely theory.'

'I believe the only way is to carry on as normal and hope that he will make a mistake.'

'You are very brave.' Gerard looked at her gravely. 'I would rather give you up than have your death on my conscience, Amelia—but, as you say, if we give way now it does not follow that you will be safe. I think it is better than we go ahead with the wedding as soon as possible so that I am in a position to take care of you.'

Amelia felt as if her heart had been squeezed. Gerard would rather give her up than have her death on his conscience. How could he say such a thing to her? She would rather die than give him up, but it seemed he did not feel the same way.

Lisette had been desperately unhappy because he did not love her. Amelia could not help but wonder if she were laying up pain for herself in the future. She loved him so very much. Would she one day feel desperate because Gerard was unable to love her? Would she ever feel so alone that she would be driven to take her own life?

No, she had known heartbreak and lived through it. She was stronger than Lisette.

'I am certain there is more to this mystery than you yet realise,' she told him. 'Your enemy knows where we are and what we are doing. He knows all about me. How can that be? We must have a mutual acquaintance. Someone close to us who knows where we intend to be.'

'Yes, that would seem to be the case. I am damned if I know who it is, though!'

'We must both think hard. Since I was the target, you cannot be certain that he is your enemy, Gerard. He might very well be mine.'

'You are sure she means to go to Coleridge?' Lieutenant Gordon asked of the woman he had met late at night in the shadows of a summerhouse. 'If I have men waiting on the road and she goes to another location, I may miss my last chance of surprising them.'

The woman's mouth curled in a sneer. 'Your fools bungled it once. Do you imagine that you still have the element of surprise? No, you lost that when you involved Northaven in your plans. Why did you not ask me? I should have told you that he would not do it. I know he spoke of hating them, but he hated only that they distrusted him—thought him a traitor. He is no angel, but neither is he a murderer. I could have told you had you asked my advice.'

'How do you know so much about him?' Gordon asked, looking at her jealously. She was his second cousin. When they were children they had played together in the meadows. She had given herself to him when she was thirteen. Wild and enchanting, she had had the power to command him, making him her slave, but when he joined the army as a young man he had broken free of her. He had fallen in love, but Lisette had betrayed him. He had searched for her when his wounds healed, and when he discovered the truth of her death he had been devastated. On his return to England some months ago, he had sought his childhood love out, discovering that her power to enslave him had become stronger. 'Is Northaven your lover?'

She laughed mockingly. 'I may once have indulged myself with the gentleman for an hour or so one summer, but I never loved him. You have no need to be jealous.' She laid her hand on his arm, giving him a seductive smile. 'Have I not helped you by telling you where you could find Miss Royston? Have I not helped you to plan your revenge on the man who stole your lover?'

'Lisette was a silly little fool. I was angry when I discovered that he had married her and made her unhappy—but I never loved her in the way I love you. I have always adored you. You are the one who hates him. Or is it Miss Royston you hate?'

'She is nothing to me. I care not whether she lives or dies, but he loves her and so her fate is sealed. You want Gerard Ravenshead dead and so do I—we are agreed on this, are we not?' He nodded, though it was she who had demanded Ravenshead's death as her price—the price he must pay to have her. 'Then there is nothing else you need to know.'

He moved towards her, reaching out to pull her hard against him. His mouth was demanding on hers, bruising and possessive. 'You know I love you. I have hated him for what he did to Lisette, but—'

'You would have let him live?' Her eyes snapped with scorn. 'She cut her wrists…bled to death…and you would let him live? You snivelling coward! I thought you had more courage. Perhaps I should find another to help me.'

'No!' Gordon caught her wrist as she would have turned away from him. 'I will see her dead and he shall witness her death, as I promised you.'

'She must be ravished and he must see it! I want him to suffer. His death is not punishment enough.'

'Why do you hate him so much? What did he do to you?'

'That is my affair,' *she* told him and her eyes blazed with bitter anger. 'I want revenge and I know how to get it. Forget your ideas of ambushing them on the road. They will have outriders and grooms and all will be armed. The rogues you employ will turn tail and flee at the first shot fired at them. No, I have a much better idea. Listen well, because this is what we shall do…'

'I wish that we were coming with you.' Susannah hugged Amelia as they parted. Christmas was over and the snow had cleared, but the overnight frost had turned the ground hard. 'I know that we shall see you at Coleridge, but I am concerned for you on the journey.'

'You must not be, dearest.' Amelia kissed her cheek. 'Thank you for giving us such a wonderful Christmas. Perhaps another year you may come to us.'

'I doubt if the relatives would give up the Christmas visit. It is tradition, you know—but I shall be very glad to stay with you at other times. The *Old Crusties*, as Toby Sinclair calls them, enjoy their stay. I shall be fortunate to get to Coleridge before the day of the ball.'

'You make them too comfortable.' Amelia laughed. 'Well, I must not keep Gerard waiting; I know he is anxious that we should make good time.'

'I shall see you soon. You must write to me as soon as you arrive.'

Amelia laughed. 'You sound like Marguerite. She is always anxious to hear my news. I must write to her again soon.'

Susannah frowned. 'Marguerite? I do not think I know her.'

'No, perhaps I did not mention her to you. We did not communicate for some years following a family tragedy, but then she wrote to me and I learned how miserable her life has become.

Since then I have written to her at least twice a month and sometimes more.'

'Is she another of your lame ducks, Amelia?' Susannah laughed teasingly.

'Marguerite's situation is more difficult. Her parents are not poor. Indeed, they have money enough to give her a Season in town if they wish—but they refuse to allow it. Marguerite never goes into company without her mama. She is kept very strictly at home.'

'That is such a shame. Poor girl! What has she done to deserve such a fate?'

'She is hardly a girl. I believe we are of a similar age. She may be a year or so older. Marguerite has done nothing to merit her fate, which is why I feel for her so strongly. Her parents blame her for something that happened to her sister and that is unfair.'

'You must ask her to stay with you,' Susannah said. 'Perhaps you could find her a husband. After all, she is old enough to marry without permission, is she not?'

'Yes, but her father is a bully. I think she is afraid of him. However, I do have something in mind, though I am not sure she would wish to accept. I did invite her to stay with me in Bath, but her father would not allow it at that time.'

'That is so unfair, especially if she has done nothing wrong,' Susannah said and hugged her again. 'She is lucky to have you as a friend, Amelia. I am sure you will do something to help her if you can.'

'I have written to Marguerite with my suggestion. I wrote as soon as I knew Lisa would need a new nanny. Marguerite's parents will not allow her to have a Season in London or Bath, but they may allow her to stay with me in the country to help to care for a motherless child. If Lisa were in her care, I should feel that we could safely leave her sometimes.'

'And you entertain a great deal so she would have company and make friends.' Susannah clapped her hands. 'How clever you are, Amelia! It is exactly the thing. I do not see how her parents could object to such a suggestion for their daughter.'

'Well, we shall see. Marguerite may not like the idea of becoming a child's nanny—but she will live as one of the family and have the opportunity to meet all my friends. In time she might meet someone suitable that she might marry.'

'I do hope it all works out for her,' Susannah said. 'And now you really must go, because I can see Gerard in the hall and he looks impatient.'

'Farewell for now, dearest Susannah. I shall write to you and you will join us at Coleridge within the week.'

Amelia parted from her friend and went into the hall where Gerard was in close conversation with Harry. He turned as soon as she came up to him, looking relieved.

'We must go, Amelia. I am sorry to hurry you, but I wish to reach Coleridge before dark. We shall change the horses, but we shall not stop for refreshments. Harry's chef has put up a picnic for us and we may eat on the road.'

'Yes, of course. I understand perfectly.' Amelia glanced at Harry. 'You will not forget what I asked of you, sir?'

'The matter is already in hand. I have the details and my agent will deal with it as a matter of urgency.'

'Thank you. I am in your debt.'

Harry bowed over her hand. 'No, no, Amelia. You brought Susannah to me. I shall forever be in your debt.'

Amelia shook her head and smiled as she followed Gerard outside. He looked at her oddly.

'What was that about, Amelia? If you need the services of an agent, I could have arranged it for you.'

'I know and I would have asked, but you have enough worries as it is—and it is a matter for someone else, Gerard. It is not personal and need not concern you.'

'Very well,' he said but there was a jut to his chin, as if it had not pleased him that she had asked Harry to execute her commission.

Amelia was prevented from saying more because Emily was standing by the carriage. She could not tell Gerard that she had asked Harry to see if he could find Emily's daughter at that moment. Besides, though she had been forced to confide the details to Harry, she had done so in confidence and would not speak of it more than she need, even to Gerard.

He looked a little serious as he handed both ladies into the carriage. Amelia wondered if she had offended him and regretted it. She did not wish anything to overshadow their wedding. Gerard's careless words had given her a restless night, but eventually she had told herself that she was being foolish. Gerard cared for her safety, which meant she was important to him. It was foolish to wish for the romantic love of their youth. Had she not already decided that a marriage of convenience would do very well?

She was impatient for their wedding so that they could begin their new life together. This threat hanging over them was un-pleasant, but she had perfect faith in Gerard and his ability to protect her. She could not help feeling relieved that he no longer believed her brother had been trying to murder her. Michael would not be pleased when she wrote to him to tell him that she intended to marry the man he had expressly forbidden her to wed. She frowned as she wondered just why her brother was so much against the marriage. He had gone to great lengths to prevent it when she was younger, but Gerard had inherited an estate he had not expected to inherit. He was not as wealthy as Harry Pendleton or Max Coleridge, but he was certainly not a pauper and his estate was free of encumbrances. It was unreasonable for Michael to be so against the marriage now.

Amelia turned to her companion as they settled in their seats. Gerard had chosen to ride behind the carriage for the first part of the journey and the ladies were alone, Amelia's maids following in the second coach with Lisa's nurse and the child.

'Nurse insisted that Lisa ride with them for a while, but I think when we stop I shall tell her to come in with us—you will not mind that, Emily?'

'Of course not. She is a delightful child, intelligent, and seems older than her years, though she is almost five now…' The shadows were in Emily's eyes, though she was no longer weepy and was clearly making an effort to be cheerful.

'Are you sure you wish to come to Coleridge? If you would prefer to go to Bath until I am settled at Ravenshead, I would understand.'

'Of course I wish to come. I am looking forward to seeing Helene.'

'You know that Toby Sinclair may be there for the ball?'

'We are bound to meet in company,' Emily said. She lifted her head; her face was proud though her mouth trembled a little. 'I have accepted that he has rejected me. I am in control of my feelings now, Amelia. I shall not break down again.'

Amelia reached for her hand and squeezed it. It was Emily's hurt that had prompted her to have a search made for her child.

If she could arrange for Emily to visit her little girl now and then, it would be something.

'I think you have behaved with dignity, my love. It is natural that you should weep for your lost hopes. I must tell you that Mr Sinclair is not the man I thought him.'

'I cannot blame him. I should have told him the truth when I first knew he was becoming interested. It was my own fault for allowing him to think me something I am not.'

'You must not think of yourself as a fallen woman, Emily. The fault was not yours.' Amelia saw that her companion was unconvinced. 'I told you of my friend Lucinda, did I not?' Emily nodded. 'Lucinda took her life because she was too ashamed to have her baby. You were braver. I am proud of you, my love.' She touched her hand. 'Now, I have a request to make of you…'

'Anything. You know I am always happy to oblige you, Amelia.'

'Lucinda had a sister. She was a year older than Lucinda and not as pretty. When Lucinda took her life and her parents understood that she had been seduced, they became much stricter with Marguerite. They refused to let her go to dances or anything where she might be alone with gentlemen. She is taken out only when her mother goes into company with her friends, which is, as you can imagine, a tedious life for a young woman.'

'Poor Marguerite.' Emily smiled. 'I can guess what you mean to ask me, Amelia. You are going to invite her to live with us.'

'I have written to her parents and asked if she may be allowed to live at Ravenshead to help care for Lisa. I am not sure Marguerite will wish to come, but if she does I hope you will make her feel at home with us.'

'Naturally I shall. It is most unfair that she should be denied the pleasures of society just because her sister was seduced…I know just how she feels.' Emily's voice quivered with passion. 'She has been treated most unfairly!'

'Of course you know, dearest,' Amelia said and smiled at her. 'I thought you could help Marguerite to find her way in society again. She may find it a little frightening after so many years of being almost a prisoner in her parents' home.'

'I shall do all I can to help her,' Emily said and looked thoughtful.

Amelia felt a warm satisfaction. Emily would find some ease for her own pain in thinking of others—and perhaps soon both of her friends would find happiness.

In the meantime, she could only hope that their journey would be accomplished peacefully. She could not help but be aware that they were surrounded by grooms, far more than she would normally dream of travelling with—and all of them armed. Gerard and Harry were taking no chances and she could only be grateful for their care of her.

They stopped briefly to change the horses, and, in the case of the ladies, to relieve themselves in private at a good posting inn. Lisa transferred to the main carriage and was as good as gold, perhaps because Amelia had thought to bring along a book filled with bright pictures. The ladies ate a picnic in the carriage and fortunately did not need to get out again at any point. In consequence, they were able to make good time and it was not yet dark when they arrived at Coleridge.

Helene came to greet them eagerly, kissing Amelia and then Emily. She looked radiant and very happy, as she told her friends that she was increasing.

'I believe Max thinks it is a little soon, but he is merely concerned for me,' she said as she led the way upstairs. 'Your rooms are adjacent and there is a connecting door should you wish to use it. I hope you will both be very comfortable with us. I have been looking forward to your visit so much. Did you enjoy yourselves at Pendleton?'

'Susannah made us very welcome, as always,' Amelia said. 'I am delighted at your news, my love. I must tell you that I have a little news myself. I am to be married.'

'Amelia! I am so pleased. You must be promised to the Earl of Ravenshead?'

'Yes. Gerard asked me to wed him at Pendleton and I agreed. However, I fear there is someone who does not wish us to marry and has already tried to prevent us.'

'Amelia?' Helene looked at her in alarm. 'Are you speaking of your brother?'

'Michael does not wish for it. Indeed, he forbade me—but this is someone else: someone who would prefer to see us dead rather than happy. As yet we are not certain of his identity, though we believe he may use the name of Lieutenant Gordon.'

'How can that be? Who would wish to see you dead?' Helene looked shocked.

'We are not certain.' Amelia frowned. 'I do not wish you to worry, Helene—especially in your condition. If you would prefer that we leave…'

'Certainly not. How could you think it? After all you have done for me, Amelia, I would never close my door to you—and I am sure that Max will wish to help Gerard in whatever way he can.'

'Thank you, dearest.' Amelia smiled her gratitude. 'I was sure you would feel that way. We have decided to announce our engagement at the ball.'

'I am so happy for you. I must admit that I thought you might never marry, but now you are to wed the earl and I know you will be content—he is a good man.' Helene turned to look at Emily. 'How are you, dearest? I have thought that you might also have some news for me.'

'No, I fear I have not,' Emily replied, avoiding Helene's bright gaze. 'Besides, I should not dream of leaving Amelia while she had need of me.'

'I could not bear to part with you,' Amelia told her, guessing how much it was costing her to keep her smile in place. Helene would never deliberately hurt Emily and she could have no idea how much her careless remark had wounded her. 'I expect you will have many guests for the ball, Helene—but I hope you will find room for one more. I mentioned Marguerite to you in my last letter, did I not?'

'Yes—and I sent her an invitation, Amelia. I have had no reply.'

'I dare say her father would not permit it. However, I have appealed to her mama to let her come to help me with my stepdaughter. You have not yet met Lisa, Helene. Her nurse took her straight upstairs, as you may have noticed. She is lovely and also a little charmer.'

'I shall look forward to meeting her,' Helene said. 'You know that I once wished to find a position as a teacher in your orphanage, Amelia. Lisa is so much luckier than the children you help, because she has you and Gerard.'

'She will also have Emily and possibly Marguerite to make a fuss of her.' Amelia laughed softly. 'It will be a wonder if she is not utterly spoiled—but she lost her mama when she was a small child and the nanny Gerard employed when he brought her to England was not kind to her. I want her to be content and

I think it will be a happy release for Marguerite to come to us. I told her we should be here until a day after the ball and then we shall go down to Ravenshead. If I find the house acceptable, and Gerard assures me I shall, we shall spend most of our time there. We shall visit Bath and London in the Season, naturally, but our home will be at Ravenshead.'

'Will you not miss your home?'

'Perhaps at first—at least the garden. However, I shall make a garden of my own at Ravenshead. We shall keep my aunt's estate for our second child.'

They had reached the upper floor, which housed the bed-chambers. Having seen Emily installed in hers, Amelia looked at her own with pleasure.

'This has been freshly refurbished in the colours I love, Helene.'

'Yes, it has. It was done especially for you—for the best friend that I could ever have.' Helene reached forwards and kissed her cheek. 'You are such a generous person, Amelia. I cannot imagine that anyone would wish to harm you.'

'Well, it may be all a storm in a teacup,' Amelia said and laughed in a dismissive manner. 'Gerard and Harry took great precautions to safeguard us on the way here, but nothing happened. I dare say having made a blunder once the rogue has decided it is not worth the effort to try anything of the sort again.'

Helene was clearly puzzled. Amelia told her about Emily being kidnapped and then restored to them by the Marquis of Northaven.

'He told you that Emily was taken in mistake for you?' Helene was amazed. 'Oh, Amelia—it is almost like when attempts were made on Max's life and we thought it might be his cousin, but in the end it turned out to be his cousin's physician. When someone wishes you harm, it is difficult to know who they are.'

Amelia nodded but looked thoughtful. 'I hope this will not distress you, my love. I wonder if perhaps it would be better if we did not stay for the ball…'

'I should be most distressed then.' Helene lifted her head proudly. 'I was not frightened when that awful man threatened to kill me in order to get to Max…at least only a little and not until it was over. I do not want you to leave, Amelia. Max will help Gerard discover who this wicked rogue is. Gerard helped us—as did Mr Sinclair…' She frowned. 'I had thought that Toby Sinclair might propose to Emily.'

Amelia hesitated, then, 'In actual fact he did at Christmas, but she turned him down.'

'Emily turned down Mr Sinclair? Why? He is perfect for her.'

'She has her reasons, I dare say. It would be best if you did not speak of him to her, Helene—unless she takes you into her confidence, which she may. I know you were good friends.'

'We still are. Emily writes to me once in a while.' Helene looked thoughtful. 'I know she has a secret. I shall not ask you or her to reveal it, but I have seen the sadness in her eyes.'

'I shall tell you only that she had had an unhappy life before she came to me. I too had hopes of Mr Sinclair for her, but it seems that it was not to be. He left the same night and we have not heard from him since.'

'Then you do not know that his father died?'

'Oh, no! That is sad news indeed. I had wondered why he went so suddenly. Susannah told me he had an urgent summons to return, but I had no idea it was so serious.'

'Extremely serious. I know Max had a letter only this morning. Toby gave us the news and said that he was not sure if he could attend the ball. His mother and sister are in great distress. I dare say he cannot leave them immediately, especially for a ball. I am sure Toby will have written to Harry and Susannah, but perhaps the letter had not reached him before you left.'

'No, I dare say it had not, for he would have mentioned it,' Amelia replied. 'It is a sad time for the family and I do not expect that Toby will feel able to attend your ball. Indeed, it would look wrong if he did. I think too that Harry's sister will need him at her side at this difficult time.'

Helene chattered on for a while, but Amelia was thoughtful. She might have misjudged Mr Sinclair somewhat. She had thought him cruel and rude to abandon Emily so abruptly, but if he had received terrible news and then arrived home only in time to see his father on his deathbed, it was not to be expected that he would write immediately to Emily.

'His mother and sister must come first—and of course there will be business to be done. He must be very distressed, I imagine.'

'Yes, very sad. I am sorry that Emily refused him—but perhaps she will reconsider.'

'I should be happy to think she might. However, at the moment I do not think it possible.'

Left to herself, Amelia took off her pelisse and fur-trimmed bonnet. The news about Mr Sinclair's father was shocking. She did not know if his family had expected it, but even so it would have devastated them. Susannah had certainly not expected it. The very fact that Toby Sinclair had intimated that he might come to Coleridge even now made Amelia think that he had not completely given up the idea of wedding Emily. She would tell her companion the sad news, but she would not speculate about Toby Sinclair's intentions.

If he had any he would make them clear himself in time.

Amelia's thoughts turned once more to Marguerite. She fully intended to make sure that Marguerite had every chance to meet a decent gentleman—and to help persuade her parents if the chance of a marriage presented itself.

Chapter Six

'Mr Sinclair's father has died?' Emily was shocked and distressed when Amelia told her the news the next morning. 'How terribly sad! I had no idea that he was so ill.'

'I do not believe anyone realised quite how precarious his health was—at least no one outside the family.'

'I thought…how selfish of me to be so upset about my own concerns.' Emily blushed. 'If Toby has been caught up in family problems—' She broke off and shook her head. 'No, I must not allow myself to hope. If he wished to communicate with me he could have sent me a letter.'

'I dare say he may have had too much on his mind.'

'You said he wrote to Helene to tell her the news—could he not have written to us?'

'He could…but perhaps he felt a letter inappropriate. What he has to say to you must be said face to face.'

'You are trying to make me feel better, but you did not see his expression when I told him about my child.' Emily raised her head. 'It would be foolish to imagine that this changes anything. If Mr Sinclair comes to the ball, I shall greet him as if nothing has happened between us, but I dare say his mama will need him with them for some time.'

'Yes, I think you may be right,' Amelia agreed. 'However, you should not give up hope entirely, dearest.'

'It was foolish of me to think that I might marry. My father told me that no decent man would want me and he is right.' The sheen of tears was in Emily's eyes, but she held them back. 'Perhaps we should go down now, Amelia. We do not wish to keep everyone waiting.'

Amelia did not answer. She knew that Emily was suffering, but there was no cure for a broken heart, as she had discovered to her cost when she was younger. Time alone would soften the hurt. She could only hope that Toby Sinclair would not visit Coleridge unless he was prepared to say something of importance to Emily.

'Now that I understand the circumstances I am prepared to make allowances for Toby,' Amelia told Gerard when they walked together in the long gallery later that day. 'However, I think that he might have made an effort to write to Emily—if only to tell her of his father's death.'

'Letters are sometimes too difficult to write,' Gerard said. He stopped walking and looked at her. 'Think of the wasted years, Amelia. Had I written to you at the time, we might have saved ourselves so much unhappiness.' He reached out to touch her face, remembered sorrow in his eyes. 'If you knew of all the tortured nights I spent thinking of you…longing for you. I should never have let your brother poison my mind against you. I should have known that he lied when he said that you had asked him to send me a message.'

'Is that what he said to you? How dared he? You must know that I would never have done something like that.'

'Afterwards, when I had time to think it over, I began to see that I had been a fool to believe him, but at first I was too bitter. I married Lisette while still resenting both you and Michael, Amelia. And then it was too late…'

Amelia took a step towards him. Her body throbbed with a deep and urgent desire, making her discard her usual reserve. 'You were not alone in your despair, Gerard. I thought that I should never know the happiness of loving…never feel the touch of a lover's hand…because I could not forget you even though others asked for me.'

'That would have been a sin.' He smiled, his eyes warm with laughter. 'I know there is passion in you.' He reached forwards, bending his head to kiss her. Amelia did not hold back, clinging to him, giving herself to him without reserve. 'I can hardly wait for our wedding night.'

'Nor I.'

'Perhaps we need not wait…' Gerard was about to kiss her again when they both heard something. He looked beyond her at a woman who stood watching them from the other end of the gallery. 'We are not alone.'

'Forgive me,' the woman said and came forwards. She was a tall woman, slim with silky blonde hair that was caught back from her face in a severe style, and her gown was a dull grey that did nothing for her complexion. 'Lady Coleridge thought I might find you here. I wanted to let you know I had arrived, Amelia—but I did not mean to intrude.'

'Marguerite!' Amelia exclaimed in surprise. 'My dear friend. I am so pleased that you came. I hoped your parents would permit it, but I was not sure. I have had no word that you were coming.'

'I have not been well. Nothing serious, merely a chill. However, Mama thought it would do me good to have a change of air—and of course she is always willing to oblige you, Amelia.'

'How is your dear mama?'

'Very well, thank you.'

'Gerard—this is Miss Marguerite Ross.' Amelia turned to him. 'I am not sure if you know each other? Marguerite's family lived near my father's home when I was a girl. You may have met her when you visited the area. You stayed with friends for some weeks one summer—Max and one other were also visiting in the district… Marguerite, this gentleman is the Earl of Ravenshead. We are engaged and it is his daughter that I have asked you to come and meet.'

Gerard extended his hand. 'I do not think we can have met. I am certain I should have remembered. It is a pleasure to meet any friend of Amelia's, Miss Ross.'

Amelia realised he was puzzled and explained, 'Marguerite's parents do not go out much in society. I asked her to come and stay with us. I believe she might enjoy helping me with Lisa. I do not think we need another nanny. Lisa has her nurse and Marguerite has often told me that she adores children—is that not so, my love?'

'Yes, indeed that is true, Amelia.' Marguerite did not take Gerard's hand. Instead she dipped a curtsy, her head bowed. 'I am sure we have not met, sir. I am delighted to be here and I hope I may be of service to Amelia and you.'

'I am certain you will.' Amelia smiled. 'You are not to think you are a servant, Marguerite, though I shall of course make you an allowance. It will be a pleasure to me to have you live with us—and I shall always be certain that Lisa is safe in your care.'

'I promise you that the child will be cared for as if she were my own,' Marguerite said. 'I shall not intrude on you longer, Amelia. I merely wanted you to know that I was here.' She turned to leave, but Amelia put out a hand to stop her, giving Gerard an apologetic glance. 'Forgive me, Gerard. I want to make sure that Marguerite is settled in—and to introduce her to Lisa…'

'Yes, of course. I must speak to Max about something. I shall see you this evening.'

'You will excuse us?'

'Yes. Please go with Miss Ross.'

Amelia held out her hand to Marguerite, who smiled and took it. She felt a little regretful as she glanced back at Gerard and saw him staring after them. They had reached a new stage of their relationship and it was a pity they had been interrupted. However, they had a whole lifetime ahead of them and she did want to make sure that Marguerite was comfortable.

Gerard stared after them as they left. He had said that he did not recognise Miss Ross; indeed, he could not recall having met her—and yet there was something at the back of his mind. She had looked at him oddly when he said that they had not met, a flicker of annoyance or resentment in her eyes.

Was it possible that they had met at some time in the past? He knew that any woman might feel offended if a gentleman they remembered claimed not to recall their meeting. The name Ross seemed to ring a chord in his subconscious, but he could not immediately find a reason for it.

He must be mistaken. Had they met before he would surely

have remembered. Miss Ross was not beautiful, but she was not unattractive. Indeed, she might look very well dressed in a different style. She reminded him of someone, but he could not place the memory.

It would come to him in time. He gave it up and went in search of Max. He had hoped to spend an hour or so with Amelia, but since she was otherwise engaged, he would seek out his friend.

'You look thoughtful.' Max, Lord Coleridge, raised his brows as Gerard entered the library. 'Has something happened to trouble you? You have not received another threat?'

'No. Though the broken doll was, according to Northaven, a warning and not a threat. As you know, I expected there might be an attempt to hold up the carriage on the way here. It would have been easy enough to make it appear the work of a highwayman. However, we were strong enough to fight off a gang of ruffians and perhaps they knew it…which begs the question: how do they know where we go and what we do?'

'A spy in our midst, you think?' Max Coleridge frowned. 'A servant, perhaps—the nanny you dismissed?'

'She could certainly have passed on information after I asked Amelia to marry me, but I doubt she knew anything of her until then.'

'Do you trust Northaven?' Max asked. 'You told me that he brought Miss Barton back to you after she was abducted—but could that not have been arranged to gain your confidence? A ruse to get close to you?'

'Harry and I thought of that, but we believed him genuine in his desire to make amends. I believe we may have misjudged him. He is by no means a knight in shining armour, but may not be the traitor we thought him in Spain.'

'You say he believed he knew where he might find this Lieutenant Gordon—if that is the rogue's real name?' Max picked a speck of fluff from his otherwise immaculate coat. 'I suppose you have heard nothing from him?'

'Not as yet,' Gerard said. 'Perhaps Gordon will give up his attempts now that he knows we are aware of him.'

'Do you really believe that? If he hates you, as seems to be the case, can you see him just giving up and walking away?'

Gerard sighed. 'If I speak truly, no. I suppose I hoped that he might have decided we are too well protected, but I dare say he will simply become more devious.'

'Exactly. We must remain alert at all times, Gerard. Helene has invited so many guests to the ball that it would be an ideal moment to strike. I shall have the grounds patrolled all night, every night—but I think we should have a man on guard outside Amelia's door at night too, just in case.'

'As long as the ladies are not aware of it. We must dress the guard as a footman or we may alarm the guests.'

'Certainly. I am sure we have enough livery to accommodate your men, Gerard.'

'Would you rather we went home and saved you the bother? It is a lot to ask of you, Max. I should not have brought this trouble to your house.'

'Damn you, Gerard! We swore to be true friends in Spain, to help each other in time of need. If it had not been for you, Helene might have died last summer. You stood by me then and I shall stand by you now.'

'Thank you. Both you and Harry have been the best friends

a man could have,' Gerard said. 'I do not know why I am so uneasy. I have a feeling that the danger is closer than we imagine—but I have no idea why…'

'Emily, my love. This lady is Marguerite Ross—I mentioned to you that she was coming to live with us.'

'Miss Ross.' Emily dipped a curtsy. 'I am so happy to meet you. I am Emily Barton—Amelia's companion. I hope you will be happy with us. Indeed, I know you must be. Amelia is the most generous of friends.'

'Miss Barton—may I call you Emily?' Marguerite gave her a nervous smile. 'I am so fortunate that Amelia wrote to Mama. My life has been…less than happy since…' She sighed and shook her head. 'No, I shall not dwell on the past. I am here now and I am looking forward to my duties and helping Amelia where I can.'

'You will not find your duties onerous,' Amelia said. 'Lisa has her nurse. Nurse Mary will continue to care for her clothes and to give Lisa her meals. All I ask of you is that you will read to Lisa, play with her—and perhaps help her to study books I shall provide for her pleasure. She is too young for a governess as yet, but she needs friends. I want you to be her friend, Marguerite.'

'She is an adorable child. It will be no hardship to be Lisa's friend,' Marguerite said. 'She is a fortunate child to have a stepmother like you, Amelia. Most women in your place would not wish to take on the daughter of their husband's first wife. They would employ a strict nanny and stay away from the nursery.'

'The earl has just dismissed one nanny for being too strict,' Emily said with a little frown.

Marguerite turned her gaze on her. 'Has he, indeed? I remember our nanny was very strict. Papa told her she must make sure we behaved ourselves. I dare say it did us no harm.'

'I am sure it did not,' Amelia said, 'but I love Lisa as if she were my own. I intend to spend some time with her myself most days. However, there will be times when I cannot and then I shall be able to relax in the knowledge that you are caring for her. I know my dear Emily would care for her, but she may have other concerns. Emily does so much for me.'

Amelia smiled at her companion. Had it not been for Emily's hopes of marriage she would probably not have thought of bringing Marguerite here, but she was pleased that she had done so. The young woman had been living a terrible life, because her parents had made her suffer for her sister's shame and it was not fair.

'However, you must not think that I asked you here simply to be Lisa's friend, Marguerite. You will live as one of the family and accompany us when we go visiting. Lady Coleridge is holding a ball this weekend. I hope you have a suitable gown?'

'I have not had a new ball gown for years.' Marguerite looked distressed. 'I have nothing suitable. I did not realise that I should need one and brought only a few things with me.'

'We are of a similar size.' Amelia's eyes went over her. 'I think that my clothes may fit you, though you may need to adjust the hems slightly. I have a new green gown that I have not worn. I think it will suit you well, Marguerite.' She glanced at her feet. 'I do not think my shoes will fit, for I have smaller feet than you do. Emily—do you have a pair of dancing slippers that might fit Marguerite?'

'Yes, I think I have a pair I have worn only once. You can try them on and see,' Emily said. 'I shall be very happy to give them to you, for I have several pairs to choose from.'

'You are both very kind.' Marguerite's eyes held a glimmer of tears. 'I do not know how to thank you.'

'When we go down to Ravenshead I will commission a seamstress and a shoemaker. I shall need a trousseau and you may as well be fitted out at the same time,' Amelia said. 'No, do not thank me, Marguerite. I have been very fortunate and it is my pleasure to help others less so. All I truly want is for us to live comfortably together.'

Marguerite dabbed at her eyes with a lace kerchief that smelled of rose water. 'I do not know what I have done to deserve such kindness from you.'

'I was distressed when Lucinda took her own life,' Amelia replied. 'She was my friend. I did not know you as well, Marguerite, but I have often thought of you. Had I realised sooner how your life had changed, I should have done more to help you. I know your mama refused to allow you to stay with me, but had I appealed to her personally, she might have done so. I shall write and thank her for allowing you to come to me.'

'Mama admires you, Amelia. I am sure she needs no thanks for agreeing to something that costs her so little.'

'Nevertheless, I shall write to her.' Amelia smiled. 'It will be so pleasant to have your company, Marguerite.' She turned to Emily, missing the odd look in Marguerite's eyes. 'Will you help Marguerite settle in, dearest? I am going to sort out a few gowns that I do not need. I shall bring them to your room later, Marguerite. You would look well in green or blue—colours will suit you so much better than that grey gown.'

'Come with me, Marguerite,' Emily invited. 'I shall show you the rooms we mostly use here—and then you may try on those dancing slippers.'

* * *

Amelia found six gowns that she thought might appeal to Marguerite. She chose a green ball gown that she had never worn, a blue evening dress, a silver-grey evening dress, two afternoon dresses and a striped green morning gown. She added a spangled shawl, two pairs of evening gloves and a velvet evening purse.

She judged that the gowns would be enough to see Marguerite through their short stay at Coleridge. Once they were at Ravenshead, she would order new gowns for all of them.

'Martha, would you take these to Miss Ross's room, please?' Amelia said when she had finished laying out the clothes. 'You may take the silver-grey gown first and the others can follow later. I am not sure whether Miss Ross has a gown pressed for this evening, but this one is ready to wear.'

'Yes, Miss Royston. Are you sure you meant to give this ball gown away, miss? It is new and your favourite colour.'

'It becomes me well, but I have many others. My friend was unable to bring much with her and she will need these gowns until new ones can be ordered.'

'Yes, miss. I just wanted to be sure.'

Amelia smiled to herself as the maid took the gown away. She was dressed ready for the evening and she wanted to go down early. She had sensed that Gerard was surprised by Marguerite's arrival and she ought to explain that she had said nothing to him only because she had not been sure her friend would come. She had not expected Marguerite to simply arrive, imagining that she would receive a letter from Mrs Ross in the first instance.

Now that she had a moment to herself, she was at last at liberty to think about the scene in the library with Gerard. He had kissed her and she had not held back. What might have happened had Marguerite not come in at that moment?

Gerard had told her more of his feelings when Michael had him thrashed and sent him away. He had spoken of his bitterness, his longing for her and lonely nights. For the first time Amelia understood how he had felt, realising that his pain had been as deep as hers, if not deeper. He had been hurt and humiliated—her brother's bullies had been too many and too strong for him to fight back.

He had married Lisette while still feeling resentful. She had thought he must care for her but it seemed he hadn't loved her. When he spoke of her he seemed deeply disturbed. He had spoken of Lisette's terrible unhappiness, which drove her to take her own life. He said that he could not give her what she needed…would it be the same when they married? Or had Gerard been unable to love his wife because in his heart he still wanted Amelia?

His kiss had been passionate and hungry. She had felt that he truly wanted her. Perhaps he did love her in his way…

'I trust your judgement completely,' Gerard said after Amelia had explained why she had asked Marguerite to come to them. They had met once again in the library so that they could be alone for a few moments before dinner. A fire had been lit and the candles burned brightly, giving the room a warm, intimate feeling. 'It is a sad thing that Miss Ross should have been treated so badly. I did not remember her when we spoke earlier, but I have been thinking and I seem to recall a young woman with a similar name.' He frowned, an odd, slightly uneasy expression in his eyes. 'Was not Lucinda Ross Marguerite's sister? I think

Lucinda Ross was the young woman who killed herself some years ago?'

'Yes, that is correct. Lucinda was in some trouble. It happened during that summer. I thought at one time—' She broke off and shook her head. 'Northaven… I know that he had been to the house a few times. I once saw him flirting with Lucinda in the gardens.'

'Both Harry and I were also invited to some functions at the home of Mr and Mrs Ross—but Harry would never dream of seducing a young woman of good family. Nor would I, come to that, but at the time I could think only of you. It was you I loved, Amelia.' He frowned, hesitated, then, 'I do recall the name, but not Lucinda's face, though I remember meeting her. I might have liked her sister more for I believe I danced with her a few times, but there was nothing more than politeness between us. Indeed, I could not recall her when we met, but she may have changed. That gown and hairstyle are not becoming to a young woman.'

'You do not mind that I have invited her to stay with us for a while? She is not beautiful, but I think she would be attractive wearing the right clothes. I hope that she may meet someone she likes who will offer for her.'

'Playing matchmaker again?' Gerard teased.

'No, for I have no one in mind for Marguerite. I merely wish to give her the chance she has been denied so long. Besides, she loves children and she will be a big help to me.'

'Then I am delighted she has come,' Gerard said and smiled. 'Are you looking forward to the ball, my love?'

'Yes, of course.' Amelia moved towards him, her breath catching as she gazed up at him. 'We shall be able to dance together as often as we wish. Once our engagement is announced no one could lift a brow if we danced all night—though I suppose it might be thought rude to ignore one's friends altogether.'

'I think it would be pistols at dawn if I dared to monopolise you completely,' Gerard said teasingly. He turned his head and frowned, then strode towards the door and threw it open.

'Is something the matter?' Amelia asked.

He turned to Amelia, frowning. 'I thought someone was eavesdropping outside the door. If someone was listening to our conversation, he or she fled before I could discover who it was.'

'Listening to our conversation?' Amelia stared at him. 'Surely not? In this house…who would spy on us, Gerard?'

'I wish I knew.' Gerard's eyes darkened. 'It is foolish, but since we came here I have grown more uneasy.'

'You expected an attack on the road, did you not?'

He nodded. 'We were prepared for it, but it did not happen. Therefore our enemy has something else planned—something more devious and perhaps more dangerous. I have men watching the grounds, Amelia. I can shoot a man who tries to abduct you, but I have a feeling that something more sinister is going on.'

'What are your reasons? What has changed?'

'I do not know, but I trust my instincts. They served me well in Spain and at other times.'

A shudder caught Amelia and for a moment she was afraid of something she could not understand. 'I must confess that frightens me…'

'Won't you withdraw before it is too late? I could go away— take the danger with me, for I feel it is directed at me. However, you may be hurt, because this person will use you to get to me.'

'No! I have already told you nothing will keep me from you. Would you go away and condemn me to a life of solitude?'

Amelia demanded. She moved towards him, clutching at the lapels of his immaculate coat. 'Will you let me die a maiden—unfulfilled and regretful?' Her eyes were fearful, desperate. 'Have you no idea of the feelings I have for you—the longings I know must seem immodest in an unmarried lady?'

'My dearest one! You cannot believe me indifferent? You are beautiful. Any man would be grateful to have such a woman as his wife.' Gerard caught her to him, kissing her with a fierce hunger that set her pulses racing. She clung to him, her body melting into his as the raging desire swept through her. 'I would leave you only to protect you, believe me.'

'If you do, I may as well die.'

'Never!' Gerard gazed down into her wild face, a thrill of laughter and triumph sweeping over him as he saw the passion he had always believed was in her. 'I shall not give you up, Amelia—and nothing shall part us for a second time.'

'Do you swear it?'

'I swear it with my life. Only my death will part us.'

Amelia pressed herself against him, lifting her face for his kiss. As he took her mouth, she parted her lips for him, meeting his tongue in a delightful dance of sweet desire. Her body flamed, tingled with the need to know him, to lie with him.

'Gerard, I want to be truly yours.'

'I burn for you, my love.' He smiled ruefully. 'I would we were at Ravenshead. I could come to you there without ruining your reputation, Amelia. Here, I hesitate to abuse our hosts' hospitality.'

'Once we are at Ravenshead we shall not wait,' Amelia said. 'Nothing must part us now, for I could not bear it.'

Gerard kissed her, but this time softly. 'We must wait for the moment, but I agree that nothing shall part us, my dearest.'

* * *

Hidden behind a heavy curtain, the eavesdropper sat curled up on a deep window ledge and listened. For a moment it had seemed that Ravenshead had discovered the presence of a third person, but he had gone to the slightly open door, thinking the listener was outside. Seeing no one, he had believed himself mistaken. He was mistaken only in the location. What good luck that quick thinking had prevented discovery the instant they entered the room!

A smile touched the lips of the hidden one. Gerard Ravenshead thought himself so clever, but revenge was close. It was like the taste of honey on the tongue of the person who hated him. A smile hovered. Soon now. Soon the debt would be paid...

Amelia went to bed feeling happier than she had been for years. She could no longer doubt that Gerard felt a strong passion for her. He might not love her as he once had, but he was certainly not indifferent. They would not lack for passion in their marriage. She longed for the time when they would be at Ravenshead...when she could at last become one with him.

She had lingered downstairs for as long as she could, but Gerard had been caught up in a discussion about politics with some of the other gentlemen. He had thrown her an apologetic glance, telling her by means of a look that he longed for some time alone with her, but it was impossible. She knew that they must be patient; in a few days they would leave Coleridge and then...

A smile on her lips, Amelia sat down at her desk and took out her writing box. She opened it and took out some sheets of vellum, then dipped her pen in the ink and began to write a letter. She was not yet ready to sleep and she wished to tell several friends her news, for she knew it would please them.

* * *

After she had been writing for some half an hour or so she sanded and sealed her letters, four in all, leaving the one addressed to Marguerite's mother on the top of the pile. In the morning she would take them down to the hall and place them with others to be franked by Max and taken to the receiving office with any other letters his guests wished sent.

Amelia brushed her hair, washed her face and hands and then went to bed. She blew out the candle and settled down to sleep, but her mind was busy and it was a while before she settled. She was resting, but not sleeping, when the sound of her door opening startled her. For a moment she lay listening, thinking that she must be mistaken. She had not locked the door to her dressing room for it was that way the maid entered in the morning, but her maid would not creep unannounced into her darkened bedchamber at this hour.

'Who is there?' she called and sat up in bed, her hand reaching for the candle by her bed. It was a moment or two before she secured it and some seconds more before she could strike the tinder. 'Who are you?' she cried as a dark shadow fled through the dressing-room door.

Amelia lit her candle and got out of bed. She went through the door to the dressing room. The intruder had left it open in his haste and she saw that the door that led from the dressing room to the servants' stairs was also open. Whoever had been in her room must have come and left by that means.

Amelia knew that her own maid would not have reacted in such a way. No other servant ought to have been there at this late hour and would not be on their lawful business. Yet someone had come to her room—why? What were they searching for? Amelia's jewellery was locked away in her dressing case, which she kept by the bed as she slept. A brief glance told her that it was still there and untouched. So what had the intruder been doing?

Amelia felt chilled, because this was something she had not expected. What might have happened had she been asleep? She wondered if she had been meant to die—or was it merely an attempt to rob her? She shivered, feeling uneasy and anxious. Ought she to send for someone? Amelia hesitated, but it was past midnight and she did not wish to make a fuss at this hour. However, in future she would make sure that the dressing-room door was locked—at least until they were safe at Ravenshead. Her maid could knock if Amelia were still asleep when she came, but it was more likely that she would be wide awake!

Amelia returned to bed. She was not unduly frightened now that the door was locked. She would not be disturbed again this night, but the incident had shocked her more than she liked. She would have to tell Gerard about the intruder in the morning—and of course Max would have to know. He would wish to make enquiries amongst his servants. It did not seem that anything had been taken, but it could quite easily have been simply a bungled robbery. He would have to warn his people to be vigilant.

'You are certain that the door to the hall was locked?' Max asked the next morning when Gerard asked him to meet in private. 'Whoever it was came from the servants' stairs?'

'Amelia tried the door leading into the hall and it was locked. She is positive that the intruder came and went by means of the servants' stairs. Indeed, she saw the shadow escape that way, though it was too dark to be certain whether it was a man or a woman.'

'It would be easy enough for anyone to come that way once

the servants have retired for the night. However, I gave strict instructions that all the outer doors and windows were to be secured at night.' Max frowned. 'I am loathe to think that any of my people would do such a thing, Gerard—but of course our guests have brought their own servants.'

'It is difficult to point the finger at anyone,' Gerard agreed. 'We had a guard outside Amelia's room and Miss Barton's room. Nothing untoward was seen.'

'And we have men patrolling the grounds…' Max swore softly. 'Are you thinking…?'

'That the intruder must have come from inside the house.' Gerard nodded. 'Amelia suggested that it could have been an attempt to steal her jewels, but I am not so sure.'

'I dare say she does not wish to think it anything more. It is fortunate that she was not asleep.'

'Very.' Gerard looked grim. 'I have been aware that something had changed, but I cannot put my finger on it, Max. I know only that I am uneasy.'

'What does Amelia feel?'

'She says that her maid must knock if she is not awake. She will lock her dressing-room door at night.'

'She is very composed about this, Gerard.'

'Perhaps too much so for her own good. Amelia trusts everyone.'

'What do you mean?' Max's gaze narrowed. 'Has something occurred to you?'

'Yes…at least it is just a little seed of doubt. Something I cannot quite place…' He shook his head as Max lifted his brows. 'I am not certain therefore I shall lay no blame, but my instincts are telling me I am right.'

'You do not wish to tell me?'

'Yes, of course. You have the right to know—but you will not tell Helene or anyone else except Harry when he arrives, for I may be wrong.'

Amelia wandered around her bedchamber. She was looking for something, but she was not sure what it was. Her dressing case was there and the contents were intact. Her silver evening purse was lying on the dressing table where she had put it last night before she undressed. What else had she done before she went to bed? Ah, yes, she had written some letters.

The letters were missing. She had left a small pile on the desk. They had gone and she had not taken them downstairs herself when she went down to speak to Gerard earlier, for she'd had other things on her mind. She frowned as the door opened and her maid entered carrying a gown she had pressed.

'Martha—did you by chance take my letters down to be franked this morning?'

'No, Miss Royston. I saw them lying on the desk when I woke you first thing, but I was not certain you wished for them to be sent yet. You would have asked had you intended me to do it for you.'

'Yes, I should,' Amelia agreed. 'It is most odd, for I did not do it myself. I wonder if Emily…'

'Miss Barton did come to your room earlier, miss. I saw her leaving as I came to collect your gown for this evening. It needed pressing and I had taken some other things to be laundered earlier so I returned to fetch the gown and Miss Barton was leaving. She asked if I knew where you were.'

'Perhaps she took them down. I shall ask her later.'

Amelia picked up a book she wished to offer Lisa as more interesting reading than those Nanny Horton had considered suitable and left the room. As she went into the nursery, she saw that both Emily and Marguerite were before her. They were playing a game of Blind Man's Buff with Lisa and another child and the children were screaming with laughter.

Amelia watched, smiling as Marguerite allowed herself to be caught by Lisa and accepted the blindfold from her hand. She stopped suddenly, as if becoming aware of Amelia.

'Oh, we are playing a game. I hope you approve?'

'Melia…' Lisa cried and came running to hug her. 'Marguerite has been teaching me games and Emily has been playing with us. Have you come to join us?'

'I came to bring you this book. It is a bestiary and there are lots of pictures of animals and birds. I thought you would like to have it—but you may look at it another day. Go on with your game, my love.'

'I would rather look at the book with you,' Lisa said and took hold of her arm, pulling her towards a sofa. 'It is just a silly game and the book is beautiful.'

Glancing at Marguerite, Amelia saw her flush and smiled, shaking her head. 'Now that is unkind, Lisa—and Marguerite was very good to play with you.'

'Thank you, Mademoiselle Ross—and Emily…' Lisa tilted her head, a beguiling smile in her eyes. 'I like to play, but I like books with pictures best.'

'Well, you have run us ragged and we must rest,' Emily said, laughing. 'Next time I shall bring a picture book, miss.'

Lisa giggled and shot a look of mischief at her. 'I like to play sometimes.'

'You won't get round me that way,' Emily teased. 'Is there anything you need, Amelia?'

'No—oh, yes, one thing. Did you by chance take my letters down to the hall this morning?'

'No. I would not without asking you first. You might not have finished them.'

'But your letters were downstairs earlier,' Marguerite said and looked at Emily oddly. 'I wrote a letter to my mother and placed it in the hall for franking, as Lady Coleridge said I might. I saw a letter from you to Mama, Amelia—and some others. If Emily did not put them there, your maid must have done so. Was there something you wished to alter?'

'No. They were ready to go, but Martha says she did not take them and I did not for I had other things on my mind…' Amelia was about to mention the intruder, but changed her mind. Emily had already suffered a bad experience and she did not wish to make her nervous. 'Someone else must have done so. Perhaps one of the other maids went in to clean and saw them there. Well, it does not matter.' She smiled at Lisa. 'When I was young I used to look at this book with my nanny. I believe you will like it.'

'Let me see…' Lisa pulled at her hand. 'Let me see.'

Amelia smiled and sat down, taking the child on to her lap. The small boy who had also been playing with them looked on shyly until Amelia beckoned to him. He came and leaned against her shoulder, his eyes fixing hungrily on the pictures she was showing to Lisa. After a few moments, both children fired questions at her and she was so engrossed with them that she did not look up for some time. She saw that Emily had gone, but Marguerite was still there, watching, a strange, half-envious expression in her eyes.

Thinking that she understood, Amelia handed the book to Lisa and allowed the children to look through it alone.

'Children are such a blessing,' she said to Marguerite and went to stand next to her by the window. 'I thought once that I should never have my own, but now I have hopes for the future—and already I have a daughter to love.'

'Yes, I dare say the care of a motherless child is as good a reason for marriage as any.'

'It is certainly one reason,' Amelia said. 'Lisa is a delightful child and Gerard did need someone to help with the care of her, but we are good friends.'

'Friendship is more than most find in marriage. Men are always so faithless…though I do not imply that the earl will be faithless to you, Amelia. After all, you will bring him a fortune when you marry.'

'Yes, that is true. I expect to be very happy in my marriage. You should not think that all men are faithless, Marguerite, though I know you think of Lucinda.'

'Lucinda was foolish to trust the man who betrayed her.'

'Perhaps she loved him and did not think further.'

'Perhaps. Can you love the child of another woman?' Marguerite's eyes were watchful. 'Will you not think of her, of his wife…?' She shook her head. 'Forgive me. I should not have spoken to you so, Amelia. It was not my place.'

'Emily knows that she may say anything to me—and so may you, Marguerite. If something is on your mind?'

'No.' She hesitated, then, 'I just wondered if the shadow of…the manner of his wife's death might hang over you.'

'I am sorry for the way she died,' Amelia replied, glancing at Lisa, who was happily absorbed in the book. She wondered how Marguerite knew of Lisette's suicide, because not even Emily knew more than that Gerard's wife had died in Spain. 'It is sad when someone dies tragically but I know that Gerard did all he could for her.'

Marguerite looked as if she would speak, gave a little shake of her head and walked to where the children were still entranced by the pictures of animals and birds. She pointed to some words beneath one of the pictures.

'Do you know what this says, Lisa?'

'It is funny writing. I cannot read it.'

'That is because it is in Latin. It says that the picture is of a parrot…'

Amelia watched for a moment as Marguerite continued to explain what the words meant. She thought that she had chosen well, for Marguerite was obviously good with children. She was surprised that Marguerite should have mentioned Gerard's first wife. It almost seemed that she knew exactly how Lisette had died, and yet Amelia was sure he had not spoken of it to many people. How could a woman he had never met know anything about Lisette's suicide?

Amelia was thoughtful as she went downstairs, but then she realised that Marguerite had not actually said anything directly about the suicide. She must, of course, have imagined that Lisette had died from the fever she'd caught after her child was born. So many women died that way that it would be easy to assume it was so. Satisfied that she had misunderstood, Amelia dismissed Marguerite's words. The look in her eyes was harder to dismiss, for it had seemed to carry a warning.

Amelia dressed that evening in a ball gown of blue satin overlaid with swathes of silver lace. It had a deep scooped neckline that revealed a tantalising glimpse of her soft breasts, and little puffed sleeves. Around her neck she had fastened a collar of lustrous pearls with a diamond clasp that had a large baroque pearl as a drop. On her wrists she wore gold-and-pearl bangles and she had a magnificent sapphire-and-diamond ring on her left hand. Gerard had given it to her after tea that afternoon, slipping it on her finger himself.

'It fits. I am relieved,' he told her, lifting her hand to kiss the palm. 'I hope you like it, my love. It was commissioned for us. In time I shall send for the family jewels and you may take your pick of them, though I know you have jewels enough of your own.'

'Most of Aunt's jewellery was not to my taste and remains in the bank. She was extremely fond of amethysts, but I prefer pearls—and of course sapphires and diamonds.' She looked at the deep blue of the sapphire oval ring surrounded by fine white diamonds. 'This is lovely, Gerard—perfect. Thank you.'

'I am glad you are pleased.' He reached out to touch her cheek. 'I care for you so very much.'

Amelia admired her beautiful ring as she went down to the ballroom. It was a long gallery that normally housed musical instruments and several sofas as well as music stands. This evening it had been cleared of furniture and the rooms connecting on either side had their double doors thrown wide so that the effect was of one very large room.

In the first room, Lord and Lady Coleridge stood waiting to receive their guests and footmen were circulating with trays bearing glasses of the best champagne. Amelia accepted a glass and went to stand with Helene. She was one of the first to appear, but she could already hear the strains of music coming from the gallery.

'May I see your ring?' Helene asked and exclaimed over it. 'How lovely, Amelia. Three stones is a shape that suits your hands very well—and I believe you already have a small sapphire-and-diamond cluster that was your mama's?'

'Yes, I do, though the shank is wearing a little thin and I did not bring it with me—for I must have it repaired.'

'That sapphire is such a deep colour,' Helene said. 'I am so happy for you, Amelia. If it had not been for you, I should never have met and married Max. I wanted you to be happy too, and now you are.'

'Yes, I am,' Amelia said and kissed her. She moved away as Emily and Marguerite entered the room, wandering into the far room where flowers from a hot house had been arranged. There were some exotic blooms and the perfume was quite heavy, making her want to sneeze.

'Are you all right, Amelia?'

Amelia heard the voice and turned as Marguerite came up to her.

'Yes, perfectly, thank you. I was feeling a little nauseous for a moment, but I think it may have been these flowers—they have a strong smell, not unpleasant but a little overpowering.'

'You looked pale,' Marguerite said. 'Are you sure you feel quite well?'

'I shall be perfectly well, but I must not linger near these flowers; they are giving me a headache.'

'Why do you not go out for a breath of air?'

'It is too cold. Besides, I am looking forward to the ball. Excuse me.' Amelia saw Gerard coming and walked to greet him. She smiled and held out her hands to him. 'You look very handsome tonight, sir.'

'And you look beautiful, Miss Royston.' Gerard's eyes went over her hungrily. 'I see some people are beginning to dance—shall we?'

'Yes, please.' Amelia took his hand. 'I have been longing to dance with you again.'

The slight feeling of nausea she had experienced earlier vanished as he took her into his arms. The dancing had begun with a waltz and Amelia felt that she was floating on air as he whirled her along the gallery and back. She felt such sweet sensation, like being carried on a wave of sparkling sea to the stars, lost to everything, but the touch of his hand against her back and the faint masculine scent of him in her nostrils. She wanted to go on and on for ever.

Too soon the dance ended and almost immediately the guests came up to them to congratulate Gerard and wish Amelia happiness. Everyone wanted to know when the wedding would be and all their best friends demanded to be invited, which Amelia assured them would be the case.

A few of her friends told her that they had gifts for her, but the engagement was a surprise to most and they exclaimed over it again and again. Some of their closest friends teased Gerard and said that he had stolen a march on them and she was swept away to dance with several of the gentlemen. It was some time before they danced together again, but she noticed that Gerard danced once with Emily, Marguerite and Helene.

'I am glad to see you have been dancing,' she told him when they danced the final waltz before supper. 'It was good of you to ask Marguerite.'

'I asked Miss Barton because she was looking sad and had hardly danced at all,' Gerard told her. 'I could not avoid asking Miss Ross because it would have seemed rude. She said that she had remembered me and reminded me of the night we met. Apparently, we danced twice that evening and I fetched her some champagne.'

'Did she remember so clearly?' Amelia frowned. She would have liked to ask Gerard if there was any way that Marguerite could have known that Lisette had taken her own life, but the evening of their engagement was not the moment. 'She has not spoken to me of knowing you—though you told me you knew her sister, Lucinda, better.'

'Lucinda was an odd girl…'

Amelia saw his expression. Something in his look made her spine prickle. 'What do you mean? I always thought her a sweet and gentle girl.'

'Did you, my love?' Gerard's forehead creased. 'I thought something different, but keep your memories, Amelia. I hardly knew her after all.'

Amelia was intrigued, vaguely disturbed. He was hiding something from her. She sensed a mystery, but again this was not the time to inquire further. A niggling doubt teased at the back of her mind, but she dismissed it almost at once. Earlier, Marguerite had almost seemed to imply that Gerard was marrying her for her fortune and that he would be faithless once they were married. Did she know something that Amelia did not? She felt cold for a moment and shivered, then squashed the unworthy doubts.

She raised her head and smiled. Nothing should be allowed to spoil her special evening.

'Are you happy, Gerard?'

His gaze seared her. 'Can you doubt it? I cannot wait until we are at Ravenshead…to be alone with you…'

Amelia felt reassured. He felt something more than friendship for her. She would be a fool to doubt it, to let her thoughts be poisoned by a casual remark.

Turning her head at that moment, she suddenly saw Marguerite looking at them. The look on her face was so strange that it sent a shiver down Amelia's spine. Marguerite looked… angry…resentful.

Why should she look as if she hated to see others happy? Amelia had an uneasy feeling that something was very wrong, and yet a moment later, as Marguerite saw her glance she smiled and the shadows were banished from her face.

Amelia decided that she had been mistaken. Marguerite's expression must have been wistful, not resentful. She was thinking of all the dances and happy times she had missed. After all, why should she resent the people who had given her this chance to enjoy herself? Of course she would not. She had several times expressed her gratitude. It would be foolish to imagine resentment where there was none.

Chapter Seven

Emily came to Amelia as she was standing by the buffet looking at a bewildering array of dishes. Her complexion was pale and there were shadows beneath her eyes.

'Are you not feeling well?' Amelia asked in concern.

'I have a headache,' Emily confessed. 'Would you mind if I left after supper and went to bed? Is there anything I can do for you before I retire?'

'I have all I want. Are you truly ill, my love—or is it because…?'

'I truly have a throbbing headache. I do not know why, for I scarcely ever have them, Amelia. I think it must be something to do with the soap that the maids used for laundering my kerchiefs. I came to ask if I might borrow one of yours this morning, because mine all had a strong perfume clinging to them, which seemed to bring on my headache. The pain has been lingering all day and is worse this evening.'

'I am so sorry. Yes, of course you must go to bed, Emily. If you are still unwell in the morning, I shall have the doctor to you—and I will have Martha launder your kerchiefs with the soap she uses for mine.'

'Thank you…' Emily hesitated. 'I did not touch your letters this morning, Amelia. I just went into your room, saw you were not there and then left—you do believe me?'

'Of course. Why should I not? You have always been honest with me.'

'Someone suggested to me that I had taken the letters and lied to you.'

'Someone…' Amelia's gaze narrowed. 'Do you mean Marguerite?'

'I do not wish to say—but I should be distressed if I thought you believed I would lie to you.'

'Well, you may rest easy, Emily. I know you too well to ever think you would lie to me.'

'Thank you.' Emily's eyes carried the sheen of tears. 'I thought…but I shall forget it. My foolish head hurts so. Excuse me, I must go. Goodnight, Amelia.'

'Goodnight, my love. Ask Martha for a tisane if you wish. I hope you feel better soon.'

Amelia frowned as she watched Emily leave the supper room. She was sorry that her friend was feeling unwell for she had enough to bear. The scent clinging to her kerchiefs was odd, for Amelia had experienced a similar thing in the room where all the exotic flowers had been displayed; overpowering perfumes could bring on headaches, especially if one were in close contact through a piece of personal lingerie.

She would ask Martha to wash all of Emily's things as well as Amelia's for the next few days. Helene's maids must be using something that was quite unsuitable.

Amelia was thoughtful as she ate a little supper. She had hoped that Emily might have something to celebrate this evening, but Toby Sinclair had not been able to tear himself away from his family at this sad time. She supposed that he could not decently attend a ball so close to his father's funeral. He was perfectly correct not to come. Perhaps he would write to Emily— or seek her out when they went down to Ravenshead in two days' time. She put her thoughts to one side as Marguerite came to sit with her and eat a syllabub.

'Are you enjoying yourself, Marguerite?'

'How could I not when everyone has been so kind?' Marguerite's mouth curved in a smile. 'Is Emily unwell? She told me she was going to bed...'

'She has a little headache. I dare say it will pass by the morning.'

'She was pale. I would have made her an infusion to help her had she mentioned her headache.'

'Oh, I dare say she will ask Martha. It is a pity that it should come this evening, for Emily seldom has headaches.'

'Perhaps she has been feeling out of sorts. Someone mentioned that she had suffered a disappointment recently. Heartache sometimes manifests itself as illness, do you not agree?'

'You should not listen to gossip,' Amelia said. 'Besides, I am sure Emily will be better soon.'

Gerard watched the woman from across the room. Why did he have the feeling that she was not all that she appeared? Her smiles made him uneasy—for she seemed to be saying that she knew something he did not. He was pleased when he saw her leave the room. He wished it was as easy to send her packing altogether, but knew that Amelia trusted her, was fond of her. To voice his suspicions would only bring a cloud to their time of happiness—and perhaps he was wrong.

For the moment all he could do was to watch and wait. He turned as Max joined him, understanding that there was something he needed to tell him.

'A few moments of your time, Gerard—in private?'

'Of course,' Gerard agreed. 'I am promised to Amelia for the next dance, but she is otherwise occupied for the moment.' His eyebrows arched. 'You have discovered something?'

'Yes. It means nothing and yet it might…' Max said. 'One of my footmen was up with a toothache early this morning and he saw something that might interest you.'

Amelia saw Gerard leave the supper room with Max. She frowned, because she had wanted a few moments alone with him. However, on further reflection she decided that what she had to say would keep for another day. She turned as Helene came up to her.

'Emily was looking pale earlier,' Helene observed. 'Has she by chance taken a chill?'

'She says that the perfumed soap your maids used for washing her kerchiefs gave her a headache. I shall ask Martha to use my soap for her in future since it seems that she is sensitive to strong perfumes, as I am myself.'

'I was not aware we were using strongly perfumed soap.' Helene looked puzzled. 'I shall ask my housekeeper and it shall be changed, Amelia. Some of the lilies used this evening had a very strong scent. I had one pot taken out this morning because it was overpowering.'

'Yes, I noticed the lilies,' Amelia said. 'I should have developed a headache had I stayed near them for long.'

'I shall not use that particular variety in the house again,'

Helene said. 'I am sorry Emily was made unwell. I had thought it might be something else.'

'You mean because Toby Sinclair did not come this evening?'

'No…' Helene hesitated, looking slightly conscious. 'Forgive me, Amelia—but I am not sure that Emily likes Miss Ross. I think they may have had words…but I may be mistaken.'

'Emily is always so thoughtful,' Amelia said. 'I cannot think she would take a girl like Marguerite, who has suffered much at the hands of her parents, as she did herself, in dislike. They hardly know one another, after all.'

'As I said, I may be mistaken—' Helene broke off as Marguerite came up to them. 'Miss Ross—have you enjoyed yourself this evening?'

'Thank you. It has been a lovely evening. Amelia was so kind as to give me this dress…' Marguerite held out the skirt of the green gown. 'It is beautiful.'

'It becomes you well,' Helene said. 'I have seen you dancing several times. I think you have made friends and admirers, Miss Ross.'

'Thank you,' Marguerite said, but did not smile. 'I passed Emily as I went to my room just now, Amelia. I believe she had been to yours. She said that she has a terrible headache. I offered to make her a tisane myself, but she refused me.'

'Emily had no doubt been in search of Martha to ask *her* to make her a tisane, as I advised,' Amelia said. 'Ah, here comes Gerard—I am promised to him for the next dance.'

Amelia said goodnight to Gerard. He had escorted her to her door, seeming reluctant to let her go inside. He kissed the palm of her hand, closing her fingers over the kiss.

'Keep that until we can be alone,' he said. 'Sleep well, my dearest. I trust that nothing will disturb your sleep this evening.'

'I dare say it will not. Martha has instructions to lock the dressing-room door when she leaves the room. Max provided her with a key and I also have one so I do not think anyone will intrude on me again.'

'Max has his footmen on duty all night so you should be quite safe,' Gerard told her. 'I shall see you in the morning, but you will sleep in and I have things to do—so you need not look for me before noon.'

Amelia nodded and went into her room. Martha came when she rang the bell and unfastened her gown at the back, helping her off with it.

'What is that smell, Miss Royston?' she asked, wrinkling her nose. 'You do not have a new perfume?'

'No…' Amelia glanced around her. 'I had just noticed it myself—it smells like lilies…the exotic ones they grow in hot houses that have strong perfume.' She took a step towards the bed, halting as the smell became overpowering. 'I think…behind the chair…is that a pot of lilies? It is not easy to see, but I believe it must be the source of that smell.'

Martha went quickly to look. 'Now how did that get here? I swear it wasn't here when I came in earlier to turn down the bed. The nasty thing!' She picked it up and went to the door, speaking to someone outside for a moment. 'I've given it to the footman to get rid of. I wonder who could have put that in here.'

'I cannot imagine for one moment,' Amelia said. 'Have a look around the room to make sure nothing else has been hidden and then you may go to bed. I am sure you have become tired waiting up for me.'

'I like to see you when you come back from a ball, miss. Have you enjoyed yourself?'

'Yes, very much,' Amelia said, watching as Martha went round the room, looking behind chests and under tables. 'I am sure you will find nothing else. Remember to lock the dressing-room door when you go out, Martha.'

'Yes, of course, miss. I have kept it locked since you told me. If someone entered your room, they must have a key or they came from the hall. You do not lock it when you leave.'

'Whoever it was must have entered from the hall. Lord Coleridge assured me that we have both keys to the dressing room. I have not been accustomed to locking my doors during the day. I have never needed to before, but I shall consider it in future.'

Before retiring, Amelia checked the door to the hall and the one to the dressing room. Both were locked. She was pensive as she pulled back the top covers on her bed and looked to see if anything unpleasant had been placed between the sheets. They were fresh and sweet smelling, just as Martha had prepared them for her.

The lilies were further evidence that someone was stirring up trouble for her. She had not dreamed up the intruder of the previous night—and there were the letters that no one would admit to having taken down to the hall. She had not bothered to ask Max if he had franked them for her, but she might do so in the morning.

She knew that if she spoke to the footman outside the door, Gerard would come to her, but she did not consider the pot of lilies reason enough to disturb him. Their perfume still lingered and she found it strong so she opened her a window a little to let in some fresh air. It seemed odd that Emily should complain of a strong soap used for washing her kerchiefs and now the lilies…

Amelia's thoughts were confused. Emily would not lie to her, but Marguerite had implied that she had taken the letters—and that she had seen her coming from Amelia's room this very evening. If she had not trusted Emily implicitly, she might have wondered if her companion had played a trick on her.

Why would anyone take some letters? Why would they hide a pot of lilies in her room? Supposing it was all part of a clever plot to make her believe that Emily was lying to her… Amelia dismissed the idea immediately. Someone was trying to unnerve her. Why? Was it to make her so distressed that she called off her wedding?

She thought it must be the most likely explanation. Yet why should anyone want to prevent her happiness? The only person she could think of who refused to accept her marriage was her brother. However, he had not been invited to Coleridge for the ball, because Helene did not like him.

Michael could certainly not be behind the odd things that had happened this past few days—though he might have paid someone to do it, of course. A servant, perhaps?

In another moment she would be thinking that Martha had placed the lilies in her room herself! This was so foolish and she would not think of it any more.

Martha had left a jug of lemon barley by her bed. She poured some into a glass and drank most of it. It was a little stronger than usual, but not unpleasant. She snuffed out the candles and closed her eyes. No one would disturb her sleep that night!

Martha awoke her by pulling back the curtains the next morning. Amelia yawned as she sat up, feeling that she could have slept a little longer, but as she looked at the pretty enamelled carriage clock she kept by her bed, she saw that it was almost noon.

'I am late this morning,' she said as she sat up and threw back the covers. 'Please pour me a cup of chocolate while I dress. Lisa will think I have deserted her.'

'I looked in twice, miss,' Martha said. 'You were sleeping so soundly that I thought it best not to wake you.'

'I must have been tired. I do not usually sleep this late even after a ball.'

Amelia went behind the dressing screen, washed and dressed in the green-striped linen gown that Martha brought her. She drank her chocolate at the dressing table, while Martha brushed her hair and wound it into a shining twist at the back of her head, securing it with pins.

'Thank you. I shall not eat, because it will be nuncheon very soon. I must hurry to spend a few minutes with Lisa before we are summoned.'

Amelia went up to the nursery. Nurse Mary was folding clothes as the children played with puzzles and books at the table.

'I am sorry to visit so late. I overslept this morning.'

'Miss Ross has been to play with the children,' Mary said. 'Miss Barton usually comes, but she hasn't been this morning. It is the first time she has missed since before Christmas.'

'She had a headache last night. Perhaps she still has it.'

Amelia spent a little time with the children. She promised Lisa that she would return later that day.

'We are going to Ravenshead tomorrow,' she said. 'I shall have more time to take you for walks then, my love.'

'Will you be my mama then? Must I call you Mama?'

'I shall always be your friend,' Amelia said. 'If you wish to call me Mama, you may, but if you would rather call me Melia, you can, Lisa.'

'Nanny said I would have to call you Mama—even though you are not my mother…' Lisa frowned. 'My mother died, didn't she?'

'Oh, darling, yes, she did, soon after you were born. Why do you ask?'

'How did my mama die? Did it hurt her?' Lisa's eyes were dark and a little fearful.

'No, she wasn't in pain. She had been ill for a long time— and she just went to sleep. You shouldn't think about it, Lisa. Your mama loved you and she would want you to be happy.'

'You won't die, will you, Melia?'

'No, my love. Not for a long time.'

Lisa clung to her hand. 'Promise me you won't go away and leave me and never come back.'

'I promise. I may go somewhere for a visit with your papa sometimes, but we shall both come back to you. We love you very much and we shall all be together as much as possible.'

'Thank you for telling me.' Lisa's eyes fixed on her intently. 'I love you, Melia.'

'I love you too, my darling.' Amelia embraced her, then looked into her face. 'Who told you that your mama died?'

'I asked Emily, because *she* said—' Lisa broke off as Marguerite entered the room. 'I want to read my book…' She ran to pick up the picture book, her head bent over the beautiful illustrations.

'Emily is unwell,' Marguerite said. 'She has vomited this morning and I think she has a fever. I believe she may be sickening for something. Perhaps we should ask for the doctor to call?'

'Yes, perhaps we should,' Amelia said. 'I must go, Lisa. I shall come again later.'

Amelia hurried from the room. She felt anxious about Emily. It must be something more than strong perfume on her kerchiefs if she had been vomiting. She would visit her and then make a decision about sending for the doctor.

'I am sorry to be so much trouble,' Emily said, looking pale and wan as she lay with her head against a pile of pillows. 'I do not know what is wrong with me. I was awake most of the night and vomited three times.'

'I am so sorry you are ill,' Amelia said. 'I shall send for the doctor. He will give you something to help with the pain.'

'I never have headaches. I thought it was the perfume on my kerchiefs, but it throbs so and I feel terrible…' Emily put a hand to her head. 'I am sorry to cause all this bother, Amelia.'

'You are not causing a bother. I shall call the doctor and hope that you are well enough to travel in the morning, Emily. However, if you are still unwell, we shall put off our journey for a few days. I have no intention of leaving you behind, my love.'

Leaving Emily to rest, Amelia went downstairs. She was late entering the dining parlour and apologised to the assembled company.

'I am sorry to keep you waiting, but Emily is most unwell—and I slept late.'

'I am so sorry Emily is unwell,' Helene said. 'Have you sent for the doctor?'

'Yes, I spoke to one of your servants, Helene. Emily is too sick to keep food down. I have asked Martha to make her a tisane and I shall go up to her as soon as I have eaten.'

'I could help nurse her,' Marguerite offered.

'It would be better if you stayed away from Miss Barton,' Gerard said from across the table. 'If she *is* sickening for something infectious, I would not wish it passed on to Lisa. Your first duty is to the child, Miss Ross.'

Marguerite's face remained impassive, but, happening to look at her, Amelia noticed that a little nerve flickered at the corner of her eye. She was not sure if Marguerite were angry or distressed.

Amelia frowned. 'I promised to visit Lisa this afternoon, Gerard. Perhaps I should not—unless Emily is merely suffering from an excess of nerves?'

Gerard stared at her for a moment in silence, then inclined his head. 'I shall bow to your good judgement, Amelia. However, it might be best if you left the nursing of Emily to Martha or one of the other maids.'

She gave him a reproving look. 'Emily is my friend. She needs me.'

'You are Lisa's mother now. She should be more important to you. I hope you will not let her down, Amelia.'

Gerard's expression was hard to read, but she thought that he was angry. Amelia was puzzled and a little hurt. How could Gerard think that she would desert Emily when she was so ill? Lisa had her nurse and Marguerite, and if Gerard was afraid of cross-infection then she would simply have to stay away from the nursery until Emily was better.

She did not like his tone or the way his words seemed to imply that Amelia's own wishes must come second to the child's. Of course she would never intentionally let Lisa down, but neither could she abandon Emily when she was so ill.

Gerard had been acting a little oddly recently. Amelia was not certain what some of his remarks were supposed to mean. She would ask him to explain, but for the moment it did not look as if she would have time to speak with him alone.

The doctor visited Emily. After examining her, he shook his head and looked grave, but said nothing until Amelia followed him into the small sitting room.

'She has no physical signs of illness other than the vomiting and the headache. There is no fever and I cannot see any sign of a rash—nor does she have any lumps in her stomach that might indicate an internal problem.' He polished his little round spectacles on a white kerchief. 'Could she be suffering from an excess of feeling, perhaps? Has she suffered a disappointment?'

'Yes, I believe she may have.' Amelia frowned. 'That happened some days ago and she was well enough then, distressed but not unwell. Are you sure there is nothing wrong with her?'

'It is my opinion that she is of a delicate constitution and, as you may know, some ladies go into a decline after suffering a severe setback.'

'I would not have thought that Emily had a delicate constitution.' Amelia wanted to say more, but held the words back. 'Thank you for your time, sir. You may send me the bill.'

'I shall send something that may help with the headache—but I believe she needs a tonic to lift her spirits. Perhaps she should go to Bath and take the waters there.'

'Yes, perhaps. I shall suggest it to her.'

Amelia returned to Emily's bedchamber after he left.

'He will send something for the headache, but I believe one of Martha's tisanes would do as well, Emily.'

'I am not sure, but I think it was the tisane that made me sick,' Emily said. 'Martha brought it to me and I left it beside my bed. I was sleepy and did not drink it then, but later…something woke me. I got up to relieve myself and then drank the tisane. Some minutes later I started to vomit.'

'Martha's tisane could not have caused you to be sick,' Amelia said. 'She has made them for me many times when I have felt a little unwell and they always do me good. It is very strange.'

'Well, perhaps it was not the tisane,' Emily said. 'I feel a little better now, but I shall not get up. I want to be well enough to come with you tomorrow, Amelia.'

'If you are not, we shall delay our departure. I shall not leave you behind, dearest. If you are not completely better once we are at Ravenshead, I shall call another doctor. I would send you to my own doctor in Bath, whom you know and like, but I cannot come with you.' Amelia was thoughtful. 'Unless you would like to go alone?'

'No, I should not. I do not want to leave you. Especially at the moment…while you may be in danger.' Emily's fingers moved nervously on the covers. 'I have not forgotten that it was you those rogues meant to snatch when I was kidnapped—the things they said…' She gave a little shiver. 'You must be careful, Amelia—even when you think there is no reason.'

'I know you care for me, Emily. We must just hope that you are soon feeling well again, my love.'

Amelia came upon Gerard as she was on her way back from the nursery. She had spent a pleasant hour reading to Lisa. The child seemed much happier than she had at Christmas, though she had clung to Amelia and was clearly reluctant to see her leave.

'You have been to visit Lisa?'

She met Gerard's questioning gaze, looking directly into his eyes.

'The doctor says that Emily may be suffering an excess of the nerves. I am not sure that he is correct, but he says there is no fever. She is not infectious. I have visited Lisa as I promised her. Had Emily been infectious, I should not have visited the nursery until it was safe.'

'Are you annoyed with me for suggesting it?'

'You have every right to protect your child. I know she is important to you.'

'It was not simply that...' Gerard frowned. 'Something odd is going on, Amelia. I am not sure what it is, but I have sensed it for a while.'

'I am not sure that I understand you, Gerard. I know Emily was abducted at Pendleton, but nothing else has happened since then. Unless you know something I do not?'

'There was the matter of the intruder in your bedchamber.' Gerard hesitated. 'A footman saw a woman leaving the back stairs that evening. She went into the hall and up the main staircase. He did not see her face clearly for it was dark and she had no candle, but he thought she wore a grey gown. He thought it odd that she did not carry a candle and reported it to Max.'

'Perhaps there was sufficient light from the stars.'

'But why not take a candle—unless she did not wish to be seen?'

'You think a woman came to my room—a woman who was not a servant?'

'I think perhaps she might have been your intruder.'

'I was not harmed and nothing was taken.'

'But someone was there and must have had a reason.' He

frowned. 'The footman thought it might have been your companion.'

'You cannot think it was Emily?'

Amelia had said nothing to Gerard of the letters taken from her desk or the pot of lilies in her room, because the incidents were merely annoying and not of consequence.

'We only have Miss Barton's word—and Northaven's, of course—that she was abducted.'

'Gerard! How could you?' Amelia raised her brows. 'What are you implying? You do not think that Emily would lie about a thing like that? Why would she pretend to be abducted?'

'At the moment I hardly know what I think. Yet something is nagging at the back of my mind.'

'You must tell me later.' Amelia smiled. 'Here comes Marguerite.' She went forwards to meet her. 'Are you on your way to the nursery? We have good news, Marguerite. Emily is not infectious, but she is far from well. I have told her that we shall not travel to Ravenshead until she is better. Indeed, if she does not recover I may have to take her to Bath to visit my own doctor. However, in that event, you would accompany Lisa to Ravenshead—she needs the comforts of her home about her.'

'I am sad to hear that Emily is ill. Is there anything I can do for her, as she is not infectious?' Marguerite's gaze flicked towards Gerard and for a moment her eyes seemed to spark with an emotion that might have been resentment.

'She would rather be left to rest. The vomiting has passed, but she still has a headache. Besides, as Gerard said, you came to us to help with Lisa, did you not?'

'Yes, of course. I just wish to be of as much help to you as I can, Amelia.' Marguerite glanced at Gerard and for a moment her eyes were hard with dislike. 'I shall not hurt or abandon you.'

'I am sure you would not.' Amelia smiled and kissed her cheek. 'I do not know when Emily will be able to resume her duties. In the meantime, I shall need your help, Marguerite.'

'You know that I am always willing to be of service to you, Amelia.'

Amelia glanced at Gerard. 'I shall see you later, sir. I have a little errand for Marguerite and I must explain what I need.' She turned to the other woman. 'Emily usually helps Martha to pack my clothes, but she is not well enough. Indeed, I believe she may need help herself if we are to leave in the morning as planned.'

She took Marguerite's arm and walked away with her, leaving Gerard to stare after them, a puzzled look in his eyes.

Amelia left Marguerite after giving her the task of helping Martha with their packing. She went to visit Emily, but found her sleeping and, after some thought, made her way downstairs to the parlour where she found some of the ladies sitting taking tea. When the ladies began to disperse, going to their rooms to change for the evening, Amelia had a few minutes alone with Helene.

It was almost six when she went up to change for dinner. Meeting Gerard on the stairs, she begged him not to delay her.

'Martha has had all the packing to do. I asked Marguerite to help her, but I must make sure everything has been done that needs to be done—and if I do not hurry I shall be late for dinner.'

'What are you playing at, Amelia?' Gerard's dark eyes narrowed, intent on her face.

'I do not know what you mean, sir.'

'When did I become sir again? I thought everything was settled between us?'

'Of course it is, Gerard,' Amelia said. 'It is true that I have something on my mind, but…' She shook her head. 'Tell me—have you made any discoveries about this Lieutenant Gordon? Has the marquis been in touch since we left Pendleton?'

'Unfortunately I am no nearer solving the mystery than I was then.' He frowned. 'As you said, nothing of significance has happened and yet my instincts tell me that the danger is very close.'

'We must all continue to be on our guard,' Amelia said. 'I admit that I should feel more comfortable if this horrid business was over, but until we know who wishes to prevent our marriage, there is nothing we can do—is there?'

'Very little except be alert. If anything puzzles you…any little incident seems odd—you must tell me, Amelia.'

'Yes…' Amelia was thoughtful. 'Tomorrow we shall be at Ravenshead if Emily is feeling well enough to travel. Things may be easier to control then, Gerard. For a while, at least, there will be only the four of us, the servants—and Lisa, of course.'

'What are you thinking?' Gerard tipped her chin with his finger, looking into her face. 'Is there anything I should know?'

'Like you, I have an odd feeling…' Amelia shook her head. 'There is nothing I can put into words. Believe me, I would tell you if I knew what to say. Tell me, if you had an enemy, Gerard, would you wish him to be in the shadows where you could not see him, or under your nose?'

'I suppose it would be best to keep him close. You cannot fight an enemy you cannot see.'

'I imagined you would say that.' Amelia nodded in agreement. 'I think I should prefer that too—but do not ask me to explain.'

She looked up at him. 'If I thought I knew the answers to your questions, I would tell you.'

'Then I suppose I must be content to wait.' He reached for her hand and kissed it. 'You are not regretting anything?'

'Certainly not. I am looking forward to our wedding,' Amelia told him. 'Besides, Lisa would be hurt if I changed my mind at this late stage, would she not? And now, if you will excuse me, I must go up for I shall almost certainly be late otherwise.'

She smiled and ran up the stairs, leaving him to continue on his way. Gerard thought she was hiding something from him, but it was not so. There were a few things that made no sense—and a feeling that had been growing on her that someone was lying to her.

The problem was that, for the moment, she could not be certain who had lied and who had spoken truly. She might know more once Helene had spoken to Max.

Gerard was thoughtful after he left Amelia. She had put up the barriers again, shutting him out. He had thought when they kissed that she was truly able to put the past behind them, believing that she still felt much of the passion she had when they were first engaged. Now he had begun to wonder.

Amelia had been giving him some odd looks. She had changed in the last day or so, as if she were no longer sure of her feelings for him.

When she entered the bedroom, Martha was folding some clothes and packing them into a large trunk. She looked a little put out and Amelia guessed the cause, but the maid did not complain, merely coming to assist her as Amelia began to change for the evening.

'The tisane you made for Emily last evening—was it the same as you make for me?'

'Yes, Miss Royston. Just an infusion of herbs and a little honey to sweeten it.' Martha gave her a direct stare. 'There was nothing in it to make her sick. I know my herbs, miss, and I would not make a mistake.'

'Did someone imply there might be a mistake?'

'It was suggested that I might have made the infusion of herbs too strong. There was no mistake, Miss Royston.' The maid frowned. 'But I shan't tell tales so don't ask me.'

'No, I am certain that you did not make a mistake, for you never do.' Amelia smiled at her. 'Tell me, Martha—what do you think of Miss Barton?'

'She is a pleasant young lady and always helpful…' Martha set her mouth. 'And if you are going to ask what I think of Miss Ross…I would rather not say.'

'Oh dear.' Amelia smothered the urge to laugh. 'Was she not helpful, Martha? I thought she would save you having so much work to do since Emily is not well enough to do her own packing.'

'The intention was there, miss—but I've had to unpack and start again or we should never find everything again. I have an order to my work, Miss Royston. Pushing things in anywhere will not do for me.'

'Then I shall go down and leave you to work in peace. I am very sorry, Martha, but Miss Ross wanted to be of use and I thought it would be something for her to do.'

Chapter Eight

'I wish I were coming with you,' Helene said as she kissed Amelia's cheek the next morning. They were in the hall and Amelia was about to leave. 'Please promise me to take care of yourself.'

'Of course I shall,' Amelia said and embraced her. 'Was Max able to answer the question I asked?'

'He said to tell you it was three.' Helene looked puzzled. 'I do not see how that helps you, Amelia.'

'I assure you that it does. It is exactly as I suspected and the answer to a small mystery. Thank you, my love. You are not to worry about me.'

'I shall try not to—though I would be happier if I knew what was going on.'

'Nothing that need concern you, my dearest,' Amelia said and squeezed her hand. 'Truly, it is a mere trifle. I shall write and tell you everything when I can. I must go now. Gerard is impatient to be off.'

'You haven't quarrelled with him? He seems...a little odd. I thought he might be angry about something.'

'I dare say he is merely anxious. I fear we are a little at odds, but that may be my fault. He thinks I am keeping something from him—and, truthfully, I am.'

'Amelia! What are you about?'

'Believe me, there is nothing to worry you, Helene.'

Amelia pressed her hand and went out to the waiting carriage. Marguerite was already inside, clearly ready to leave. Emily was sitting in one corner, looking pale, dark shadows beneath her eyes and clutching a kerchief soaked with healing lavender water. The scent of it wafted through the carriage, but was quite pleasant. Amelia had asked earlier if she would like to stay on at Coleridge for a while, but she had refused, insisting that she was well enough to make the journey.

Gerard gave Amelia his hand to help her inside, but said nothing, his mouth set in a grim line. He moved away as the groom put up the steps and turned to mount his horse. Lisa was travelling in the second coach with her nurse and Martha.

'I fear the earl grows angry, Amelia. He seems impatient to get away.' Marguerite's words broke Amelia's reverie.

'Yes. I believe he wishes to be home by this evening.'

'I wonder that you can bear his ill humour…' Marguerite clapped a gloved hand to her mouth. 'Forgive me. I should not have said that…I am sure it is simply a natural impatience to be home. Yet it is not pleasant to live with a man of uncertain temper. My father is such a man and I have suffered from his rages.'

'I am sorry for that, my dear.'

'I have learned to accept it, but I should not wish you to be unhappy, Amelia. Many ladies are unhappy in their marriages, I think. Men are so faithless—at least many are.'

'Yes, I believe so.' Amelia was silent for a moment. 'Gerard can seem harsh at times, I know, though he is usually good natured.'

'Yes, of course. I did not mean to imply…' Marguerite looked as if she wanted to say more, but was apprehensive. 'You will bring so much to the marriage; he must surely be grateful. Of course he would never do anything to harm you.'

'No, he would not. Why should he?'

'I meant nothing. My words were ill considered and foolish.' Marguerite fiddled with her gloves, twisting them nervously in her hands and then putting them on. 'I hope I have not offended.'

'I told you when you came that you might say anything to me. If you have something to say about the earl, please do so now.'

'Oh, no…' Marguerite shook her head. 'One hears rumours, of course—but I would never repeat anything I did not know for sure.'

'It is always best not to do so. Perhaps I know the rumour you speak of—concerning his wife?'

'Well, yes, I did hear something about the way she died.' She glanced at Emily, who was holding her kerchief to her nose. 'I am not sure who told me.'

'You ought not listen to gossip,' Amelia said and frowned. 'I hope you will forget it—the earl did nothing to harm Lisette.'

'No? Then it was a malicious lie and I am glad I did not repeat it to anyone.'

Marguerite sat back against the squabs, her expression subdued. Obviously, she felt that she had spoken out of turn. She ought not to have repeated gossip, of course. Amelia was glad that Gerard had told her how his wife died, otherwise she might have wondered.

Marguerite had hinted several times that Gerard might be marrying her because of her fortune. Amelia had not considered it, because he had told her that he was not interested in her money. She did not know why Marguerite seemed to dislike

Gerard, but she was afraid there was some resentment on Marguerite's part. At the beginning neither one had been prepared to admit they had met before, though later both had remembered that they had known each other in the past.

What did Marguerite know that Amelia didn't? What was she hinting at when she suggested that men were unfaithful?

Amelia frowned. Gerard had left her without a word that summer. He said it was because her brother had warned him off, but could she be certain he had not left for another reason entirely? He had sworn he loved her that summer, but within a few months he had married Lisette.

Had he truly loved Amelia? Or was the truth that he had never—and could never—love anyone? Was he the kind of man who loved lightly and moved on?

No! It was wicked of her to think such things. She did not know why she had allowed the thoughts to creep in. She would put them from her mind at once.

It was late in the evening when they arrived at Ravenshead. However, lights blazed in all the front windows, for the candles had been lit in anticipation of their arrival. The butler and housekeeper came out to welcome them, and Gerard's servants were lined up inside the house to meet them. Amelia was introduced to them all and then the housekeeper took her, Emily and Marguerite up to their rooms.

'I've put Miss Ross in one of the guest rooms, as the earl instructed,' Mrs Mowbray said when they were alone. 'Miss Barton has a room nearer the nursery. I hope that is acceptable?'

'Yes, of course—though perhaps…' Amelia shook her head. If Gerard had asked for the rooms to be allocated that way, she would not interfere. She had hardly glanced at the hall downstairs, though she had received an impression of marble tiles on the floor and elegant mahogany furniture, but here she was aware that the décor was new and the colour variations of the pale aquamarine she liked so much. 'Have these rooms been recently refurbished?'

'The earl had them done in October, Miss Royston. I hope you will be comfortable here?'

'Yes, thank you—they are everything I could wish.'

Amelia sighed and took off her bonnet and pelisse. She had come straight up to her apartments so had not taken them off in the hall. It was obvious that Gerard had had the rooms done specially for her. She wished that she could thank him in the way she would like, but something warned her that she must be careful.

She was exploring the bedchamber, discovering the space in the large armoire, when she heard something behind her. Turning, she saw that Gerard had entered through the dressing-room door. For a moment she was surprised, then realised that these apartments had been planned for when they married. As long as the key was his side, he could come and go as he pleased.

'Gerard…you startled me. I was not aware that we had adjoining apartments.'

'You do not object? Should I have knocked at the hall door?'

'No, of course not. It will be convenient when we wish to talk.'

'And at other times…' Gerard moved closer. He reached out to touch her cheek. 'We spoke of being together in a special way when we came to Ravenshead? You have not changed your mind?'

'I think we should be careful for the moment.' Amelia saw his quick frown. 'I have good reason for what I do and say, Gerard—but please do not doubt my feelings for you.'

'I do not understand you…' Gerard began, but someone knocked at the door. Amelia gave him a little push towards the dressing room. He went through and closed the door.

'Just a moment,' Amelia called. 'Come in, please.'

The door opened and then Marguerite entered. She glanced round, her eyes absorbing the décor. 'What a beautiful room, Amelia. Did I hear voices? I am sorry if I interrupted something…'

'You did not,' Amelia replied. 'Did you need something, Marguerite?'

'Nothing. I have a very adequate room. I merely came to see if I might be of service to you?'

'Martha will see to my unpacking. I am ready to go down if you are, Marguerite. Mrs Mowbray will have a light supper prepared for us, I am sure. Emily told us that she requires no supper so we shall leave her to rest for the moment.'

'Well, if you are certain I can do nothing,' Marguerite said and turned to leave. 'Just remember that I am always ready to help you. Especially as Emily is not well enough to run errands for you. If ever you are unhappy or in distress, you may rely on me for help.'

'I am sure you will make yourself indispensable,' Amelia told her with a smile. 'I am very pleased you came to me, Marguerite—and I am sure Lisa adores you already.'

'She is a pretty little thing and she has good manners. I dare say she is very like her mother.'

'Yes, perhaps. I suppose you did not know her mama?'

Marguerite looked startled for a moment, then shook her head. 'She was French, was she not? I have few friends, Amelia. You know that it was almost impossible for me to meet anyone after Lucinda…' Her voice cracked on a little sob. 'Mama and Papa broke their hearts when she died. She was so foolish. She should have named her seducer and faced her shame. He might have been forced to marry her. His desertion broke her heart.' Marguerite's eyes flashed with sudden anger. 'If I could, I would make him pay for what he did to her.'

'She would not tell me his name. Did she never say anything to you, Marguerite?'

'She hinted once or twice…' Marguerite shook her head. 'I do not know his name, Amelia—just that it was a gentleman we all knew. Someone who ought to have known better than to seduce an innocent girl.'

'That is a wide field. I was so sorry when Lucinda took her own life.'

'If she did…' Marguerite's eyes flashed with sudden anger. 'How can we be sure that she did kill herself?'

'I thought there was no doubt?'

'I have sometimes thought…' Marguerite hesitated. 'Just before she died she was happy. She hinted that she might have something exciting to tell me soon…and then she disappeared and they dragged her body from the river. Her dress had been torn and…a ring she had been wearing had gone from her hand. I think her lover gave her the ring and…I suspect he took it from her before he…killed her…'

'Marguerite!' Amelia stared at her in horror. Prickles of ice danced along her spine. 'You think her lover killed her—but why?'

'I know he killed her! Even if she had taken her own life it would have been his fault. He would still have been her murderer,' Marguerite said bitterly. 'She was but a child and he took advantage. I think when she threatened to reveal his name, he pushed her into the river and watched her drown. She could not swim.'

'How can you know that? You do not even know his name.'

'I know most of what happened.' Marguerite lifted her head defiantly. Something flickered in her eyes. 'If I knew his name…I should not rest until he was punished.'

Amelia touched her arm. 'I understand your pain and distress, but hate will not bring her back, Marguerite. You cannot change the past.'

'I have suffered for her stupid lack of morality. If she had behaved as she ought, none of this would have happened. Why did she give herself to a faithless rogue? She ruined her own life and mine.'

'You must try to forget it. You are here now, Marguerite. You will meet my friends and Gerard's. You have every opportunity to find happiness.'

'My parents would not allow me to marry.'

'I think they might if it was a good match,' Amelia said. 'I believe I might be able to persuade them if you found someone you thought you could love.'

'Men are not to be trusted,' Marguerite flashed at her. 'They seduce you with their smiles and sweet words and then they destroy your life. Be careful who you trust, Amelia. Even marriage does not mean you are guaranteed happiness.'

'Are you suggesting that the earl cannot be trusted?'

'His first wife was unhappy enough to take her own life…' Marguerite said and then put a hand to her mouth in horror. 'I should not have said that…now you will send me home. Yet it is true and you should be careful, Amelia. Be sure that he truly cares for you or you may be hurt too.'

'No, I shall not send you home,' Amelia said, looking at her steadily. 'Tell me, do you really believe that Lisette's death happened because Gerard made her unhappy? Are you saying that he was cruel to her?'

'I only know what someone told me.' Marguerite looked at her oddly. 'What do you think, Amelia? Why would she take her own life if she were happy?'

'I know the truth of it and I know it was not Gerard's fault,' Amelia said. 'But perhaps I shall ask him about it again.'

'You should.' Marguerite gripped her wrist. 'For your own sake, Amelia. I should be so sorry if something were to happen to you because of him.'

'You are hurting me.'

'Forgive me. I did not realise what I did…'

Amelia drew away and Marguerite let go of her wrist. Amelia rubbed at it. 'There is nothing to forgive. I know you are thinking of me—but we shall not speak of this again.'

'I am sorry. You have been so good to me. I had no right to speak but I care about you.'

'I know you do.' Amelia smiled at her. 'Do not look so anxious, Marguerite. I am not going to send you away.'

'You are too forgiving,' Marguerite said. 'People take advantage of you. Emily told me what you did for Lady Pendleton and Lady Coleridge.'

'Had I known how unhappy you were, I should have asked for your company before this,' Amelia told her. 'However, it is not too late for you to make a new life. Nothing that has happened so far should make it impossible for you to find happiness—if you can let go of the past.'

Marguerite stared at her in silence. Amelia nodded at her encouragingly, hoping she might respond to the invitation, but Marguerite turned her face away, going ahead of her down the stairs.

Amelia thought she understood why Marguerite thought so badly of Gerard. She was still grieving for her sister and did not trust any man. When she came to know him better, she would realise that she was wrong to distrust him.

Amelia was seated at her dressing table later that night when the door to the dressing room opened and Gerard entered. He went to the hall door and tried the handle, nodding his satisfaction when he discovered it was locked. Amelia stood up. Her hair had been taken down from its customary style and hung loosely on her shoulders, and she was wearing a pale blue lace peignoir over a matching silk nightgown. Her feet were bare. She picked up a perfume flask and dabbed a drop behind her ears.

'Why did you check the door?'

'Because I wanted to make certain we were not interrupted this time, Amelia.'

Amelia saw that he was still fully clothed, though he had taken off his boots. 'To what do I owe the pleasure of this visit, Gerard?'

'I have not been able to speak to you alone for days,' he said, looking frustrated. 'We need to talk.'

'Yes, I agree. I think you should tell me the whole truth about Lisette, Gerard. You told me something, but I do not believe it was all—was it?'

'What do you wish to know?' Gerard's gaze narrowed.

'You told me that you married her while still angry with my brother and me—but did you love her?'

'No. As I told you, she had been raped and was lying by the side of the road, beaten and close to death. I nursed her back to health and then she told me her lover was dead. She was having his child. I married her to protect her and the child—and because I thought I could never have you.'

She gazed up at him. 'I know you said something died in you

the night Michael had you beaten, but do you think you can learn to love me?'

'Did I say that to you?' Gerard looked puzzled. 'I felt that way for a long time, but you cannot believe it now? You must know that I care for you, my dear one.'

'I hoped that you might in time…'

'Believe me, you are the only woman I want as my wife.'

'You truly mean that?'

'Yes, of course.'

'Why did you come to me tonight?'

'So that we could talk. Why?' His eyebrows arched.

'I thought you might have come for another reason,' she said and moved closer to him, the scent of her body inviting and tempting.

Gerard looked at her steadily. 'You told me you thought we should be careful—and I have noticed something odd in your manner of late. You asked me about Lisette and I have answered you truthfully. Will you tell me what is troubling you?'

'Yes, perhaps I should,' she agreed. 'But do not expect me to solve the mystery, Gerard. I am concerned because I think… Emily and Marguerite do not truly like one another. Helene noticed it and…Marguerite has hinted that Emily is lying to me.'

'Good grief!' Gerard frowned. 'What has she said exactly?'

'Some letters were taken from my room. I asked Martha, Emily and Marguerite if they had taken them. They all said no, but Marguerite told me she had seen letters in my hand on the salver in the hall. As you know, Max always franks his guests' letters to save their families the expense of some sixpences.'

'Letters…' Gerard wrinkled his brow. 'I can see nothing wrong in anyone taking them down for you. What is strange in this?'

'Nothing—except that one of them must have taken the letters, but none of them will admit it.'

'You have questioned your maid?'

'Yes. Martha would only take the letters if I told her. Marguerite told me that Emily had been to my room that morning. She still denied having taken them—and Max told Helene that he had franked three letters for me. I wrote four.'

'Four…you are certain?' Amelia inclined her head and Gerard pursed his lips. 'Was there anything of value in any of the letters? Were they important?'

'They were thank-you letters for Christmas gifts—and one to my brother to inform him of our marriage.'

'You do not know which one was taken?'

'I cannot know for certain. Max recalled the number, but he would not have remembered to whom they were addressed—but one was to Marguerite's mother, to thank her for allowing her daughter to come to us.'

'You think it may have been the letter that went astray?'

'I do not know…' Amelia hesitated. 'And there were the lilies…a pot of them in my room. Martha noticed the smell and took them away. If we had not noticed it, they might have given me a headache for they were very strong. It was a silly incident—but something Marguerite said has led me to believe that it might have been Emily. Unless…' She sighed. 'It is quite ridiculous. I have wondered if Marguerite wishes to take Emily's place in my affections…and if Emily feigned illness because she is perhaps a little jealous.'

'This is all trivial stuff,' Gerard said. He reached out to lift her chin with his finger. 'You are certain this is all, Amelia?'

'There have been other hints…things said that I felt not quite as I would like, but nothing that means anything. Someone spoke of Lisa's mother dying to her. She was upset until I told her that her mother died peacefully with no pain.' She saw him flinch. 'It would be wrong to tell her the truth, Gerard. I believe she was afraid that I might die or leave her. I told her it would not happen for a long time.'

She said nothing of Marguerite's hints that he might be unfaithful to her. He had told her the truth about Lisette and to question about the summer he had courted her would seem as if she distrusted him.

'Who told her? You should speak to whoever it was, Amelia. Make it clear that you will not tolerate this kind of thing.'

'Emily has been unwell. I shall speak to her when she is better.'

'You think it was Miss Barton?' Gerard's gaze narrowed, became intent. 'Did Miss Ross tell you it was Emily?'

'No. Lisa started to tell me something, but after I explained, she seemed content and wanted to look at her book. To question her would make more of an incident best forgotten. I shall talk to Emily once she has fully recovered from whatever ails her.'

'Perhaps you would do better to let them both go,' Gerard suggested. 'We could find a governess for Lisa—'

'Gerard! They are my friends. I could not be so cruel as to dismiss either of them for such trivial things.'

'Are you sure they are trivial?'

'No more, Gerard.' Amelia reached up to touch his cheek. 'Now you know why I hesitated to tell you in the beginning. Someone has lied to me—and someone said things they should not—but at the moment I can make no sense of it all. Emily's abduction has turned everything upside down. It is easy to start at shadows, to imagine fault where there is none. Besides, if there was something…we need to know the truth, Gerard. To send the guilty person away might mean that we should never be free of this shadow.'

'If I thought either of them meant harm to you or Lisa…' A glint of anger leapt in his eyes.

Amelia placed her fingers to his lips. 'Lisa is safe, my dearest. Why should anyone wish to harm her? Besides, they both love her. I am sure they do.'

'Why should anyone wish to stop our marriage?'

'It could not benefit either Emily or Marguerite. No, I am certain this is just because of a little jealousy.'

'Then we are no nearer to discovering our enemy.'

'I think we may be,' Amelia said. 'I cannot give you a reason, but I feel that things have moved forwards, though why is not clear. Something is at the back of my mind, but I cannot tell you what it is.'

'You are not holding back from me?' Gerard's eyes seemed to look deep into her soul. Wordlessly, she shook her head. He smiled oddly and reached for her, drawing her close so that she felt the heat of his body and the urgency of his need. 'I should not be here. You are too tempting, my love. I want to sweep you up in my arms and carry you to that bed. I want to kiss and know every inch of your lovely body.'

Amelia's lips parted invitingly, her breath sweet and quick. 'You know how much I want to be with you, Gerard—to be yours. I should not deny you if you took me now.'

'I am tempted beyond bearing, but something is warning me that I ought not to take advantage—that I should wait…' His fingers traced the arch of her white throat. He bent his head to lick the little pulse spot at the base of her neck. Amelia quivered, pressing herself against him, her body surrendering to the need inside.

'Gerard...forget the shadows...forget caution. I want to be yours.'

'Supposing something happens to me...if there should be a child...' he warned as he caught her to him; his mouth pressed against her neck, warm and moist as he nibbled gently. She arched into him, melting in the heat of their mutual desire, lifting her face for his kiss. 'Amelia, my love. I want you so much...'

'If something happened to part us, I should have known your love,' she whispered passionately. 'I am not a green girl, Gerard. I am a woman, but I have never known a man's love—never felt the happiness of being one with you. Do not let me go to my grave never having known what it is to be loved, I beg you. If either of us should die before we wed, we should at least have had this night.'

Gerard's resolve melted as she pressed herself against him. There was a wild, wanton look in her eyes; the barriers were down and he could not resist their mutual need.

He moaned softly in his throat, bending to sweep her up in his arms and carry her to the bed. She smiled up at him trustingly as he lay her down amongst the soft sheets, her peignoir falling open to reveal the sweet swell of her breasts. His body throbbed with the need to have her and he began to strip away his shirt, ripping the fine material carelessly. Amelia undid her peignoir, pushing it back from her shoulders, slipping her arms out so that all she wore was the thin nightdress that did nothing to hide the contours of her shapely body.

Gerard stripped off the rest of his clothing. Amelia's eyes travelled over the lean length of him, his strong legs and arms, his smooth chest and the sprinkling of dark hair that arrowed to his aroused manhood. The sight of his beautiful naked body was shocking and breathtaking, making her quiver with anticipation as he raised her so that he could pull her nightgown over her head and dispose of it with his clothes.

Then he was lying beside her on the sheets. He faced her, his mouth close to hers. He could smell the sweetness of her breath, the light taste of wine on her lips, and the perfume of her hair was intoxicating. His hands stroked down her back, smoothing the arch, cupping her buttocks and pressing her against him. She moaned softly, lips parting for the invasion of his tongue. He sucked at her, tasting her, their tongues meeting in little experimental darts of sensation, seeking, finding pleasure beyond all expectation.

He caressed her back and her shoulders, stroking firmly until she quivered and moaned with pleasure. Bending his head, he sucked at her nipples, taking first one and then the other into his mouth, the roughness of his tongue against them sending jolts of pleasure through her. His hand stroked her thigh. His tongue traced its way over her navel to her mound, and then his hand parted her legs. He stroked the sensitive inner thigh for some minutes, making her pant with endless, aching need to feel his fingers touching her inner citadel.

When he touched her there she gasped, her back arching as the sensation of fierce pleasure shot through her. She opened wide, allowing him to stroke and then to enter her moistness. His mouth returned to hers, kissing her as his body slid over hers, and then the hot, hard probing of his manhood entered her with gentle thrusts, deeper and deeper until he found what he was seeking.

Amelia cried out as he broke through her maidenhead. For one moment the pain was sharp, but then his kiss was taking it away, soothing her. His hands stroked and pleasured, bringing her back to a state of blissful desire so that the moisture ran and she opened, taking him deep inside her. Their bodies moved together in a sensuous rhythm, the almost unbearable sensation making Amelia's breath come in quick gasps and then all at once Gerard gave a shout and she felt his release. She clung to him as the powerful spasm took her, making her cry out and arch beneath him.

After the intense sensations had faded to a pleasant feeling of satisfaction, Amelia turned her face into his shoulder as he lay beside her, still stroking the silken arch of her back. Her cheeks were wet with tears for she had not expected to feel anything as wonderful…as fulfilling as this sweet certainty of belonging.

'I dreamed…' she whispered. 'I dreamed so many nights…but I could not guess at what it would be…so beautiful…'

'You made it beautiful,' Gerard told her. 'I have never loved anyone else…never known such completeness…such happiness.'

'Gerard…' she murmured against his shoulder. 'We are one, together. No one can part us now.'

'I shall not let them,' he vowed fiercely as he lifted himself on one elbow to gaze down into her face. 'You are mine. Nothing and no one can come between us now.'

They held each other, falling asleep wrapped in each other's arms.

Amelia had not drawn her curtains completely. The light of the candles clearly showed the outline of two people as they moved together and embraced.

The woman watched for a few moments. In the light of the moon, which had just moved out from behind some clouds, the anger and bitterness was stamped on her features. So intent on what was happening in that room was she that she did not hear the man approach and jumped as he touched her shoulder. She whirled round, fingers clawing at his face. He gave a shout of alarm, jerking back and grabbing her wrists.

'What do you think you are doing? It is me—Gordon.'

'You startled me. Creeping up on me like that! I thought I was being attacked.'

'Wild cat,' he said and grinned as he caught her to him. He kissed her hungrily, but she pushed him away with an angry cry.

'I told you! Not until I have what I want. Gerard Ravenshead must die.'

'What of her?' Lieutenant Gordon nodded his head at the window. 'You said she must be raped and he must watch. I'm not your man for that…I'll gladly put a ball into his black heart, but she has done me no harm. I've never killed a woman and the idea has bothered me.'

'I wanted her to suffer as someone else suffered, but that no longer matters. Now all I want is that he should see her dead. He must suffer—he must know what it feels like to lose everything.' Her eyes glittered with hatred. 'His death is not enough for what he has done. If you want me, you must take revenge for me—and for yourself.' She smiled at him, suddenly luring him with a look that took his breath. 'I know you want me…but first I need my revenge.'

'You shall have it. I'll kill him for you and willingly,' he vowed. 'I heard that they are to be married soon. Shall it be before or after the wedding?'

She glanced back towards the bedroom window. There was no sign of the couple embracing now. She imagined them lying together…making love. At that moment her anger was so intense that she shook, but she fought the rage, knowing she must not give way to one of her fits. She was so close now—so close to the revenge she craved.

'It must be soon,' she said. 'There is no reason to wait longer. I have been making plans. Where can I reach you if I need you quickly?'

'At the inn in the village. Send a letter—or find a stable lad to bring your message.'

'Meet me here again in one week and then I shall tell you what I plan.'

Amelia woke to find the bed cold beside her. She looked at the indentation in the pillow where his head had lain, touching it, inhaling the scent of him that still clung to the sheets. Gerard had left her before the servants were about, because he was still trying to protect her reputation. She smiled, stretching, aware of how good she felt. The night had been filled with pleasure as they explored each other's bodies, touching, kissing, reaching a place that Amelia had never been. Gerard had told her it was the same for him.

'No other woman has ever made me feel as you do, my love,' he'd told her just before she fell deeply asleep.

She had slept so soundly that she had not felt him leave their bed. Perhaps he had tried not to wake her. Amelia was a little amused at his gallantry for her maid would know when she changed the sheets. Amelia's blood had stained them, and the masculine smell of Gerard clung to them. Martha would know. She might keep the knowledge to herself, but it would not be long before it became common knowledge below stairs.

Once, Amelia might have worried that her good name might be soiled, but she was too much in love to care. She was engaged to the man she loved and in a few weeks she would be Gerard's wife. Nothing else really mattered…but life went on. She had obligations she must fulfil.

Amelia rose, washed in the water that remained from the night before in the jug on the washstand and dressed in a serviceable gown, leaving her room before Martha arrived to open the curtains. She walked along the passage and up one short flight of stairs to the rooms nearer the nursery. When she reached Emily's door, she knocked and called softly, 'May I come in, my love?'

'The door is open,' Emily replied. 'Please enter, Amelia.'

Amelia went into the bedroom to discover that Emily was already up and dressed, her bed neatly made. However, she was still a little pale and it was obvious that she had not slept well.

'How are you feeling, my love?'

'I am about the same as yesterday. I have not been sick, but my head still aches a little.'

'I am so sorry.' Amelia looked at her anxiously. 'Shall I ask Gerard to send for the doctor, my love?'

'No, I do not wish to trouble him,' Emily said. 'I am sure it is nothing serious, Amelia. I shall be better soon.' She fiddled with the sash of her gown, pulling at a slight crease. 'I should wish to be of use to you. Is there anything I can do…help you with the wedding invitations? You will have much to do if the wedding is to be soon.'

'I should prefer that you rest as much as possible. I do not like to see you so low, Emily. Marguerite may help for the moment— and you may join me when you are feeling more the thing.'

'I am much recovered—and I would rather help you than stay in my room.'

'Very well. I have drawn up a list. You may look through it with me and see if I have forgotten anyone. When it is complete, Gerard will have the invitations printed and I shall sign them. I dare say you will be well enough to address some envelopes for me. And there will be thank-you letters to friends, for I believe his notice to *The Times* should be inserted any day now.'

'You look so happy,' Emily said and smiled. 'Please do not worry about me, dearest Amelia. This should be a happy time for you—and I shall be well enough in a few days.'

'I hope so, my love. Meet me in the little parlour at the back of the house at eleven, Emily. I am going to visit the nursery first—and then I shall accompany Mrs Mowbray on a tour of the house, but I should be finished by eleven o'clock.'

As Amelia had expected, she found Lisa wide awake and ready to play. She spent a delightful hour reading to her and helping her to draw pictures on her slate. Lisa drew a credible picture of a dog and then looked at Amelia.

'Will Papa remember I wanted a puppy?'

'I should think he might, but if he doesn't I will remind him.'

'You are so good to me! *She* told me he would forget… *She* said that he did not truly love me, because he did not love my mama…' Lisa's eyes were dark with anxiety. 'Papa does love me…he says he does.'

'Who said that to you, Lisa? Was it Emily?' Amelia frowned. 'Was it Emily who told you that your mama was dead?'

Lisa shook her head. She shuffled her feet and glanced over

her shoulder. '*She* said if I told you Nanny would come back and punish me.'

'Nanny will never come back. I promised you that, Lisa.'

'But I saw her…I saw her outside in the gardens last night. I saw her from the window. I like to look out at the moon, you see…'

'You saw Nanny? Miss Horton—you saw her here in the gardens last night?'

'Yes. Nanny was talking to a man—and then they both walked away.'

'I shall tell your papa about this,' Amelia said. 'Nanny has no right to be here and she will be sent away. Who told you that Nanny would come back, Lisa?'

Lisa opened her mouth and then shut it as someone entered the nursery, but her eyes flew to Amelia's face and something in them answered her question. Amelia held her hand and smiled at her reassuringly.

'Papa will not forget, my love,' she said, holding her close to whisper in her ear. 'Whatever anyone else tells you, I shall not let you be hurt or neglected.'

Lisa hugged her, clinging to her as if she did not want to let her go.

'Run to your nurse now, my love. I have other things to do this morning, but I shall return later and we will go for a little walk in the garden this afternoon.'

Amelia turned and greeted Marguerite with a smile. 'You are up early,' she said. 'Perhaps like me you like to be up with the lark?'

'I often rise early. It is the best part of the day. I like to walk before anyone else is about.'

'Excuse me, my dear. I have things I must do this morning…' Amelia said.

Chapter Ten

After completing a tour of the house with Mrs Mowbray, Amelia consulted with her on various things. She was asked if everything was to her satisfaction and if there were any changes to the routine that she would like to instigate.

'For the moment I think I am pleased with everything,' she said. 'However, I believe Nurse Mary needs more help in the nursery. She cannot do everything and I do not want Lisa to be left alone at any time.'

'I thought Miss Ross was to have charge of the nursery, Miss Royston?'

'Miss Ross is part-governess, part-friend,' Amelia said. 'She will spend time with Lisa—but I want another sensible girl to work with Mary. Someone who would know what to do in the event of an emergency. Do you have a suitable girl—or should we employ another?'

'There is Beattie…' Mrs Mowbray frowned. 'She is a good-hearted lass and has eight brothers and sisters younger than herself at home—but she isn't a clever girl. Beattie is very loyal, but she can't help with Miss Ravenshead's studies or anything of the sort.'

'I think Beattie may be just the girl I am looking for,' Amelia said. 'Will you send her to my room in a few minutes, please?'

'Yes, of course, miss. This will be a step up for the girl, Miss Royston. She will be pleased.'

'She must have a rise in her wages. I leave it to you to decide what would be appropriate, Mrs Mowbray.'

'Now that is generous.' The housekeeper beamed her approval. 'Beattie gives most of her money to her mother and this will be a help to them. I think five shillings a month would be fair.'

'Then we are agreed,' Amelia said. 'I am going up to change my gown now. Please send Beattie to me as soon as you can.'

Amelia left the housekeeper and went up to her room.

She had finished changing her gown and was struggling with a hook at the nape of her neck when a knock at the door announced Beattie's arrival.

'Ah, there you are,' Amelia said. 'Could you do this up for me, please?'

'Yes, miss, of course.'

Beattie fastened the hook and then stood before Amelia, her hands clasped in front of her.

'Do you like children, Beattie?'

'Oh, yes, miss. I love them. It's as well I do, miss. Ma has nine of us at home and I helped with the young ones until I came to work here.'

'Then you would enjoy looking after Lisa?'

'Yes, miss. She is a lovely little thing.' Beattie was beaming all over her face.

She was a plump, homely girl with curly hair and blue eyes,

but there was something sturdy about her and Amelia could see why the housekeeper had recommended her.

'I am asking you to help Nurse Mary, because I do not wish Lisa to be left alone at any time. Either you or Nurse Mary will accompany her at all times—in the nursery or when she goes out. The only exception is when the earl or I take her out ourselves. Nurse Mary is in charge of the nursery, but if there is anything that worries you at any time, you may ask to speak to me.'

'Yes, miss. I understand,' Beattie said. 'You can trust me to keep an eye on her.'

'Yes,' Amelia said and nodded. 'That is exactly what I need, Beattie…'

Amelia was in a small parlour that overlooked the rose gardens when Gerard entered. She had been going through the list of guests for the wedding with Emily, but when he entered Emily stood up.

'If you will excuse me, Amelia. I shall go up to my room. I have a headache coming on and I think I shall lie down for half an hour before nuncheon.'

'You must not come down for the rest of the day if you are unwell, my love. Something can be brought to you on a tray.'

'Thank you. Martha will make me a tisane and I shall be better soon.'

Gerard frowned as Emily left the room. 'Do you think Miss Barton is pining? I could write to Sinclair if you wish—ask him to explain himself.'

'No. He had his reasons for what he did,' Amelia said. 'I dare say he will come here when he feels ready. Besides, I am not sure that is the reason for Emily's headaches.'

'If she is really ill, we should have the doctor.'

'I shall send for one if she does not improve within a day or so.' Amelia smiled and got to her feet as he came to her. 'How are you this beautiful morning, Gerard?'

'It may have escaped your notice, but it is raining and there is a gale blowing.' Gerard laughed softly and held out his hands to her. 'Yes, it is a beautiful morning, my dearest one.' He took her hands, gazing down into her eyes. 'You have no regrets?'

'None. Have you?'

'You know the answer to that, Amelia.' He bent his head to kiss her softly on the mouth. 'I loved you before last night—but now I worship you, my lovely, passionate woman.'

Amelia blushed faintly. 'I dare say you think me wanton?'

'Deliciously so. I think myself the most fortunate man alive this morning, my love.'

'Oh, Gerard…it was so wonderful…all that I had dreamed of, longed for, for so many years.'

'And so many years wasted.' Gerard frowned. 'I was a damned fool to let your brother send me away. Nothing will stand between us now, Amelia. The only thing that can prevent our marriage is death.'

'And your men will patrol the grounds, Gerard. Are they in place?'

'Yes. I have given orders this morning. Why do you ask?'

'Because Lisa saw Nanny Horton and a man in the garden last night…'

Gerard swore. 'We must have been followed here. I had men riding behind us, some distance apart. None of them reported a shadow. I thought it would take a few days before anyone realised where we were.' His brow wrinkled. 'But why would Nanny Horton be here in the garden? I do not understand.'

'I think I begin to—' Amelia broke off as the door opened and someone entered. 'Good morning, Marguerite. Have you just come from the nursery?'

'Yes. I spent an hour reading to Lisa. She has a new maid. The girl refused to leave the room when I asked her to fetch something. I think she may prove insolent, Amelia. You may have to replace her.'

'Oh, I think not,' Amelia replied with a smile. 'Beattie has been told that Lisa is not to be left alone.' She glanced at Gerard, her eyes seeming to convey a message. 'I think I should reveal something to you, Marguerite. The earl received a warning—a broken doll. We believe this may constitute a threat against his daughter. Perhaps an abduction for a ransom? Therefore I have asked that one of the maids is always at hand. If an attempt at abduction were to be made, you might be overcome if you were alone, but if two of you are there I think she should be safe for one may raise the alarm—do you not agree?'

'A threat to abduct Lisa?' Marguerite was clearly shocked. 'That is terrible, Amelia. How upsetting for you! I understand why you have given orders that Lisa should never be left alone. I do not know how anyone can be wicked enough to threaten a child—and she is adorable!'

'Yes, she is,' Amelia said. 'I think I would prefer to be threatened myself. If anyone harmed Lisa, I would never forgive them.'

'Indeed, no,' Marguerite said. 'How could you?'

'Was there something you needed?' Amelia asked. 'You came in search of me—for a particular reason?'

'Oh… Emily told me that she is unwell again,' Marguerite

said. 'She said that she would ask Martha for a tisane. I do not know what herbs your maid uses, Amelia—but some can cause headaches in certain people. However, I find camomile tea very soothing. Would you like me to make some for Emily?'

'Did you ask her?'

'She refused me, but perhaps if I took it to her room…'

'That would be very kind of you, Marguerite. Emily might find it soothing. I do myself.'

'Then I shall.' Marguerite inclined her head towards Gerard and went out, closing the door behind her.

'What was that about…?' Gerard began, but Amelia shook her head. She went to the door and opened it, looking out. Gerard watched her, brows raised in inquiry. 'What are you up to, Amelia? You did not tell me that you had arranged for another maid for Lisa.'

'I should have done so in a moment had we not been interrupted. It was a precaution after Lisa told me about Nanny Horton.'

'But the tale about the doll? We already know that it came from Northaven.'

'I know that—but I wish others to believe that we think it a threat to Lisa.'

'By "others" I take it you mean Marguerite Ross?' He stared at her hard. 'Something about her has been nagging at me, but I cannot think what…' He stopped, his gaze intent on her face. 'You know something—tell me.'

'I am not certain, but I believe that Alice Horton may once have been in the employ of Mr and Mrs Ross…as a nanny when the girls were young. I believe she was dismissed when they were older, but she may have kept in touch with Marguerite…' Amelia paused. 'Marguerite likes to write letters, as I do myself.

I think it possible that they have never lost touch.' She looked at him. 'Tell me, how came you to employ Alice Horton?'

'I made inquiries at an agency...and she was one of those who applied for the post. She had letters of recommendation. I checked her last employer and they said she was reliable.'

'I dare say she is in many ways, but too strict for my liking.'

'I do not see the connection.' Gerard looked puzzled. 'You said Marguerite was a friend. You invited her here because you felt sympathy for her plight.'

'Her sister was my friend. After Lucinda died I wrote to console the family. Mrs Ross wrote to me a few times and I responded—then Marguerite wrote to me and told me of her plight. She begged me to say nothing to her mother, because Mrs Ross's health was precarious at that time.'

'None of this makes sense. Why did Miss Ross come here?'

'I believed she came to help us. I know that she has longed for a child, but did not expect to have one. She told me that she had no hope of marriage for she seldom mixed in society and the only gentlemen she met were her father's friends and too old.' Amelia frowned. 'When I invited her here I was not sure she would be allowed to come. As I told you, I wrote to her mother to thank her for allowing it, but now I am sure that letter was not sent.'

'So you think you've solved the mystery of the missing letters?' His brow arched.

'Precisely. I could not see why anyone would want to steal one of my letters. I wondered if perhaps one of them had been damaged and the ruse was to cover up carelessness on the part of someone. I was not sure if it was Emily, Martha—or Marguerite.'

'And now you think it was Marguerite? Why? Why would she wish to prevent your letter to her mother reaching her?'

'I wish I knew. I think Nanny Horton knew we were coming here and perhaps came on ahead. If Lisa is right, Nanny Horton spoke to a man last night in the gardens. I do not know who the man was, but…' She paused and gave him a significant look.

'You are wondering if it could have been Lieutenant Gordon?' Gerard pursed his lips as Amelia nodded. 'It would explain some of the mystery.'

'Yes, it would explain how they knew where we would be. I have been writing to Marguerite for more than a year now.'

'So she knew you were at Pendleton the summer before last?'

'Yes, she did.'

'Damn it!' Gerard took a turn around the room. 'We may have invited our enemy into our home, Amelia.'

'Marguerite would never harm a child.' Amelia frowned. 'If she has come under the influence of this man…'

'You think he has turned her mind…that she has been giving him information? She may be infatuated with him.'

'Perhaps.' Amelia frowned. 'I am not sure if she understands what he means to do.'

'I wish that I understood,' Gerard said in a tone of frustration. 'Everything is speculation. We have heard nothing of Northaven—' He broke off as they heard the ring of more than one person's footsteps in the hall and then the door was opened and Mrs Mowbray entered. 'Yes?'

'Excuse me for interrupting, sir—but there is a gentleman…' She had hardly finished when Toby Sinclair walked past her.

'Forgive me,' he said. 'Amelia—I must speak with Emily. It is important.'

'Toby!' Amelia gave Gerard an apologetic look and moved towards him. They were being interrupted once more, but she could not deny Toby—she knew how important this might be to Emily. 'I am glad to see you here. We were all so sorry to hear of your loss.'

A shadow passed across his face. 'It was expected and yet it was sudden. Father knew he had only a few months, but in the end we thought it would not be quite so soon. Mama was distraught. I could not leave her before this—but I must and will see Emily.'

'Of course you must. Why should you not?'

'I was told that I could not see her because she is ill.' Toby's face was white, his manner desperate. 'I cannot blame her if she hates me—but still I must see her. I know something that she must be told.'

'You have news for Emily?' Amelia stared at him, seeing the excitement, the triumph in his eyes. Her intuition told her what the news must be. 'Did Harry find the child?'

'His agents were able to help point me in the right direction, but I found her myself only yesterday. I would have been here sooner, but the circumstances…and then I heard news that delayed me.'

'You have come to tell Emily that you've found the child?' Amelia stared at him in dawning delight.

'Yes, I am pleased to say I have—but first Harry bid me speak to you, Gerard.' Toby turned towards him. 'He has learned that an attempt to murder Northaven was made three days ago. He was shot in the back, but the assassin's aim was poor and the ball merely grazed his shoulder. Harry told me that Emily was abducted and that Northaven helped her…and that may be the reason why he was shot.'

'Good grief! Has Harry spoken to him?'

'He told me that he would do so today—and then he will come here. He may bring Northaven with him.'

'Thank you for coming to me.' Gerard's mouth thinned. 'This becomes serious…if Northaven was shot because of what I asked him to do, it means they will stop at nothing.'

'Gerard…' Amelia's eyes sought his in concern. 'This is far worse than I imagined. If they would kill the marquis because he helped Emily escape…'

Gerard turned to her. 'Go up to Emily. See if you can persuade her to come down,' he said. 'I would have a few words alone with Toby.'

'Yes, of course.' Amelia glanced at Toby. 'Emily is lying down with a headache, but I will ask her to see you in the front parlour. Tell me, is the news good for her?'

'I hope she will think it excellent.'

'Very well. I shall let you tell her yourself.'

Amelia ran upstairs. For the moment her suspicions must be shelved. She was not sure when she had begun to suspect that something was not quite as it ought to be in Marguerite's manner—perhaps only in the last day or so, or this very morning. Now she was feeling concerned, for though she was certain that the woman would never harm a child, she could not be trusted if she were under the influence of a man who would kill anyone who stood in his way.

She had been unwilling to send Marguerite away until she had proof and had taken the precaution she thought necessary, but this latest news had made her uneasy. If Gerard wished to dismiss Marguerite, she could not deny him.

She paused at Emily's door to compose herself. Emily answered her knock, her eyes suspiciously red.

'Amelia…please don't ask me to see him. I cannot…'

'You would be foolish not to do so, my love. He has come here to see you—and he has something important to tell you.' She saw the doubt and fear in Emily's eyes and touched her hand. 'Do not look so nervous, Emily. I think you must hear what he has to say. It may turn out better than you imagine. I believe he has your happiness at heart.'

Emily raised her head, a glimmer of hope in her face. 'If you think I must see him…'

'Yes, you must. He has done you a service. It was something I hoped to do for you, but Toby has news. I shall let him tell you. Wash your face and go down to him now…' Amelia paused. 'Did Marguerite bring you some camomile tea?'

'Yes, but I poured it away.'

'Good. I expected you would do so. I think you have been suspicious of her from the start. Now tidy yourself and go down to the front parlour, my love. I shall tell Toby you are willing to see him.'

When Amelia returned to the back parlour, she discovered that Toby was alone. He turned to her eagerly, smiling in relief as she inclined her head.

'Emily will come down to the front parlour in a few minutes.'

'I cannot thank you enough,' Toby said and looked awkward. 'I know I have hurt her. You must think badly of me.'

'Your apology must be to her. I trust you do not intend to hurt her again?'

'Not for the world!'

'Then you need say no more to me, sir.' Amelia smiled and glanced round. 'Did Gerard say where he was going?'

'He said he must speak to Max and told me to wait for you here. He said to tell you that he would explain later.'

'Yes, I am sure he will, thank you. Tell me, has the child been well cared for?'

His smile faded. 'I fear she has not been treated as she ought, but she is in good hands now. I left her with my mother, who is preparing to spoil her.'

'Does Lady Sinclair know whose child she is?'

'Mama has been told all she needs to know for now. Excuse me—I must not keep Emily waiting.'

'Of course.' Amelia smiled as he left the room hurriedly. She had not asked his intentions, but she could only feel that Emily's future was assured. Toby Sinclair had acted in his usual impulsive way. His reaction to the news that Emily had given birth to a child had been one of shock, but the time accorded him by his father's death had clearly brought him to understand what was important. The fact that he had found the child and taken her to his home said all that needed to be said in Amelia's opinion.

She wished that her own affairs might be settled as easily. It would not sit easily with her conscience if she had brought danger to Lisa by inviting a woman she had thought of as a friend to this house. Yet even though her mind was tortured with doubts, she could not imagine why Marguerite would wish to harm any of them. Unless, of course, she had fallen under a man's spell…

Feeling uneasy, she decided to visit the nursery again even though it was well past the time for nuncheon.

As it happened, only Marguerite was in the small dining parlour when Amelia entered it after a brief visit to the nursery. She had discovered Beattie playing a game with strands of wool bound about the child's fingers. Lisa had been perfectly happy, absorbed in the game. Amelia watched for a few minutes and left them to it. Beattie obviously knew how to amuse children. A governess would need to be found in time, but for the moment Lisa was safe and happy.

Marguerite stood up as Amelia entered. 'No one else has come to nuncheon, Amelia. I sent the maid away for I can serve myself. Would you like me to serve you?'

'No, thank you.' Amelia went to the sideboard where an array of cold meats, cheese and bread with butter and savoury preserves had been laid out. 'I do not wish for very much. Please continue with your meal, Marguerite. I have just spoken to Emily. She told me that the tea you made for her was helpful.'

'I am so pleased. I am sure that it was the tisane that upset her before. Some people are more sensitive to herbs than others.'

'Do you often make tisanes yourself?'

'I made them for Mama,' Marguerite said. 'After Lucinda died, she often suffered with irritation of the nerves. She could not sleep without her tisanes.'

'I sometimes have nights when I do not sleep well, but Martha's tisanes have helped me.'

'I hope she does not use laudanum. It can be dangerous if you use too much. I have known it to kill.'

'No, I think she merely uses herbs.' Amelia sat down at the table with her plate in front of her. 'Is your mother better now?'

'Oh, yes. I could not have left her otherwise.' Marguerite sipped a glass of water.

'I am sure she relies on you, Marguerite. If she should need you, you must not hesitate to tell me.'

'I am sure she will not.' A closed expression had come

over Marguerite's face. 'Would you wish me to take some food up to Emily?'

'Oh, no, I do not think she wishes for food at the moment.' Amelia forked a small piece of ham. 'I know that you love children, for you have told me so often—has there never been anyone you would like to marry?'

Marguerite hesitated. Her eyes did not meet Amelia's as she said, 'There was once someone I liked, but Lucinda ruined my chances. He went away and I did not see him again. Papa would not have allowed it even had he asked me.'

'I am sorry, my dear. That was sad for you. You have had a hard time of it since your sister died.'

'Lucinda was a fool.' Marguerite stood up. 'Besides, men can never be trusted. You should remember that, Amelia. Do not put too much faith in the man you marry or you may be hurt. Excuse me. I must see to some lessons for Lisa. If you need me, I shall be in my room.'

'Yes, of course.'

Amelia ate her solitary lunch. She was not sure whether or not she had driven Marguerite away with her questions, but she had felt it necessary to ask them. It was as she stood up to leave the dining parlour that she heard the ring of boots on marble tiles. She looked towards the door, waiting, expecting Gerard, and gasped as instead she saw her brother enter.

'Michael—what are you doing here?'

'Did you expect me to ignore your letter?' He glared at her. 'You cannot truly intend to marry that scoundrel, Amelia? After all the warnings I have given you…'

'Please, come into the back parlour where we may be private,' Amelia told him. 'I would be glad if you speak in a softer tone,

Michael. If we are to quarrel, it should not carry to the servants. I do not care to have my private business open knowledge.'

'It will be known soon enough if I have my way. This marriage cannot go ahead. I forbid it.'

She led the way into the small parlour she had begun to make her own. It overlooked pleasant gardens and had a French window, which she could have open when the weather permitted, enabling her to walk on to a stone terrace. The room itself was furnished comfortably with wing chairs, occasional tables and a desk where she could see herself writing letters in the future. She might make a few changes, bring some of her personal effects into the room, but for the moment it served very well. A fire had been lit and it was warm despite the bitter cold day.

When the door was closed, she turned to face her brother. His neck was red with temper and she noticed the fine purple lines mottling his nose and cheeks. His temper and his lifestyle had not improved his looks, for he had been handsome as a young man.

'I shall be honest with you. I hoped you would not come, Michael. Let me tell you at once that you cannot change my mind. I do not see why you should wish to. Gerard may not have come up to your standards when he was younger, but he is the Earl of Ravenshead now and his fortune is sufficient for his needs.'

'Can you not see that it is your fortune that interests him now? You are an old maid, Amelia. If he wished for a wife, he might find a dozen young girls to catch his interest. Depend upon it, he wants your money. The man is a scoundrel and not to be trusted.'

Amelia's expression remained unchanged despite his deliberately hurtful words, which were uncannily similar to Marguerite's.

'You are wrong, Michael. Gerard has told me that I may order my fortune as I wish. We shall secure much of it to my children; the rest will pay for the upkeep of my orphanage and be at my disposal if I need it.'

'And you believe him? The man is a rogue. Listen to me, sister—or you may be sorry. I have had a letter informing me that his first wife took her own life because of his cruelty. It was not signed, but I believe it to be true.'

'It is a wicked lie. I know what happened. Lisette took her own life, it is true, but it was not Gerard's fault.' Amelia lifted her eyes to his. 'If you have a good cause for your objection to my marriage, tell me—otherwise please leave me in peace.'

'You have got above yourself, miss. If you had done your duty to your family and allowed me the control of your fortune, none of this need have happened.'

'If my aunt had wished you to control my fortune, she would have left it to you.' Amelia glared at him. 'You have not answered my questions—why do you so dislike Gerard?'

'You will force me to tell you.' Sir Michael glared at her. 'I have tried to bring you to your senses, Amelia. I do not wish to break your heart—'

'Indeed? You had no such scruples when you had Gerard beaten and sent him away.'

'I had him beaten for good reason. I believed—I still believe—that he was Lucinda Ross's lover. I also think that he may have had a hand in her death…that he threw her into the river when he discovered that she was with child. Even then, you were a better match.'

Amelia staggered as if he had struck her, reeling from the shock. 'No! You accuse him of such wickedness to spite us. It is not true. It cannot be true. I shall not listen to your lies. What proof have you that any of this is true?' Her face had drained of colour and she could only stare at him in horror. 'No…it is not so…'

It must be a wicked lie and yet, if it were true, all the things Marguerite had been saying to her would make sense. She had been trying to warn Amelia from the moment she came and found her with Gerard, about to kiss.

'I do not believe it. He could not…he loved me.'

'Damn you, listen to me.' Michael scowled at her. 'I know that I saw them together in the woods some weeks before she died. She was in his arms, kissing him as if her life depended upon it—and I believe that he may have been near the river the day she died.'

'I do not believe you—this is all lies. Gerard could not…he would not…' Amelia shook her head and sat down as her legs threatened to give way. Supposing Gerard had never loved her…that he had seduced Lucinda at the same time as he had courted Amelia? He had married only a short time after their parting. He swore he had never loved Lisette…but was it all lies? Her heart would not believe it, but her mind told her that there must be a grain of truth in her brother's words. Yet still she continued to deny it. 'Gerard was visiting his uncle at that time. Besides, he would not have done such a wicked thing! Gerard would not…' A little sob broke from her. 'He would not…'

'What would I not do?'

Amelia turned her head and saw him standing in the doorway. He was staring at her, his eyes narrowed, angry. 'Gerard—how much did you hear?'

'Only your last words.' His gaze narrowed, moved to her brother. 'To what do we owe this pleasure, sir?'

'It does not please me to visit under your roof.' Sir Michael glared at him. 'Well, I have spoken my piece. I shall not linger.'

'Leaving already?' Gerard barred his way as he would have left them. 'You will oblige me by telling me what you have said to Amelia. I know that you despise me, sir. I would hear your reasons from your own lips.'

'Very well,' Sir Michael said. 'I know your evil heart, Ravenshead. You were Lucinda Ross's lover—and it is my belief that when she told you she was with child, you killed her.'

Gerard's face went white with shock. 'That is a foul lie! How can you make such an accusation? You have no proof. It is without foundation.'

'I saw you kissing Lucinda in the woods—my woods,' Sir Michael said. 'It was the kind of kiss a young woman gives only to her lover—and it is my belief that you killed her when she threatened to tell everyone that you were her lover.'

'Lucinda kissed me once in the woods—that I shall not deny,' Gerard replied, a little nerve flicking at his right temple. He glanced at Amelia. 'I had forgot it, but it came back to me recently. She declared that she loved me and threw her arms about me. I pushed her away and told her not to be foolish. At no time was she my lover—nor did she ever threaten to reveal that I was the father of her child. She could not, for I did not lie with her. Whatever you may have heard to the contrary, I was visiting friends elsewhere when she killed herself. I returned to ask for Amelia's hand—and you were waiting for me, Royston.' He lifted his head, nostrils flared, proud, angry. 'I had no idea of what had happened to a girl I hardly knew until some time later.'

Amelia's eyes were on his face. Guilt mixed with the anger. He was hiding something from her. She felt as if a dagger had been plunged into her heart.

'Do you expect me to believe that?' Sir Michael sneered. 'I

saw you together in the woods some weeks before she died. I witnessed the kiss. You did not throw her off immediately.'

'I was gentle with her,' Gerard admitted. 'I may have been flattered for she declared she loved me. I swear that I did nothing to encourage her. She meant nothing to me.' His gaze moved to Amelia. He frowned as he saw she was pale, her eyes dark with horror. 'You cannot believe his lies? You must believe me, Amelia. I was not Lucinda's lover—nor did I kill her.'

'If you tell me it was not so, I believe you.' Amelia's gaze went from him to her brother. She felt bewildered and she was hurting, trying not to believe that Gerard had lied to her. She had sensed there was something he was hiding when he had hinted that Lucinda was not as innocent as Amelia believed. Had he lain with her? No, no, she could not believe such ill of him. It would destroy her. 'You are wrong, Michael…you must be.'

'Why must he be wrong?'

Amelia spun round as she heard Marguerite's voice. She was standing in the doorway, her eyes wild, full of bitterness, her mouth curling in a snarl of hatred as she stared at Gerard.

'Lucinda told me. She boasted of it to me. Everyone thinks that she took her secret to the grave with her—but that is not true. She told me that Gerard Ravenshead was the father of her child and that she would marry him. I warned her that he was not suitable. Father would not have agreed for he hoped then that we should both make advantageous matches. It was only after her shame was known that he told us we would never be allowed to marry.'

'No!' Amelia looked at Gerard; the doubts were in her eyes now. She did not want to believe what Marguerite was saying, but Michael also believed that Gerard was Lucinda's lover—and for a moment she had seen guilt in Gerard's eyes. He had broken her heart once—how could she be sure that he was not lying to her now? 'Please—it cannot be true.'

'I tried to warn you,' Marguerite cried. 'I told you that he was not to be trusted but you would not listen.'

'Damn you!' Gerard moved towards her in a threatening manner. 'You will leave my house, witch. Your sister was a wanton, but I was not her lover. I believe that she did not know the name of her child's father, for she had more than one lover—'

'Gerard!' Amelia moved to protect Marguerite from his anger. 'Do not speak to her thus. Lucinda was my friend. She could not have been as you describe her.'

'You would take her word above mine?' Gerard's eyes blazed with fury. 'I shall not tolerate that woman in my house another day, Amelia. I will arrange for my coach to take her home, but she leaves today.'

'Do not bother to defend me, Amelia,' Marguerite said. 'I was coming to tell you that I was leaving. Mama has need of me.' She turned and walked from the room, leaving silence behind her.

'Well—' Gerard's tone was harsh as he looked at Amelia '—do you believe her or me?'

Amelia was silent. He was so angry…bitter almost. She hardly knew him. This was not the charming man she had fallen in love with. Her tender lover of the previous night had disappeared, in his place a cold and angry stranger. She wanted to believe him, because if she did not her love became ashes—but she had seen a flicker of guilt in his eyes. He had admitted that he had kissed Lucinda.

'Gerard, I…' She faltered, the words stuck in her throat and she could not go on.

'If she believes you, she is a fool,' Sir Michael said. He glared at them both. 'I've said my piece, Amelia. If you choose to marry him now, I wash my hands of you. Do not expect me to attend your wedding.'

Amelia blinked away the foolish tears, looking at him proudly. 'You will always be welcome in my house—providing you behave as a gentleman.'

Sir Michael inclined his head, turned and walked from the room. Amelia moved away, looking out of the window at the view. The rain had stopped and the sky was getting lighter but it was as if a dark cloud hung over her.

'I am waiting for an answer.'

Amelia could not look at him. 'I am trying to believe you, Gerard,' she said, without turning her head.

'Trying!' He took hold of her shoulders, swinging her round to face him. His eyes blazed with fury. 'Good grief! You cannot think that I would ravish a young girl of good birth and then kill her when she tells me she is with child? What kind of a monster do you think I am?'

'She told Marguerite you were her lover…' Amelia drew a trembling breath. 'I know you would not kill her. I believe she took her own life, but—'

'You think that perhaps I was her lover? You think I played with her emotions, took a despicable advantage at the same time as I courted you—and then destroyed her? You believe that I drove her to her death.' Gerard's face was grey with shock, horror in his eyes. 'You swore you did not blame me for Lisette's death, but perhaps you lied? You do think me capable of these things…and Lisette did die because I hurt her, because I could not love her. I am innocent of all else, but perhaps you prefer to believe your friend?' His tone was scathing, flicking her on the raw.

Amelia shook her head. It was impossible to answer. She did not want to believe that Gerard had done the things he was accused of, but the seed of doubt had been planted. She was too shocked, too stunned to think clearly.

'I am sorry—' she began, but was interrupted by the arrival of Emily followed by Toby. One look at their faces was enough to tell the world how they felt. 'Emily…' Amelia wanted to tell her that this was not the time but before she could speak Gerard had walked from the room. 'Gerard…'

Amelia choked on the words. She wanted to call him back, but did not know what she would say if she did, because she was still reeling from the shock of Marguerite's accusation. Had it been only her brother, she would have dismissed his claim, but Marguerite's accusation had the ring of truth. Oh, but she did not want to believe her! She must be lying…

Smothering her desire to weep, Amelia turned to face Emily. She forced herself to smile.

'So, my love—is it all settled?'

'Toby has found my daughter,' Emily told her. Her face was glowing, her eyes lit from within. 'He says she has not been well treated, but she is quite healthy. She was neglected, but not harmed physically. Her adopted parents did not love her, because they had children of their own and they had long spent the money they were given to take her. They gave her up readily and Toby has taken Beth to his parents. He says that his mother will adopt her. I shall be able to see her every day. I shall look after her, love her and teach her to be happy—but her birth will remain our secret.' Her cheeks turned pink as she glanced up at

Toby a little shyly. 'He has explained it is for my sake and not because he is ashamed of me...he loves me truly...'

'If you wish it, we will tell the world,' Toby said stoutly. 'But for your sake, my love, it will be better if Beth is brought up as Mama's adopted daughter. No one will think anything of it if you love her—and one day you may tell her the truth if you wish.'

'And does Toby know the truth of what happened to you now?' Amelia asked.

'When I thought about it, I guessed what must have happened,' Toby answered for her, his hand reaching to take Emily's in his own. 'I love her. I should not stop loving her whatever the truth, but when I discovered how she had been treated, I knew what I must do.'

'And how did you discover that?'

'Harry Pendleton wrote to me. He knew how I felt about Emily and once you told him her story, he thought I should be informed. It was simple enough to find the child, for no one had bothered to conceal her whereabouts. Harry's agent met me and told me what he knew and the rest was easy.' He reached for Emily's hand and kissed it. 'I am taking Emily home to Mama. We shall stay for a couple of weeks and then come back for your wedding, Amelia. Emily would not want to miss that for the world.'

Amelia wondered if there would be a wedding. She was not certain how she felt, but she could not cast a cloud over her friend's shining happiness.

'I am very pleased for you both,' she said. 'When are you leaving?'

'Almost immediately. I thought Emily could pack a small bag for now. Perhaps you would have her things sent to her at my mother's home?' Toby said with his customary eagerness.

'Yes, of course. I shall be happy to do so. Martha will see to her packing.' She moved to kiss Emily on the cheek and then Toby. 'I hope I shall be invited to the wedding?'

'You will be the guest of honour,' Emily told her. 'Toby says we shall hold a ball and announce our engagement in a few months from now. We may be married in the summer. It should not be sooner, because of his father's death. Besides, I am going to live with his mama and we shall see each other all the time…' She hesitated, looking anxious. 'You will not need me, Amelia? I know it is short notice, but you have Marguerite to keep you company now.'

It was impossible to tell Emily that Marguerite was leaving under a cloud—or that she might be forced to return home alone. 'Yes, of course. You must not worry about me, my dearest. I am delighted at the way things have turned out for you. I wish you both every happiness.'

'I am so very fond of you,' Emily said and embraced her. 'I would not leave so suddenly, but I know that you are happy and settled.'

'Yes, of course I am,' Amelia said. 'Go and pack your bag now, dearest.'

'My mother is anxious to become acquainted with Emily,' Toby said after she had gone. 'Harry told me that you intended to search for Emily's child. I am grateful, because his agent was able to save me some time in locating the child.'

'She was so very unhappy after you left. I felt I must do something.'

Toby looked a little uncomfortable. 'I did not behave well, but I must admit Emily's revelation came as a bolt of lightning. Had my father not died, I should have returned sooner. As soon as I could, I went to Pendleton and then in search of the child.'

'I dare say Emily will forgive you. She has not been well, but I believe she will soon be better now.'

Amelia left Toby to prepare his curricle for the journey. She went upstairs to her room. Discovering that the key to the dressing-room door had been put her side, she locked it. She sat down on the bed, bending her head and covering her face with her hands.

Amelia did not cry. Her distress was too deep for tears. She did not know how she felt about things at the moment. She had begun the day feeling on top of the world, but a few spiteful words had turned her world upside down. Her thoughts went round and round in her head as she tried to come to terms with what she had been told. She raised her head, a look of determination in her eyes. She must think about this calmly. It would be foolish to give way to emotion.

Michael had been certain enough of his beliefs to have Gerard beaten. He had acted in a high-handed manner to prevent her marriage at that time, but it seemed he had meant to protect her from a man he believed a rogue. He ought to have told her the story and let her discover the truth for herself. Yet perhaps he had acted as he thought best.

Amelia stood up and began to pace the room. The most terrible accusations had come from Lucinda's own sister! Marguerite was convinced that Gerard was her sister's lover. She had not been lying. She truly believed it.

Marguerite had sworn that her sister had told her that Gerard was her lover. The evidence seemed damning. Amelia had always known it was possible that it could have been Gerard who was Lucinda's lover, if only because he was one of several men visiting the area at that time, but, as time went on, she had completely exonerated him. She had believed that Lucinda's lover was Northaven, but then she had begun to wonder if she had misjudged him too. Now two people had told her that Gerard had seduced and deserted Lucinda at the time he was supposed to be courting Amelia. A shudder of horror went through her, for if Gerard were capable of such an act he would not be the man she loved. No, no, it could not be true! Everything she knew of him denied it. Besides, something was deeply wrong here…

If Marguerite believed that Gerard had seduced her sister and then driven her to her death—why had she come to this house? She had known that Amelia was going to marry him, for she had told her, asked her to come and help take care of his child. Why would she do that if she were convinced of his guilt?

Amelia frowned as she began to revise the theory she had previously held. She had believed that Gerard's enemy was Lieutenant Gordon—that he wanted revenge because of the way Lisette had met her death. She had imagined that he was the instigator of the plot to kidnap her, possibly persuading Marguerite to help him. She had wondered if Marguerite had fallen in love with Gordon. However, if Marguerite had had reasons of her own to hate Gerard…

She would never rest unless she knew the truth!

Amelia decided she would speak to Marguerite before she left. She went along the landing to Marguerite's room, knocked at the door and then went in. She saw at once that things had been snatched from the armoire and from the chest. A stocking lay abandoned on the floor and the gowns Amelia had given Marguerite were lying on the bed—each of them had been torn with a sharp instrument, rendering them useless. The glass dressing-table set had been knocked to the floor and some silver items were missing. The mess caused had clearly been done out of spite. Marguerite had vented her anger on anything to hand.

Amelia felt slightly sick at the sight of such wanton destruction. She was seized with fear and hurried to the nursery. Relief swept over her as she found Beattie playing with Lisa while Mary stood folding a pile of clean linen and smiled as the child laughed. Lisa was safe! Amelia schooled her features to a pleasant smile.

'Have either of you seen Miss Ross in the past hour?'

'No. She came earlier, but not in the last hour,' Nurse Mary said. 'Is something the matter, Miss Royston?'

'Miss Ross is leaving us. I do not want her near Lisa again.'

'I'm glad she's gone and that's a fact,' Beattie said. 'She gave me the creeps—and that's the truth.'

Amelia didn't ask her to elaborate. She accepted that she had made a mistake in asking Marguerite to come here on the basis of a few letters. Had anything happened to Lisa because of her error she would not have forgiven herself. If Marguerite was consumed with hate for Lisa's father, she might well have constituted a danger to the child. Amelia felt guilty for having brought her to the house.

She was on her way back to her room when she saw Emily walking towards her with a bag in her hand and a cloak over her arm.

'I wanted to say goodbye,' she said. 'This is your cloak, Amelia. You were kind to lend it to me, but after I was kidnapped while wearing it I did not wear it again.'

'I do not think I shall wear it,' Amelia said. 'I may give it to one of the maids, for it is warm and comfortable.' She leaned forwards to kiss Emily's cheek. 'I wish you lots of happiness, my love.'

'I am very happy—but a little nervous. Supposing Beth does not like me…?'

'How could that be?' Amelia shook her head. 'She will come to love you, as I have, dearest. Go on now. Toby has his horses waiting.'

'Yes, I must not keep him. I shall write often—and we shall be here for the wedding.'

Amelia nodded and let her go. She took her cloak into the bedroom and threw it over a chair. She glanced uncertainly at the locked dressing-room door. As she did so, she saw the handle move.

'Amelia…are you in there? Open the door please. I would like to talk to you.'

Amelia hesitated. She wasn't ready to talk to Gerard yet because she was not sure what to say to him. Picking up the cloak she had discarded, she put it around her shoulders and went out of her room. She ran down the stairs and left the house by a side door. The rain had stopped and the wind had blown itself out, though the sky was dark and it was very cold.

She did not mind the cold. She wanted some fresh air—and she needed to be alone for a while.

Chapter Ten

Damn it! How could she think him capable of seducing a young woman and deserting her—and at the same time as he was courting Amelia herself?

Gerard was so angry when he left the room that he was afraid he might do or say something he ought not if he remained. When he saw Toby and Emily come in, he had felt there was no other option than to leave, because he could not speak as he wished with them present. Amelia was clearly in a state of shock and distress. He could only hope that she would come to her senses after a moment or two of reflection.

He was in his own bedchamber when he thought he heard sounds coming from Amelia's room. He went through the dressing closet and tried the handle of the connecting door, calling out to her. She did not answer, yet he was certain she was there. Why would she not speak to him?

It was an impossible situation! How could she believe those vile allegations? She could not if she loved him.

Gerard vaguely remembered the scene in the woods near Amelia's home some years previously. He had been on his way to visit Amelia when he met a young woman. She had been visiting her friend, for she told him that she had just come from the Roystons' house. She was carrying her bonnet by its ribbons, her long fair hair loose on her shoulders. The sunshine suited her—her skin had turned a pale gold and she wore no pelisse, her muslin gown clinging to her shapely form.

'I have been visiting Amelia,' she told him, laughing up at him with her soft ripe lips and her blue eyes filled with mischief. 'It is so warm today. I think I shall go for a swim in the river.'

Gerard struggled to recall his reply. It was something like, *'It is certainly warm enough. You should take care, Miss Ross. The river is deep and there are reeds that might catch your skirts and drag you down.'* Yes, he remembered saying something of the sort. The scene was becoming clearer now. He had dismissed it as unimportant, but now he thought it imperative that he should remember exactly.

'I shall not be wearing clothes…' She licked her lips, an invitation in her eyes. 'Why do you not come with me? We could swim and…' Her laughter was husky and seductive. 'Who knows what else we might find to do, Gerard?' She moved towards him, the perfume of roses wafting from her skin. 'I have always thought you one of the most handsome men I know.'

'You should not say such things, Lucinda.' Gerard could not help smiling, for she was a lovely young woman. He was in love with Amelia, but a light dalliance was no sin on a summer afternoon. 'Some men might take you at your word.'

Had his manner challenged her—encouraged her? He had not meant it to, but perhaps he had been at fault for her reply had been swift and bold.

'I should like you to take me at my word…' Lucinda threw

herself at him, winding her arms about his neck and pressing herself against his body. He put up his hands to hold her arms and push her away, but she pressed her lips against his in a wild, passionate kiss that shocked him and for just one moment he had responded. He was, after all, a young man with red blood in his veins. 'Take me swimming…lie with me this afternoon…make love to me, Gerard.'

'No!' Gerard had pushed her away as the moment passed and he realised what she was asking. He did not want her. He was in love with Amelia Royston. This wanton girl was beautiful and he had been tempted by her kiss, but now her boldness revolted him. 'Behave yourself! Think of the disgrace to your family if you were seen swimming naked.'

Lucinda laughed mockingly. 'I do not know why Marguerite thinks herself in love with you. You are such a righteous bore, Gerard Ravenshead. I do not want you. I already have a lover and he does not scruple to take me swimming and then lie with me on a summer afternoon.'

She had laughed again and then run off through the woods. Gerard had laughed too, because he thought it the foolish boasting of a young woman who felt herself scorned. He had forgotten it until he heard about the scandal and the shocking tragedy of her death.

He had never spoken to anyone of that afternoon. He had never realised that they had been seen in what must have looked like a passionate embrace. He had certainly never thought it the true reason for the beating he had been given by Sir Michael Royston's bully-boys.

'I do not know why Marguerite thinks herself in love with you.'

Gerard frowned. He had known there was something he

ought to remember from the first moment Miss Ross arrived at Pendleton.

He had not even considered Lucinda's words serious at the time. Remembering now, he thought there had been something a little spiteful in the way Lucinda had spoken of her sister. Why should Marguerite Ross have thought herself in love with him? He hardly knew her. They had danced once or twice—three times at most. He had sat next to her one evening at dinner and made polite conversation, but he had hardly noticed her. He had already been in love with Amelia.

His mind turned back to the scene earlier when Marguerite had thrown those vile accusations at him. He had been looking at Amelia, willing her to trust him, to love him as he loved her—but he had seen the doubts in her eyes.

Marguerite's accusations, the way she looked at him, had seemed angry…almost bitter. Why did she hate him? It seemed clear that she must—for why else would she meet Lieutenant Gordon and plot with him? He was certain now that the two had worked together. Gordon must have had his information from Marguerite. Amelia's innocent letters had told her all she needed to know.

Amelia had begun to suspect it even before Marguerite's outburst. She had thought the woman under Gordon's influence but…supposing *she* were the instigator of the plot to abduct Amelia and kill her? It made perfect sense. Gordon might hate him because of Lisette's death, but he had not looked for revenge at the start. Something—or someone—had made him decide that he would punish Gerard through Amelia. If that someone were Marguerite, it explained why she had suddenly arrived at Pendleton.

Gerard felt cold. They had harboured a viper in their midst! His first thought was for Lisa, because she was an innocent, unsuspecting child. Receiving no answer from Amelia's room, he went immediately to the nursery, where he found the same peaceful scene that Amelia had found earlier. His relief was soon overcome with anger.

Damn it! He would not put up with this nonsense. Gerard returned to the master suite and opened the door to Amelia's room from the hall. A brief search told him that she was not there. He left and walked towards the stairs. Down in the hall, he asked the footman on duty if he had seen Miss Royston recently.

'She went out a few minutes ago, my lord. Perhaps a quarter of an hour. I watched her for a moment, because she seemed unlike herself—a little distracted, if you will forgive my saying so. I think she walked towards the lake.'

'Thank you.'

Gerard frowned. He was not dressed for walking. It would take but a moment to fetch his greatcoat. He would follow her and hope that they could settle this nonsense!

The cold air stung her cheeks and eyes, but Amelia pulled the hood of her cloak over her head, determined not to be put off her walk. She knew it was foolish of her to run away from Gerard, because they would have to talk sooner or later. However, she was feeling too raw to face him just yet. Had the accusation come from just one person she might have dismissed it—but both her brother and Marguerite had blamed Gerard for Lucinda's downfall and her death. Until the previous night she had been unsure of his feelings for her, but after their lovemaking she had felt secure in his love. Now all those niggling doubts had come flooding back.

If Gerard loved her, why had he married so soon after they

parted? Why hadn't he come to her and told her what her brother had done? Amelia's thoughts went round and round as she battled her tears.

Was it possible that Gerard had seduced her friend while at the same time swearing eternal love for Amelia? Could he truly be so ruthless…so cold and uncaring? Could he make love to her so tenderly if he were the man her brother and Marguerite claimed?

No, of course not! Now that she could think clearly, Amelia began to see how wrong it was. Gerard loved her. It was true that he had married another woman, and Lisette had taken her own life—perhaps because Gerard had told her that he could not love her. She had exonerated him freely of blame for that—could she not show as much faith again? She must if she trusted her own senses, her own heart—because she loved him.

She still loved him! Despite all the doubts and accusations thrown at him, she loved him. She would always love him. Without Gerard her life would be empty, a sterile pointless existence that would lead to bitter old age.

Amelia frowned. If she accepted that her brother had been mistaken in what he had seen, she must believe Gerard. He had told her that Lucinda was wanton…that *she* had kissed him. It was this that she had found so hard to accept. A light, flirtatious kiss in a moment of fun—yes, that she could accept—but Lucinda a wanton?

Was it possible that she had never really known her? They had been friends, but had Lucinda kept secrets from her? The answer must be that she had, because she had never told Amelia that she had a lover. Only when she discovered that she was with child and confessed to her parents that her lover would not marry her, had she told anyone of her shame.

Amelia wished that she knew the truth. She had always felt sad about Lucinda's suicide…but Marguerite had hinted that Gerard had killed her because she threatened to name him.

No, he would never do something like that! Amelia could not accept that he was a murderer. Everything that was in her protested his innocence. If he was innocent of her death, it followed that Lucinda had either taken her own life in a moment of despair—or someone else had killed her. So if Amelia believed Gerard was innocent of murder, she ought to believe him innocent of seduction and desertion.

She did believe him! Amelia felt the doubts fall away, a weight lifting from her shoulders as her mind cleared. Gerard would not lie to her! How could he after what they had been to one another? She had hurt and angered him because she had not instantly accepted his word. She ought to have known at once, of course, but the accusations had shocked her so deeply that she hardly knew what she was saying. She had had to deal with Emily and Toby, forcing herself to behave naturally, and it was only now that she had been able to see things clearly.

Why had Marguerite come to the house if she believed that Gerard had seduced and murdered her sister?

There could be only one answer. She was in league with Lieutenant Gordon. He craved revenge for Lisette's death and Marguerite wanted revenge for her sister's shame.

Why did she believe that Lucinda had been forced into the river? Amelia had always thought that she must have flung herself from the bridge because she could not face her shame…why did Marguerite think otherwise?

It was puzzling for until now she had never heard anyone speak of such a possibility. Even Mrs Ross had spoken of her daughter's suicide.

'I was angry with her for her foolish behaviour but I would have taken care of her. She had no need to take her own life,' the grieving mother declared. *'Her papa was angry, but I loved her.'*

Amelia recalled the mother's tears. She frowned as she tried to picture the scene that afternoon. She had gone to the Rosses' house to visit and pay her condolences. Mrs Ross had received her alone and then…Marguerite had come in. Amelia had glanced at her face and…she had been so angry…

Angry. Marguerite had not looked as if she were grieving. Her eyes were not ringed with red, as her mother's were—she was angry.

'Marguerite…' Amelia unconsciously spoke the words aloud. 'She was jealous of her sister—and angry…' Why was she so angry? Amelia could not quite grasp the last pieces of the puzzle.

She had reached the lake. She stood for a moment, staring down the steep bank at the dark grey water, which reflected the clouds above. On a summer day it would be pleasant here, but today there was a feeling of isolation as a light mist began to curl across the water. Amelia sighed, feeling lonely, uneasy. Then, as she heard a twig snap beneath someone's foot, she turned and looked into Marguerite's face. She was as angry now as she had been on the day Amelia visited her home.

'What are you doing here?' she asked her. 'I thought you had left?'

'I met someone and we decided we would wait for a while.' Marguerite's eyes flicked past Amelia to someone who had approached from the right. 'It seems we were lucky, Nanny. You said that she would walk out alone if she was upset—and you were right.'

Amelia looked round and saw Alice Horton. She was dressed in a black cloak, the hood covering her head and most of her face—but her eyes were cold, filled with malice.

A sliver of fear ran down Amelia's spine. She was completely alone here, for few were out on a day like this. Even the labourers would hurry home to eat their dinner in a warm kitchen.

'This is private land. You have no right here. The earl dismissed you.'

'Because you told him to,' Alice Horton said bitterly. 'You stole my girl's admirer and then wrote pitying letters to her…asking her to be a governess. She is a lady…better than you…'

'What are you talking about? I have stolen no one's lover.' Amelia stared at Marguerite, trying to make some sense of the accusation. 'Is she speaking about you? I did not mean to patronise you by offering you a place in my household—only to help you find happiness.'

'He liked me before you made eyes at him…' Marguerite's eyes glittered with hatred. 'Lucinda knew how I felt. She laughed at me when she told me he was courting you…but then she stopped laughing.'

Amelia felt icy cold as she looked into the other woman's face. Anger and hatred—and something more…something dangerous.

'What happened to Lucinda? Why do you think she did not commit suicide?'

Marguerite's lips curved in a sneer. 'She could swim like a fish. Lucinda used to swim in the river all the time. She learned when she was five years old. She was always laughing at me because I dare not follow her into the deep water. She had no fear of anything.'

'If Lucinda could swim, why did she drown?'

'She fell from the bridge and hit her head on an iron strut. It was an accident…' Marguerite's eyes looked strange. 'She was laughing…and then she stopped laughing because I pushed her and she fell.' A queer, high laugh escaped Marguerite. 'I shouldn't have told you that, should I? You will guess now and that means you have to die…but it doesn't matter because you were going to die anyway.' She looked at Alice Horton and giggled. 'Shall I push her in the lake? Everyone will think she killed herself because he betrayed her with that slut of a sister of mine. I got away with it once, I can do it again.'

'Now then, pet, you mustn't get so upset,' Alice Horton soothed. 'Lucinda was a silly girl, but you didn't mean to kill her. It was an accident.'

'Oh, but I did…' Marguerite's eyes blazed. 'I wanted her to die. She boasted that he was her lover. She knew that I loved him. It was why she wanted him. She had the other one—the one who had given her a child—but she wanted *him* too, because she knew I loved him. She always had to have everything, but this time I stopped her.'

'Who was the other one?' Amelia asked. She curled her nails into her palms, willing herself to keep calm. She must hear the truth now! 'What was his name?'

'Surely you know?' Marguerite glared at her. 'He was so angry because he saw her with Gerard that he wouldn't help her. He had promised to leave his wife. He was besotted with Lucinda, gave her presents of jewellery. He told her that Louisa was a nag and a scold and he would get a divorce, but after he saw her with Gerard he raged at her, told her she was a slut and he wouldn't see her again. Lucinda told me it all before I—'

'My brother?' Amelia stared at her in horror. Suddenly, it all made sense. It wasn't to protect her that Michael had had Gerard thrashed—it was jealousy, because he believed the woman he loved had betrayed him with Gerard Ravenshead! His hatred stemmed from the belief that Gerard had taken Lucinda from him!

The sickness rose in her throat as she saw it all so clearly. Michael had been Lucinda's lover, not Gerard, but he had seen them kiss. It was just a moment of light flirtation, as Gerard claimed, but Michael had lost his head. He had had Gerard beaten and broken Amelia's heart because he was jealous.

Amelia's head was whirling as she tried to take all the new information in. Her brother had seduced Lucinda. He was the father of her child. He had promised to leave his wife, but then he'd seen her in Gerard's arms that summer afternoon and he had believed they were lovers. Amelia didn't know what had happened that day, but she imagined it was just a piece of nonsense on a warm afternoon—*because of it Michael had had Gerard thrashed and ruined her life. But what had Marguerite done?*

'Did you kill Lucinda because you believed she had taken Gerard from you?'

Marguerite's eyes had gone blank, but now they focused on Amelia once more. 'You stole him from me. I thought it was her, but it was you. She laughed at me and told me he was going to marry you. I flew at her and we struggled and then…she fell and hit her head. I saw her floating with her face in the water.'

'Why didn't you fetch help or try to get her out?'

'I couldn't swim. I'm afraid of the deep water and—' Suddenly, Marguerite's eyes narrowed, became crafty, evil. 'I wanted her to die. I want you to die. Why should you have everything while I have nothing? My father said I would never marry…it was her fault…your fault…' Marguerite advanced on her, her hands going for Amelia's throat. 'If you drown, they will blame him…and he will die too. He will know what it is like to lose everything.'

'No!' Amelia tried to throw her off, but Marguerite was too strong. 'Help me! Help me…'

Alice Horton stood for a moment, seeming undecided, then she pulled at Marguerite's arm.

'Stop this, sweeting. It isn't her fault that you can't marry. You know what your papa said—'

'Get off me!' Marguerite swung her arm back, throwing the older woman off balance so that she fell to her knees. In that moment Amelia struggled free and started to run. Marguerite came after her, grabbing her by the waist and somehow bringing her down. 'You've got to die. You can't live now that you know. *He* was supposed to help me, but he is a weak coward. So I must do it myself.'

Amelia screamed and struggled to throw Marguerite off, but she was very strong. Her hands were tightening their hold about Amelia's throat and she couldn't breathe. Everything was going black and then she heard a shout…several voices shouting. People were racing towards them.

'Damn you! You murdering bitch!'

Gerard's voice! Amelia heard it through a haze of mist, as if she were far away. Several men were shouting and there were the sounds of a struggle. She heard Marguerite screaming and then water splashing, more screaming, shouting and then sobbing. A woman was weeping bitterly.

'Is she dead, sir? My poor little mad girl.'

Amelia's throat hurt, but she struggled to sit up. She couldn't see clearly, but she knew that Gerard wasn't alone. There were other men there...some of them had guns. She thought one voice might have belonged to the Marquis of Northaven, but she wasn't sure, because it was distant, blurred. Everything was going hazy again as she fell back on the damp ground.

The woman was still sobbing. She thought it was Alice Horton. Men were talking, calling for someone to go for the doctor. Things seemed to be going on around her. She was being lifted and carried in someone's arms, but she couldn't see or hear any more...

Gerard stood looking down, his heart wrenched as he saw Amelia throw out her arm and cry out something he could not hear. Her body was drenched in sweat. However many times they changed the sheets she became wet through again and the doctor was worried that her fever would turn to pneumonia.

'If the fever turns putrid, she may die,' he had told Gerard before he left. 'All you can do is to watch over her and pray.'

'Don't let her die...' The anguished words were torn from him. 'If I have sinned, vent your anger on me—let me take her place. I beg you, do not let her die.'

Gerard was not sure who he was praying to, for long ago he had felt that God was a myth, a fairy story. How could a gentle God allow the things he had seen in battle?

Tears trickled down his cheeks as he bent over Amelia and kissed her damp brow. 'Live for me, my darling,' he whispered. 'Live for me. I cannot bear it if you leave me...forgive me...forgive me...'

His expression was wintry. This was his fault. If he had spoken to Amelia earlier she would not have gone out alone. He should have made her believe that he'd had nothing to do with Lucinda.

* * *

Amelia opened her eyes to see a woman bending over her. The mist cleared for long enough for her to see that it was someone she knew…Susannah. She tried to speak, but the words wouldn't come. Her throat hurt too badly and every part of her body ached. Susannah touched her hand, a tear sliding down her cheek.

'You've been so ill, dearest,' she said. 'You had a fever. The doctor said it was a putrid infection of the lungs. We thought we were going to lose you. Gerard has been out of his mind.'

'Marguerite…' The word was a harsh whisper.

Susannah gripped her hand. 'Do not worry, dearest. She can't hurt anyone again. Her father has agreed to have her sent to a secure place where she will be properly cared for as long as she lives. He says he should have done it years ago, but her mother would not have it.'

'Not dead? I thought…' Amelia sighed.

'No…she tried to drown herself, but the Marquis of Northaven pulled her out of the lake. Gerard met him a few minutes earlier as he left the house to search for you. He had brought news and they were talking as they walked to the lake—and then they saw what was happening. Some of Gerard's men were already racing to your rescue, but he was the first to reach you.'

'She wanted to kill me…' Amelia's head was spinning as she tried to remember. 'She was so…strong…'

'She was ill, Amelia. Northaven has discovered the truth from Lieutenant Gordon. She is his cousin and he has always loved her, though he knew she was wild even as a girl. Miss Horton has told us more. As a child Marguerite was prone to tantrums. That is why they had a strict nanny for her. When she grew up she seemed better, calmer, but when Lucinda became pregnant their father started to forbid the girls to go anywhere—and Marguerite had become moody. She sneaked out at night, walking in the woods alone and she was prone to bouts of melancholy. Mr Ross suspected that she had killed her own sister and decided that she ought never to marry, though he was too proud of his good name to admit it to the world.'

Amelia closed her eyes for a moment. 'She was the one who planned all this, the abduction of me that went wrong and the rest…wasn't she?'

'Lieutenant Gordon says that she persuaded him; she said that he had to abduct you and kill you in front of Gerard—and then kill him. Only then would she give him what he wanted from her. He believed that Gerard was responsible for Lisette's death and agreed, because she had bewitched him, manipulated him—but in the end he couldn't go through with all the things she asked of him. When Northaven accused him of trying to shoot him in the back, he broke down and confessed that he had taken a pot shot at him, but swears it was more in the hope of scaring him off than killing him.'

'You mean the marquis forced him to confess?' Amelia's head was clearing a little. She sat up with Susannah's help and sipped a little water. 'I wonder why Marguerite decided she would kill me herself.'

'It was an impulse. You were in an isolated spot, alone—and she took her chance. She was always a little unstable…her nurse knew it. She said that both the Ross girls were inclined to be wild at times, but Marguerite got much worse after Lucinda's death. Perhaps it was her guilt because she killed her.'

'Poor Marguerite…'

'Do not pity her, Amelia.'

'I can only feel pity for her despite what she did.'

'Alice Horton was resentful because you had her dismissed, but when Marguerite tried to kill you, she attempted to stop her. She might have agreed to help with an abduction for a ransom, but she drew the line at murder.'

'Did she?' Amelia's brow wrinkled. 'I cannot remember…'

'You have been very ill, Amelia.'

'Did they send for you?'

'As soon as I heard what had happened, I was determined to come. Helene is here—and so is Emily. She put off her visit to Sinclair's. We all love you, dearest Amelia.'

'Helene should not be worrying over me. She must take care of herself and her baby.'

'We haven't let her nurse you. Emily and I have done most of it—and Martha, of course. Everyone wanted to do their best and Lisa has been crying for you. Gerard has been here much of the time, but today he had to see some people. Lieutenant Gordon has made a full confession. They are deciding what should be done with him—whether he should be sent abroad or given up to the magistrates.'

Amelia nodded. She closed her eyes. She was so very tired.

'Thank you for explaining…but I think I should like to sleep now.'

'Yes, of course,' Susannah said and kissed her cheek. 'Go to sleep, dearest. You will soon begin to feel better now…'

'Well, it is over,' Harry said as they sat together in the library. 'I am of the opinion that Gordon has learned his lesson. When he discovered that Marguerite had murdered her own sister, I thought he would be sick. The look of revulsion on his face tells me that he will not be drawn into such an affair again.'

'I still think he should have stood his trial,' Max said. 'You were too lenient with him, Gerard—he was behind the attempted kidnap on Amelia and the abduction of Miss Barton—and that shot outside the church at Pendleton, though he says it was no more than a warning.'

'The shot might have been meant for me. Amelia suffered no ill effects and Emily was returned unhurt thanks to Northaven. I have a great deal to thank Northaven for…and I believe we all owe him an apology.'

'Not certain of that,' Harry objected. 'His careless talk was almost certainly to blame for what happened in Spain.'

'Yes, I am sure it was—but he did not deliberately betray us and we ought to show some mercy. I let Gordon go because he is genuinely remorseful. Besides, it was Marguerite who planned it all. He was merely her tool.'

'I hope you have forgiven yourself too.' Max laid a hand on his shoulder. 'Lisette had been through a great deal, losing her lover, the rapes and then giving birth. Her mind was disturbed when she took her own life.'

'And I refused her when she asked me for love.' Gerard looked grave. 'Perhaps that is why I am being punished. If I lose Amelia…'

'Ridiculous!' Harry said. 'You cannot blame yourself for what happened to Amelia the other day. She invited that mad woman into your home.'

'If she had not, I might not have been there when she needed me. She could have been attacked at any time…perhaps months after we were married.'

'Amelia will pull through,' Max told him. 'She is surrounded

by people who love her, and they will all do whatever they can
to help. Just give it time, Gerard.'

'Yes, I know—thank you.' Gerard forced a smile. 'You are the
best friends a man could have at such a time.'

Gerard said no more. It was impossible to explain that he was
afraid that when Amelia recovered her senses, she would not
wish to marry him—that she might still believe the lies
Marguerite had told her.

Amelia was dreaming. She was in the water and something
was dragging her down. When she looked beneath the surface,
she saw the eyes of a dead girl staring at her. Then the girl's
skinny claws reached out to pull her to the bottom. She could
feel the air draining from her lungs…

'Amelia…' A gentle hand shook her shoulder. 'It's just a nightmare, my love. I am so sorry she hurt you. Please forgive me.'

Amelia opened her eyes. For a moment she could not focus,
but then she saw Gerard. His face were pale in the candlelight
and tears were wetting his cheeks. He was crying…for her. She
lifted her hand as he bent over her, touching his face.

'Don't cry,' she said. 'I am better now, Gerard…' She shuddered
as she remembered. 'It was just a dream…just a horrid dream.'

Gerard sat on the edge of the bed. He reached for her hand,
holding it as if it were made of fine porcelain. 'When I saw what
Marguerite was doing I was so afraid. I thought I might be too
late. My men had held off because they did not realise what she
meant to do. She was your guest, not a stranger, so they hesitated and then it was almost too late.'

'How could anyone have guessed what she would do? I had
noticed small things that seemed odd, but I thought she was

merely suffering from melancholy because of the life she led. Indeed, I suspect that her father may have pushed her over the edge by depriving her of her freedom.'

'She tried to kill you, Amelia. You were lying there so still… I thought you were dead.' His voice broke with emotion.

'I think I almost was,' Amelia said with a wry smile. 'If you had not come…you and Northaven and the others… I owe the marquis an apology, Gerard. I once thought he was responsible for Lucinda's death, because I thought him her seducer—but now I know that he is blameless. I know who seduced her and then left her to face her shame alone.'

'He is a rake and more, but he is blameless in this instance.' Gerard's gaze narrowed. 'You do not truly think that I…?' Amelia shook her head. 'Then who…?'

Amelia reached for his hand. 'Before she tried to kill me, Marguerite told me it was Michael.'

'Your brother…but he accused me…the morning he came here—he accused me…'

'Of seducing her and then deserting her. Yes, he did—and he drove us apart, Gerard—because he was mad with jealousy. He was besotted with Lucinda. I see it all so clearly now. Things I should have noticed when she came to the house. She pretended to visit me, but it was Michael she wanted to see. He bought her things…promised to divorce Louisa—and then he saw her kissing you. In his rage and disappointment he blamed you. He loved her, still wanted her even though they quarrelled. If she had not died, he might still have kept his word to her in the end. She may have known it in her heart. She did not take her own life.'

'You are sure Marguerite was not lying?'

'It all makes sense, Gerard—and Michael changed after that

time. Before Lucinda died he was not so bad tempered. He has become worse over the years. He does not care for his wife or she for him. He is a disappointed, bitter man.'

'Lucinda kissed me. I may have let her for a moment. It was a summer day and she was pretty that day, lit up from inside—but when she wanted me to lie with her I said no. At no time did I encourage her—or Marguerite. I hardly saw either of them. I was in love with you. You do believe me?' His fingers tightened around hers.

'Yes, I do. I think that was why Marguerite wanted to kill me. In her rage, she told me that Lucinda laughed at her, told her that you would marry me—and she went for her. It may have been an accident, but in Marguerite's mind she killed her sister. I think it played on her conscience. Her father had made her a virtual prisoner and she dwelled on her wrongs. You did not want her, so you became Lucinda's murderer though she knew she had done it—but she wanted to punish you. When she suspected we were likely to marry it made her angry and somehow she persuaded Lieutenant Gordon to help her.'

Gerard nodded. 'Alice Horton came to see me this morning. She apologised for what happened and told me that a couple of months ago Marguerite's mother was taken by a stroke and can no longer speak. Because his wife was so ill, her father allowed Marguerite to help with the nursing. She took some of the sleeping draught the doctor had left for her mother and put it in her father's ale—and then she left the house to come to us. He had no idea where she had gone. She had to take the letter you wrote to her mother—if her father had known where she was, he would have come after her.'

'I suspected that something must be wrong at her home when

I realised she must have taken the letter. I feel so guilty,' Amelia said. 'She might have harmed Lisa.'

'How could you know what was in her mind? Besides, she did not hurt the child. Alice told me that Marguerite desperately wanted a child of her own. I think if Marguerite had succeeded in her plans to be rid of us, she might have spirited Lisa away. We found silver from her room at Ravenshead and also some diamond earrings of yours, Amelia. No doubt she would have taken whatever she needed before she disappeared with my daughter. Imagine what might have been Lisa's fate then…living with that woman…growing up as her child.'

'It does not bear thinking of!' Amelia closed her eyes for a moment. Gerard's fingers tightened over hers. She looked at him. 'Forgive me. I had no idea that she was unstable. Her letters were so sad…so pitiful…'

'The work of a clever if deranged mind. Her father may have suspected that she had killed her sister, but no one could prove it. She had brooded on her wrongs. When Gordon came home from France and went to visit, he told her about Lisette and how she died. She saw her chance to take revenge on me.

'Gordon was angry, but he had no thought of murder until she prompted him. He says that he resisted at first, but she was too strong for him. He had loved her since they were children, and she knew how to make him do her bidding. He wanted her, but she made him promise her that he would kill us both.'

Amelia shuddered. 'And I invited her to come here.'

'You could not have known what was in her mind.'

'What will happen to Lieutenant Gordon?'

'He is to live abroad. I have given him a letter of recommendation to a plantation owner in Jamaica. I met Jacques in France and he offered me help if I should go there.'

'Should Lieutenant Gordon not go to prison?' Amelia looked at him steadily. 'Many would seek revenge, Gerard.'

'I think he has suffered enough. He lost the woman he loved.'

'Does he know that Lisa is his child?'

'No. Perhaps it was harsh, but I thought it best for her to stay with us. She could not be more loved than she is now.'

'I am glad—for her sake. You are her true papa, Gerard.'

'Yes, I am—and you are her mama. We shall both love her and care for her, and she will remain our daughter even when we have children of our own.'

'Yes, we shall always love her.' Amelia smiled. 'Can you forgive me for doubting you even for a moment? I am so sorry, Gerard. I should have known, but I was stunned...I could not think clearly. Once I had time to let my mind clear, I knew you were innocent of all their accusations.'

'Can you forgive me for letting you walk into danger? You were close to death, Amelia.'

'That was entirely my own fault. I had completely forgotten everything else when I left the house. Besides, it is over—it is over, isn't it?' She lifted her eyes to meet his anxiously.

'Yes, my dearest. I am certain it is.'

'Then there is nothing to stop our marriage—is there?'

'Your brother...shall you tell him what you know?'

'I shall tell him all of it, Gerard. You were blameless. His jealousy and anger were misplaced. I think he may have blamed himself for Lucinda's suicide, because he told her he would not help her after he saw her kiss you—and he may find peace in the knowledge that she did not jump into the river because of his harshness. Perhaps he can find peace at last, and it may be the saving of him.'

'Yes, he may find some comfort in that,' Gerard agreed. 'He may still not forgive us—either of us.'

'If Michael wishes to remain a stranger to me, it is his choice. He may apologise and put an end to this feud if he wishes—if not…' Amelia shook her head. 'I cannot condone the way he behaved with a young woman he knew to be my friend. Besides, he made me so unhappy when he sent you away, Gerard. I have you and Lisa and all my friends—why should I need anyone else?'

Amelia stood at the church door, her arm resting lightly on Gerard's. The bells were ringing out joyfully and a large crowd of friends and local people had gathered outside to watch the bride and groom leave. Rice and dried rose petals were showered over them as they ran for the carriage.

Once inside out of the bitter February wind, Gerard drew her to him, kissing her softly, his hand moving at the nape of her neck. His eyes seemed to search her face.

'What is it?'

'You are happy? Truly happy?'

'You know I am. How could I not be on such a day? We are married and we have our friends about us. I have all that I ever wanted.'

'Your brother did not attend the wedding.'

'No, but my nephew, John, did—and he brought me a gift from my brother.' She touched the simple but beautiful baroque pearl that hung from a fine gold chain about her throat. 'This is the pendant my mother wore when she married. Michael sent it to me. It is the closest he could come to an apology.'

'Your mother's…' Gerard nodded. 'I wondered why you chose something so simple, though it is a fine pearl.'

'Mama's jewellery was divided between us after she died. Michael was allowed to choose first. He realised afterwards that I would have liked the pendant and he told me I should have it on my wedding day. Sending it for my wedding was a symbol of forgiveness…an olive branch. I wore it to show I had accepted his offering. I shall have many occasions to wear the diamonds you gave me, my dearest.'

'You hardly need diamonds,' Gerard told her and kissed her once more. 'Whatever you wear, whatever you do, you are lovely inside and out, my darling Amelia.'

'I love you so much…'

'I am the luckiest man to have found you.' Gerard took her hand as the carriage drew to a halt outside the house. 'Only you would have asked that Lisa should accompany us on our wedding trip to Paris. You are a pearl amongst women, Amelia. Your brother's gift was appropriate.'

'Thank you for being so understanding. Most men would hold a grudge after what Michael did…but you don't…do you?'

'I may never forgive him completely for what he did to us. It truly broke my heart and I wanted to die. I was reckless on the field of battle in the hope of death. However, I want you to be happy, Amelia. I know it would not suit you to cut your brother or his family entirely. I dare say I can greet him in a civil manner if it comes to it, though we shall never be friends.'

'It is enough,' she murmured as the carriage door was opened and a groom let down the steps. 'We must not keep our guests waiting, Gerard.'

* * *

Gerard watched as his wife moved amongst her friends at the lavish reception they had given. He felt a swelling of pride as he saw the way people greeted her. She was liked, respected and loved by everyone here. Known for her generosity, her dignity and her character, she was a truly great lady and he felt privileged that she was his to love and protect for the rest of their lives.

'Father wanted to come, you know.' Captain John Royston spoke from behind him, making Gerard turn his head. 'He is often bad tempered and lets his tongue run away with him—but he was upset when he heard what happened. Amelia looks well enough now, though.'

'Thankfully, she has made a full recovery,' Gerard said. 'You may tell your father he may visit us in Hanover Square when he chooses. I dare say Amelia will wish for a ball when we go to town next Season. I should be pleased to see him and your mother and brother—and you, of course, should you be on leave from your regiment.'

'Thank you. I'll make that known to my father.' John offered his hand and shook on it, then he nodded and moved away.

Harry Pendleton came up to him. 'So we are all three wed,' he observed. 'I think we have done well for ourselves, Gerard. There was a time in Spain when I believed none of us would ever see this day.'

'We were lucky to escape with our lives.' Gerard's mouth formed a grim line. 'And we have all had our troubles since. However, I believe we can all look forward to a more peaceful future.'

'With Napoleon safely tucked up in his island prison, I dare say England will be at peace—and I think the same may be said for us.' Harry looked thoughtful. 'I wrote to Northaven and thanked him for the part he played in this last affair, Gerard. You were right—the past is gone and should be forgotten.'

'It was harder for you to forgive, because of what happened to Susannah, but, from something he said when we talked, I believe that when he saw her fall with his ball in her shoulder it changed him. I dare say, given the chance, he may lead a better life in future.'

Harry shrugged and then grinned. 'Susannah wanted me to write the letter. It is amazing what we do for love, Gerard.'

'Indeed, I agree with that,' Gerard said and laughed. 'Excuse me, my dear fellow, but I believe they are about to play a waltz and I should like to dance with my wife…'

Amelia turned in her husband's arms. She thought he was sleeping and she smiled as she traced the line of his mouth with her fingertip. Sometimes he could look stern, forbidding, but in sleep he looked younger and at peace, very like the young man she had first fallen in love with so many years ago. The previous night, he had made love to her passionately, hungrily, but with such tenderness that she had wept tears of happiness. She bent her head to kiss his lips softly and found herself caught in an imprisoning embrace.

'I thought you were asleep,' she said and smiled down at him.

'Were you trying to take advantage of me?' His eyes mocked her lovingly.

'Foolish man…' She tried to pull away but he moved swiftly, rolling her beneath him, gazing down at her. Her hair was loose and tumbling about her face in disarray, her skin pearly pink and smooth as his eyes feasted on her sweetness. 'Gerard…it is almost time to get up.'

'This is our honeymoon and I may not leave this bed for a week.'

'Is that a threat or a promise?' she teased, touching his beloved face. 'I think I should be quite happy to stay right here for as long as you wish.'

'I shall take that as an invitation,' he murmured huskily, bending his head to suck gently at her nipples, which peaked at his touch. 'You are so beautiful, my love. I think I can never have enough of you.'

Amelia moaned softly, her body arching, tingling as he stroked her, coming vibrantly alive as the desire pooled inside her. She ran her hands over his back, loving the satin feel of his skin, the hardness of toned muscles. His maleness felt hard and hot against her inner thigh as he sought the sweet moistness of her femininity, entering her with a deep thrust that made her cry out with pleasure.

They moved together, slowly, taking their time as their bodies matched and met in equal need—a need that took them soaring into realms of pleasure known only to true lovers. Carried and tossed by raging passion, they ended on a far shore where the soft sea spray kissed a sunlit breach and the scent of blooms wafted on a warm breeze.

'I am in paradise...' she murmured against his shoulder, tasting the salt of his sweat. 'I am truly happy, Gerard.'

'We are both in paradise then,' he murmured and smiled down at her. 'For I am in a place I never thought to be.'

Amelia lay back, content to feel him lying beside her. She thought that he had fallen asleep or perhaps he was just pretending again.

'I was thinking,' she said. 'We have so much, Gerard. We must find a way to share some of our good fortune. I realise that I made a mistake with Marguerite, but there is a young woman I know who really does need a little good fortune. Her name is Jane and I thought we might give her a Season in town this year.'

Gerard did not answer. He must truly be asleep this time. Amelia smiled. Somewhere within the house she could hear a longcase clock striking. She felt sleepy, at peace with herself. There was no hurry for anything. When they returned to England, she would write to the young woman and invite her to stay with them at their house in Hanover Square…